# CRY FREEDOM

UNIVERSAL PICTURES PRESENTS

A MARBLE ARCH PRODUCTION

KEVIN KLINE · PENELOPE WILTON · DENZEL WASHINGTON IN

· RICHARD ATTENBOROUGH'S FILM "CRY FREEDOM"

BASED ON THE BOOKS "BIKO" AND "ASKING FOR TROUBLE" BY DONALD WOODS

MUSIC GEORGE FENTON AND JONAS GWANGWA

COSTUMES DESIGNED BY JOHN MOLLO   PRODUCTION DESIGNER STUART CRAIG   EDITOR LESLEY WALKER

CO-PRODUCERS NORMAN SPENCER AND JOHN BRILEY

DIRECTOR OF PHOTOGRAPHY RONNIE TAYLOR, B.S.C.   IN CHARGE OF PRODUCTION TERENCE CLEGG

SCREENPLAY BY JOHN BRILEY   PRODUCED AND DIRECTED BY RICHARD ATTENBOROUGH

A UNIVERSAL PICTURE

# CRY FREEDOM

A NOVEL BY
JOHN BRILEY

**B**

BERKLEY BOOKS, NEW YORK

CRY FREEDOM

A Berkley Book / published by arrangement with
MCA Publishing Rights, a Division of MCA, Inc.

**PRINTING HISTORY**
Berkley edition / November 1987

For information address: MCA Publishing Rights,
a Division of MCA, Inc.
100 Universal City Plaza
Universal City, California 91608

ISBN: 0-425-10776-0

A BERKLEY BOOK ® TM 757,375
Berkley Books are published by The Berkley Publishing Group,
200 Madison Avenue, New York, New York 10016.
The name "BERKLEY" and the "B" logo
are trademarks belonging to Berkley Publishing Corporation.

PRINTED IN THE UNITED STATES OF AMERICA

10 9 8 7 6 5 4 3 2

To Mary and Shaun —
   who lived through so much
   of this with me

# Foreword

A novel—like a film—has a life of its own. So much can be done on the screen by a gesture, a look, the way a person is dressed, that a dozen subtle points can be made just by the way a character walks into a room . . . not only insights about that character but about the other characters, too, in the ways they react to his entrance, or his clothes, or his mood.

A film's "realism" can (and I believe *does* in the case of *Cry Freedom*) create an electric immediacy and, when shared with others in a packed theater, emotions of overwhelming power.

But the novel has its advantages too. Its pace is *your* pace, and its "reality" doesn't depend on performance, or music, or design. Its reality is inside your head.

This novel is based on the screenplay for *Cry Freedom*, which has its origins in two factual books by Donald Woods, *Biko* and *Asking for Trouble*. It is not a literal transcription of those books or, indeed, of the film script. It often moves in response to its own life, but it takes the reader on the same journey, with, I hope, much the same emotions.

The screenplay for *Cry Freedom* offered a blueprint for other storytellers (the director, the actors, the editor) to follow. This novel tries to take your hand and say "Follow me" into the biggest and smallest theater of all—that theater of the imagination we all carry around in the recesses of our mind.

# i

THE DAY BEGAN before sunrise. It always did. If you had a job in Capetown, the *baas* expected you there by seven or eight. No excuses. Just be there. And if you weren't, there were plenty to take your place.

So the haze of smoke from the crude huts of tin and packing crates was already thick when the great hulk of Table Mountain began to emerge from the darkness in the cold gray of early dawn. Its dark mass was visible both from the quiet white streets of Capetown several miles away and from the stirring dirt paths of the illegal black shantytown of Crossroads.

The leaden, early-morning routine of the township masked its precarious existence. In any section of its sprawling, chaotic pathways you could find an old woman calmly brushing her teeth in a cup as she stood in the doorway of a little shack; see a young, barefoot boy sleepily stuffing wood chips into a kitchen stove; a wrinkled grandmotherly figure stirring a cornmeal mush; a yawning teen-

age girl in a cotton wrap coming from an outhouse; a dot-
ing mother placidly feeding a baby at her breast; a little girl
carefully lighting a kerosene lamp on a crude kitchen table;
a man shaving intently at a cracked mirror; a woman putting a clean chamber pot back under a rumpled bed.

The only indication of Crossroads squatters' illegality
was a young adolescent sitting on the top platform of an
abandoned drilling well, the highest point in the whole
wretched maze. Wrapped in a dirty blanket, he was
propped against a broken support post, dozing fitfully, but
around his neck there gleamed a large, bright whistle . . .
and his sleepy eyes would open occasionally to glimpse
down the long road winding to Capetown.

His sentinel duty was part of the uneasy game the government played with the shabby residents of Crossroads.
The Cape area had always bred the most independent and
the least compliant of all the blacks in South Africa. A port
city always has its underseam, and in Capetown it thrived
in the atmosphere of part-time work and the sudden needs
for ample cheap labor. Blacks were drawn to it by forces as
elemental as hunger and thirst. Employers would hire you
in Capetown even if you didn't have a work permit. And if
you stayed out of the police's way when you traveled, you
could sneak your family into the area with you, then build
a shack in Crossroads and survive on somebody's labor—
yours, your wife's, your daughter's.

The police closed only half an eye to it. They couldn't
afford to drive all of you away because the *baas,* he needed
you. And he knew that he could pay you less and work you
harder if you didn't have a work permit, so he wanted
some of you around. But nobody wanted you to get settled;
nobody wanted you to think you had a right to be there,
so—

2

A sudden, distant sound cut through the growing bustle of the morning routine, and the young man with the whistle sprang to wakefulness as though he had been doused by cold water. He stood and peered off along the dark gray of the twisting road . . . and he saw them almost on the instant the sound of their heavy motors came clearly through the damp morning air: A line of huge, gray behemoths: Army "hippos," steel-clad monsters that could transport fifty troops through a barrage of rocks and even small-arms fire —and in their wake a long string of police vehicles, all with their lights out, all closing on the makeshift settlement with relentless speed, the cloud of dust they raised becoming more visible as each second lightened the ash-gray sky.

The boy's whistle pierced the area. Its shriek echoed almost immediately from a dozen other whistles. And the somnolent township shuddered like a frightened horse. Women grabbed their babies and scurried for cover; men darted for anything valuable, a watch, a wallet, a radio; young men raced through the dirt paths, leaping puddles of water, shouting warnings, hurrying others along with a vigilant bravado but darting looks of fearful apprehension over their shoulders as the roar of the military vehicles grew louder and louder.

But the attack by the System this day rendered useless all the efforts to hide and protect. From three angles, police Land Rovers hurtled into the cluttered byways of the settlement, each of them bearing a huge tear-gas machine mounted on the back—giant, raucous contraptions that looked like early jet engines and spewed out huge volumes of burning tear gas. Each Land Rover twisted and turned down the dirt and mud alleyways, chasing bodies before them and leaving behind clouds of choking gas.

Moving with practiced swiftness, many of the blacks

managed to cover their mouths with wet rags, but there was no way to keep the smoke from burning your eyes, and if that wasn't enough to drive you into the open, police with gas masks followed the Land Rovers on foot, racing from shack to shack, smashing with whips and billy clubs, driving everyone into the open and lashing into anything that looked worth breaking. The little pathways became a chaos of people running in all directions, coughing, lunging from the whips, trying to protect small children—and the screams of pain and terror could be heard even above the whirring blast of the tear-gas machines, the police whistles, the roaring commands from the bullhorns spouting Afrikaans.

And as the smoke began to clear, police with dogs stampeded the area, and this time their goal was clear as they lunged and charged after the men, not hesitating to club an obstreperous woman out of the way but saving the heat of their fury for the males—young and old. There was no way that even the most fleet-footed could escape, and gradually they were all herded and beaten into an area where military buses with sealed windows waited to take away those who, for one reason or another, displeased their attackers.

The women and children, many with wet rags still clinging to their faces, many with eyes still inflamed from the tear gas, then watched helplessly as the police proceeded to tear apart their "houses" of crates and cardboard, of ropes and tin and canvas, bulldozers lumbering through the structures, flattening the tatty furniture, ripping away walls, crushing stoves and beds and clothes. The wide-eyed children stared, torn between fear and fascination. Most of the women just stood, clutching their most valuable possessions to them, a few shouting defiance, most taking the assault with stoic resignation and unheeded tears.

And as the inside walls of the shacks were exposed, many revealed posters picturing Nelson Mandela, some with his name printed boldly beneath with the letters "ANC." Others showed poster pictures of Robert Sobukwe, the Pan-African leader, but on some walls there were two or three of a younger face. A serious, handsome face with solemn, penetrating eyes. Most of these simply bore the words "Steve Biko," but here and there, thick, bold lettering beneath Biko's name spelled out the phrase "Black Consciousness." With angry purpose the bulldozers went back and forth over these walls, their huge scrapers reducing them to shreds.

# ii

SOME EIGHT HUNDRED miles away, a young woman was just awakening in a small, neat room. The morning was still fresh, and the sounds around her were those of the country. She stretched her lithe figure, then went to a small table where she poured water into a basin and splashed the sleep from her eyes, letting the water run down her cheeks and onto her neck. She had huge almond eyes, a sensuous mouth, but even in the relaxed languor of early morning, her beautiful face bore the stamp of intellect, of a mind that seldom relaxed totally.

She wiped the water from her face with a towel and reached up to the one expensive item in her modest quarters—an ultramodern radio with twin steel aerials. Except for a vase of flowers, the only other adornment in the room was a poster picture of Steve Biko—one exactly like those being crushed and shredded in Crossroads.

Mamphela Ramphele was a doctor. A few years before, Steve Biko had been a medical student, just as she was.

But Steve had moved from medicine to black politics—such as they were in South Africa. And now Dr. Mamphela Ramphele was the sole doctor in a small black clinic for which Steve had somehow managed to raise the money—even though he was "banned" by the South African government, forbidden to be in the presence of more than one person at a time, forbidden to write or speak publicly.

Like Steve, Mamphela was light of color and, under the Byzantine laws of race in South Africa, could have applied to be listed as "colored" rather than "black." Coloreds were descendants of mixed races. Black and Dutch, black and English, black and Portuguese. The South African government preferred them, primarily because there were even fewer of them than there were white South Africans, and by granting them some small privileges that were denied blacks, they served as a lightning rod for black anger. If the blacks grew jealous enough of the marginally higher wages and marginally better jobs allowed coloreds, their minds were diverted from their more justified anger at what the government was doing to them.

But like Steve, Mamphela was too bright not to see the malign purpose behind such classifications, too ethical to want "advantages" that split black South Africa into feuding camps. So her passbook, like Steve's, continued to identify her racial stock as "black."

Slipping from her dun-colored nightdress to wash, Mamphela suddenly froze in mid-movement. The deep voice of a radio newscaster had been relaying the morning news, and having covered the state of the dollar and the rand, the latest from the Middle East, the Common Market, and the East-West conflict, he calmly began an account of a police raid on an illegal township outside Capetown that morning. "A number of people were found without work permits, and many are being sent back to their respective homelands," he reported imperturbably. "There was no resistance to the policing action, and many of the illegals voluntarily presented themselves to the police and military authorities." His voice then changed to sunny enthusiasm. "The Springboks ended their rugby series against the visiting Argentinians with a sparkling 33–10 victory. The Springboks' pack—"

Mamphela reached up and switched the radio off.

Her eyes went slowly to the poster with Steve's picture.

Back at Crossroads, the last of the military vehicles was leaving—a giant hippo packed with sweating and laughing police. It rode off across the plain toward Capetown, leaving a little cloud of dust in its wake. For a time the women and those men left behind watched it depart with a numb stoicism . . . and then slowly, one after another, they began to reassemble what was left of their possessions.

A pall of dust and smoke still hung over the area, but patiently, doggedly, the damaged walls were reassembled and patched. It had all happened before. It would happen again—in a month, a week, three months—maybe not so severely, maybe more so. It was the price you paid for work—for being black. The only indication that it left rankling seeds of bitterness was a hand here and there that fiercely slapped a picture of Mandela or Biko back onto a piece of tin or crating board that would again become a living-room wall.

At the clinic—it was named Zanempilo, meaning "place of healing"—Mamphela was making her early-morning rounds. She was dressed in a white surgical coat, as clean and simple as the ward itself. All the patients in this ward were children, most suffering from diseases a pure water supply and ordinary sanitation would have prevented. But clean water and ordinary sanitation weren't available for the great majority of Africans, and the child mortality rate was one of the greatest indictments of the white government of South Africa.

A tiny room that housed the critically ill was at the end of the ward. Tenjy Mtintso had been the night nurse, and when Mamphela entered, she was in the room taking the temperature of a little girl who displayed a bad infection that covered part of one eye and ran down the side of her face and shoulder. Tenjy, a tiny, pretty young woman of twenty who looked younger and far more vulnerable than she really was, glanced up anxiously at Mamphela, but Mamphela went straight to the small desk by the door and began examining the night records.

Tenjy removed the thermometer from the child's mouth, recorded the temperature, then began to change the child's diaper. Mamphela moved to her side. "Her temperature is down," Tenjy said, "but she still isn't holding any food."

Mamphela bent to the child, first feeling her pulse, then listening to her heartbeat. But all the time Tenjy's eyes dwelled on her. Finally Tenjy could wait no longer. "Did you hear the news this morning?" she asked quietly.

Mamphela didn't move her attention from the child. "If they'd caught him," she said flatly, "we'd have heard. They would have boasted of it." Its finality surprised Tenjy, but it didn't convince her.

Later, at breakfast in the small kitchen, others on the staff argued the same point. Mapetla Mohapi, a tough, earnest colleague of Steve's who helped at the clinic, was as convinced as Mamphela that if Steve had been arrested, the news would be out. "The police find him—maybe with posters in the car—you think that wouldn't be the *first* item on the news?" he yelled, going out the back door to fetch wood for the stove.

"No!" Tenjy shouted. "They'd try to get him to confess to something first! Because if people *know* the police have him, they have to be more careful about the way they treat him!"

As usual, Mamphela was reading as she ate, but she was listening to the argument. She tapped Tenjy on the shoulder and pointed out the window. *"They* think he's here," she said. She was pointing to the police Land Rover parked along the dirt road leading to the clinic. It contained the two local policemen who trailed Biko throughout each day. They were sprawled in the car in their usual way, watching everything through half-closed eyes, secure in the knowledge that anything coming or going would have to pass them. "If the police in Capetown had taken him, surely that lot'd be the first to know," Mamphela continued. "And they wouldn't be hanging around here."

Ntsiki Biko, Steve's attractive, somewhat buxom wife, was keeping herself busy by emptying medicines from a delivery box, carefully placing them by category in the refrigerator and checking them off against an inventory list. She, too, had been listening to the argument, fraught with anxiety herself but trying to weigh both sides against the worry in her heart. "I think he's hiding," she offered with more conviction than she felt. "He was there with Peter Jones, and Peter has a work permit. If Steve was arrested, Peter would have called me." It stilled everyone for a moment. Even Tenjy didn't want to win the argument at the price of increasing the anxiety they all heard in Ntsiki's voice.

Tabby, a young ten-year-old who sat in one of the windows keeping a constant eye on the police while he ate his breakfast, finally broke the silence. "They're coming," he said.

Mamphela looked up again from her book. A few people were already coming up the road toward the clinic. She knew some would have been walking all night. A few for days. "All right, let's finish up and get the dayroom ready," she said, folding her book and pushing away from the table. She glanced at Ntsiki before she left. "You know Steve," Mamphela said, "he'll be all right."

"He will, for sure," Ntsiki replied, and forced a smile. Mamphela touched her arm gently and moved off briskly to start her day.

# iii

EAST LONDON IS a port city on the Indian Ocean, seven hundred and fifty miles or so from Capetown. It's a provincial city, no great metropolis, but it had gained a degree of notoriety because Donald Woods, the editor of its paper, the *Daily Dispatch*, had shown uncommon courage in publicly taking the government to task for some of its major absurdities over the race laws. Woods was a sixth-generation South African who believed, like almost every other white in the country, that South Africa belonged easily as much to them as it did to any black. But he had been trained as a lawyer and he was born with enough imagination to leap over walls of schooling and culture to understand that the government was being neither ethical nor humane in its rule of the voteless blacks.

He did not believe blacks should be given the full right to vote. He certainly did not believe they were capable of administering the government, or even of having a significant say in its administration. But he did believe in justice

as he saw it, and he did believe that all humans have some
inalienable rights. When he caught the government violating those basic ethical premises, he struck at them with a
pen so sharp and so precise that his paper was quoted from
one part of South Africa to the other. It also made his paper
and himself a target for several government actions in the
courts. But his legal training, and the government's para-
doxical deference to its independent judges, saved him
time and again from fines that could have crippled the
paper, and at times from prison itself.

One of the things he attacked most vehemently was the
practice of police raids on black townships—legal *and* illegal. He had grown up accepting the laws that forced
blacks and whites to live apart, and that blacks should be
housed in townships removed from the white cities. But
that those blacks should be subject to arbitrary harassment
—and worse—at the hands of those who were supposed to
uphold the law, inflamed him as a man and as a lawyer.

It was true that blacks living in illegal townships were
violating residency regulations, but if the government
wanted to act on those violations, they should take specific
cases to court, not subject numberless men, women, and
children to wanton assault and battery. But he knew, like
everyone else in South Africa, that the illegal townships
were tolerated because white employers benefited from the
cheap labor they provided, so he found the raids on them
hypocritical as well as immoral.

On this day in November 1975, he had seized on the
news of the raid on Crossroads and decided to make it his
headline story—and the subject of his lead editorial. He
called in his front-page makeup man, Tony Morris, and
together they started shifting stories around on the page-
one mock-up. The previous lead story on Ford's pardon for

Nixon on Watergate would go to the left-hand side of the page, and the government's refusal of the new appeal to release Nelson Mandela would go center, where it would juxtapose the story on Crossroads. The prospect of a Japanese auto-assembly plant in Durban would have to be moved to the back page.

Woods was in the midst of it, his blue pencil circling the headline areas and scrawling tentative typefaces, when Ken Robertson, one of his most laid-back but productive newsmen, pushed into the office past Alec, the elderly black "tea boy."

"Boss," was Ken's only word. But he slapped a stack of pictures on Woods' desk. Woods turned to look at them as Ken confidently took a cigarette from the pack on Woods' desk and lit up.

They were pictures of the raid on Crossroads—some of them blurred but all of them dramatic: a weeping woman clutching a baby in her arms as she stands helplessly in front of her ruined shack; a young boy being clubbed by two soldiers; an old man sitting, dazed and numb, in a ragged armchair, the walls around him smashed and broken; a young girl being chased by a whip-wielding policeman; a bulldozer smashing through a tiny, makeshift kitchen.

Woods looked up at Ken in amazement. Ken smiled. He was slightly overweight, more than a little irreverent, and he had neither the education nor the intellect of his boss, but he had street smarts and an eye for trouble, and he knew Woods looked on him as protégé and favorite.

"How'd you get these?" Woods asked challengingly.

Ken puffed smoke and smiled. "I got them. Do we dare *print* them?"

Woods examined the pictures again. He was an intense

man when he was working. His glasses and his mane of thick gray hair made him look a bit older than his forty-two years, but he was fit and youthful in his movements. A man in his prime. Suddenly his face broke into a sly grin. "For these I'll risk it," he said with finality. "I'll even give you a byline."

"You're a prince," Ken retorted. "If they put me away, yours'll be the first name on my lips." They both knew that South African "freedom" of the press was a maze of paradoxes, hedged by dozens of laws and regulations, and that printing pictures of police beating blacks could bring both official and "unofficial" reaction. But the paradox was, if you had enough of them and they were bad enough, the government sometimes felt it was better to let the matter drop than to keep it in the public eye by pressing charges. It was the kind of thin line Woods and Ken both liked to tread.

Ken scooped up the pictures to write the captions, his face still creased with a self-congratulatory grin.

"Come on, tell me. How the hell did you get those and get back here?" Woods demanded.

"It's the twentieth century, boss—wait till you see my expense sheets."

"And who tipped you off?"

"The same guy who took 'em. You see, you keep accusing me of drinking for pleasure, but it's really the hardest part of my job. If you drink long enough, you're bound to find *one* cop who's read your editorials, boss, and once in a while, one who actually agrees with them." He smiled archly at Woods and held up one of the pictures. In the foreground there was a flattened wall—and on it was an array of the Biko posters. "What about 'Mr. Biko'?" he asked. "Use his name in the story? My boy said his picture was everywhere."

And that shifted the tone of the exchange. "Do you think there was a meeting or something?" Woods asked.

"From what he said, I'd think there must have been," Ken replied. "Biko couldn't have been there, but one of his people shooting his mouth off about Black Consciousness —that, I'd say, was almost a certainty."

Woods mulled it over for a moment, then shook his head. "No, leave him out of it. I want the authorities blamed for that raid. I'll take care of Biko in an editorial. With one bunch of nut-cases saying *white* supremacy justifies anything, all we need is a black nut-case saying *black* supremacy will save the world."

Ken nodded agreement to that and swung out the door. Woods turned back to Tony Morris and the page-one mock-up. "Okay," he said, "we'll put one of those pictures right at the top in the center." And his blue pencil circled in the area.

The edition produced the explosion Woods had anticipated. The pictures were reprinted in papers all over the country, and Woods received the usual battery of phone calls—veiled threats from the police, the Office of Bantu (Black) Affairs, the Minister of Information, violent threats on his life from anonymous callers, male and female, and occasional words of congratulations from a fellow editor.

The one thing that ultimately seemed to save him from prosecution in this case was the editorial he wrote on Biko. It was titled "Bantu Stephen Biko—the Ugly Menace of Black Racism," and it won approval from even the direst enemies of the paper.

And that made Mamphela's uninvited visit to the *Daily*

*Dispatch* even more surprising. She came dressed in jeans and a white sweater, and she looked stunning.

She strode through the long corridor to Woods' office with a confident hauteur that drew as much attention as her physical attributes. Blacks did not walk that way in provincial cities in South Africa. When she came up to Ann Hobart's receptionist desk, she slammed a newspaper over the typing on Ann's blotter. "I would like to know who's responsible for this?" she demanded.

Ann, as baffled by her manner as the question, glanced down at the paper. It had been folded to Woods' editorial on Biko. Ann looked back up, but before she could stammer a reply, Mamphela put a card crisply on the paper. *"Dr.* Mamphela Ramphele," she said forcefully. "And if he won't see me, you'd better call the police, because I don't intend to leave until he does."

Ann hesitated, still a little dumbstruck by the impact of Mamphela, but she was beginning to recover enough to be annoyed at a black woman with that much effrontery. She let that annoyance register, then picked up the phone.

"There's a *Doctor* Ramphele wishing to speak to you, Mr. Woods," she said coldly.

Woods was used to Ann's reaction to blacks, especially her reaction to blacks with pretensions. He assumed Dr. Ramphele was an elderly doctor of divinity with some story to tell. "Please send him in," he said equably, and turned back to the piece he was writing for the day's edition.

Ann opened his door. *"Doctor* Ramphele," she announced acerbically. For a second Woods did not look up from his work, then he swung around and was confronted by this black Athena striding angrily toward him. The thing that registered first was her anger, but it was closely followed by an awareness of a figure that did not belong to any doctors of divinity Woods knew.

He glanced disconcertedly at Ann. She read the appeal in the look, bowed crisply, and went out the door.

Mamphela placed the editorial before Woods. "I've read this paper long enough to know you're not one of the worst," she said tartly, "so it's all the more baffling that you would try to pass off this vicious *fiction* as reasoned fact!"

Woods had recovered enough from his initial shock to react to that as any decent writer would. "Well, Doctor"— he glanced at the name he had scrawled when Ann called —"*Ramphele,* you're right. I've stuck my neck out to take a stand against *white* prejudice, but if you think that means I'm going to go soft on some sensationalist pushing *black* prejudice, you've brought your complaint to the wrong man!"

It was the kind of attacking forcefulness that reduced most antagonists to a little respect, at least. But it had no such effect on Mamphela. "Black *prejudice?*" she exclaimed. "That's not what Steve's all about at all! Don't you even bother about the facts before you rush into print?"

"Your Mr. Biko's building a wall of black hatred in South Africa," Woods retorted, "and I'll fight him as long as I sit in this chair!"

"What you do in that chair is put words in his mouth, and you know he can't answer because he's banned! If—"

"I believe I understand what 'Mr. Biko' is about!" Woods interrupted hot-temperedly. "And I am not—"

She cut him off as sharply as he had her. "Well, you believe *wrong!*" she continued. "And he *can't* come to you. If you're the honest newsman you claim to be, you ought to go and see *him!*"

"Look——" Woods began in fury, but then he caught hold of himself. What was he doing engaging in a shouting match with some woman...and a black woman, at that? He looked at her again, beautiful, intelligent beyond doubt, cocky as a white millionairess. "Where are you from?" he muttered at last.

Mamphela only lowered the pitch of her voice slightly. "From *South Africa,*" she replied sardonically. "But I was one of two from my tribal area to be granted a scholarship to Natal Medical School. I'm a token of your white paternalistic concern for the natives of this land."

It was goading, and for a second Woods almost took the bait and started to respond with a sarcasm to match hers, but he caught himself, sighed, leaned back, and tossed his pencil on the desk. "Well," he said wryly, "I'm glad we didn't waste our money."

Mamphela smiled slightly. If there was one thing that could disarm her anger, it was humor. She backed away from the desk and slouched in a chair, staring at him all the time, taking his measure as a human being at last, not just as the author of a piece she considered erroneous and malicious. Woods didn't break the silence. There was no doubt she was appraising him. The only question was what her evaluation would ultimately be. Finally she spoke, and this time it was without defiance. "I know you're not a fool, Mr. Woods, but you *are* uninformed. Steve Biko is one of the few people who can still save South Africa. He's in King William's Town right now——that's his banning area. You ought to see him. . . ."

And her quiet sincerity struck Woods with every bit as much impact as her flamboyant anger.

# iv

KING WILLIAM'S TOWN was not more than forty miles north of East London and was one of South Africa's many pretty little towns. The town itself, of course, was reserved for whites. The blacks lived in a township about five miles from the center of town. The little matchbox houses looked as dismal as the houses in other townships, but the country-side around was so gentle and inviting, it seemed something less than a hardship to be forced to live in such a place.

Woods drove up in his white Mercedes. He passed the township first and wondered again about the address Mamphela had given him. It was in the town itself. Blacks were allowed in the town to shop and work during the day, but it was still an odd place to meet a banned person.

When he reached the street she'd named, it proved to be a broad, sedate, tree-lined avenue. Woods checked the address, growing more and more surprised at the choice of a rendezvous point. He slowed as he neared the number, and then he saw it. It was an old, rather run-down church, half buried in shrubbery and surrounded by bits of crumbling fencing. He pulled in across the street and stared at it for a moment before he got out of the car. It was then that he noticed the two security policemen parked under a tree a little behind him. They were obviously Biko's "minders." He smiled and waved to them. It wasn't often that he was in agreement with banning orders, but if there was any black in the nation he thought bore watching, it was Biko. One of the hopeful ironies of South Africa was that, much as they might have cause, blacks were by and large without prejudice toward whites. If there was ever to be a peaceful solution to the country's racial problems, that was one positive that had to be maintained. It was one of the reasons he was so relentless in damning the government for its abuses of authority in the townships. And suddenly there had arisen this figure from the world of black students who had devised the diabolic "principle" of Black Consciousness.

They wanted nothing to do with white liberals. In fact, liberals were their chief target, because "they created a false sense of progress." They wanted to build *black* organizations, *black* politics. And Woods knew damn well that what was needed was *South African* organizations— black *and* white. *South African* politics, black *and* white. In fact, one of his proudest accomplishments was that he had succeeded in getting blacks accepted into his local chess club, and even got a black alternate on the national team he took to Switzerland. So in his mind, if there was ever a man who ought to be banned, it was Steve Biko.

As he walked across the street toward the old church, he saw two blacks repairing a weathered window at the side of the church. One of them saw Woods and rapped on the window. Woods just walked up to the door.

He rang the rusted bell and the door opened immediately. A smiling Ntsiki greeted him. "Mr. Donald Woods?" she inquired in that formal, ingratiating way that made you feel welcome and important at the same time. It was a gift black women had, and it could not help but take the edge off Woods' animosity.

"Yes. I'm Donald Woods," he answered.

A little boy ran to her side, grabbing her skirt and staring shyly up at the white man. His charm and Ntsiki's smile were reminding Woods of his youth, when his father ran a general store in one of the homelands and women like Ntsiki and clinging little boys were regular customers. He wanted to keep those kind of memories at a distance on this occasion. "I'm here to see Steve Biko," he said as firmly as he could.

"I'm Steve's wife," Ntsiki replied. "He's expecting you." And she opened the door wide and signaled him in.

They say you can judge a man by his wife, and Woods was more than a little surprised. Ntsiki was maternal, warm, seemingly uncomplicated. Not what Woods had expected at all.

The inside of the church was another surprise. Wallboard had been used to make a corridor from one end to the other. Some men and women were at work painting the walls and putting up interior partitions. Its open space had been converted into several small areas, each one a center for some kind of activity. Some girls were learning dressmaking in one; a flue was being fitted for a pottery kiln in another, where a young man was already turning clay on a wheel; another was a small library full of secondhand books and old magazines; there was a little workshop where two older men were making children's toys; and what had been the altar was being converted into a small stage.

Ntsiki paused each time Woods showed any interest and let him get his fill. "Father Russell got it for us," she explained. Woods had heard of Russell, a young Anglican priest who risked a lot of trouble to push black issues. "We're trying to make a kind of center where black people can meet in the day and maybe have classes; and maybe have a job board so people'll know where they can get work."

Woods nodded, more impressed than he wanted to show. He tousled the head of the little boy who was still clinging to Ntsiki's skirt but who stared, big-eyed and grinning, at Woods the whole time. The boy ducked from Woods' playful tease and buried himself in Ntsiki's skirt, but his grin grew broader. "And who's this one?" Woods asked.

"Oh, this is Nkosinathi. He's a rascal like his father," Ntsiki replied as she roughed his back affectionately. "And sometimes even more trouble."

Despite the manifest love in it, Woods detected the somewhat martyred implication that perhaps both father and son were sometimes a little too much for Ntsiki's straightforward nature.

She diverted Woods to a side door near the altar. She opened it, then turned back to Woods. "He's waiting for you. It was a pleasure to meet you, Mr. Woods." And with another warm smile she ushered him out into the yard beside the church.

When Woods stepped out, the door closed immediately behind him. He looked around but saw no sign of anyone. The chattering "busyness" of the church had been replaced

by a silence that only the wind disturbed. The yard itself
was overgrown with weeds, and there was one giant old
tree in the center, trailing a waterfall of green tendrils that
tumbled to the ground. Beyond it, in the corner of the lot,
Woods could see a small building—but still no sign of
anyone. He moved off the step down into the yard, looking
around. The wind shifted the fronds of the spreading tree,
dappling the yard with sun and shade, making it difficult to
pick things out, but still there was no sign of anyone.
Woods turned around, mystified, and grew annoyed again
—then something near the tree caught his eye. He peered
through the waving fronds, and there, in the ever-changing
light, standing as still as a tree trunk, was a tall black
figure, his eyes fixed on Woods, watching him without
emotion as he had apparently been doing since Woods
came out the door.

"Biko? Are you Steve Biko?" Woods called out.

The figure didn't answer, but after a moment he simply
turned toward the small building and gestured with his
hand, "Come, follow me."

From a black man, this annoyed Woods even more. He
sighed heavily and, muttering about the inanity of ever
coming at all, started to work his way delicately through
the heavy weeds in his expensive shoes and equally expensive suit.

The black figure went into the small building. Was it
Biko, or someone leading him to Biko? When Woods
worked his way opposite the open door, he paused and
peered in. He could see the figure standing in the shadows
behind a desk in what he could now tell was only a small
office shed. But he still could not see enough of the face to
recognize whether it was the same face he had seen on the
Biko posters.

He stood for a moment, waiting for some word of acknowledgment or welcome, but it didn't come. All he could see were the two large eyes appraising him with what seemed to Woods to be infinite patience and detachment. What did he want him to do?

"May I come in?" Woods finally asked with as much irony as he could muster. The figure nodded, and sighing heavily again, Woods took the step up into the little office. "I don't really have all day to play games, and I—"

"I would have met you in the church, but as you know, I can only be with one person at a time—and the System are just across the road." Up close, Woods could see that it *was* Biko, and he also knew that "the System" was the black term for any white authority—the police, the army, the rent officer. Those police across the street would want only the slightest infraction to pull Biko in. But now that they were face-to-face, it was Woods' turn to stare. He could see that the man looked both younger and more handsome than his pictures, because his face was unlined and his deep, dark eyes were alive, clearly windows to a complex and sensitive mind. Biko smiled suddenly, devilishly, and Woods could also see the rascal in those eyes that Ntsiki had hinted at.

"But of course," Biko continued wryly, "you would approve of my banning."

Woods' temptation was to say, "You're damned right!" but he hedged. After all, he had been talked into coming to hear what the man had to say. "I think your ideas are dangerous," he said, "but no, I don't approve of banning."

"A true liberal," Biko declared with a hint of mockery.

"It's not a title I'm ashamed of," Woods responded sharply, "though I understand you regard it with some contempt."

Biko grinned. From the moment they began speaking, he had had a dry, amused air, and it deepened as Woods grew more and more belligerently *un*amused. "Oh, that's too strong," Biko protested. "I just think that a white liberal who clings to all the advantages of his white world, jobs, education, housing, *Mercedes*"—Woods blinked involuntarily at that thrust—"is perhaps not the person best qualified to tell blacks how they should react to apartheid."

Woods nodded coolly. "I wonder what kind of liberal *you* would make, Mr. Biko, if *you* were the one who possessed the house, the job, and the Mercedes, and the *whites* lived in the townships."

And this produced a burst of laughter from Biko—at the inversion *and* the assessment of his own character, because there was no denying that a certain swagger and masculine display were fundamental parts of his personality. "Now, that *is* a charming idea," he said. "Whites in the townships and me in a Mercedes." And then, with a smile that was as warm and genuine as his wife's, he stuck out his hand. "It was good of you to come, Mr. Woods. I've wanted to meet you for a long time."

Woods hesitated for a moment, absorbing the swift change in mood, the intelligence, the unexpected sincerity in the eyes and the smile. Then he took the proffered hand.

It was the beginning.

# V

LATER THAT MORNING, they drove out to the Zanempilo
Clinic. It was about fifteen miles from King William's
Town, located in arid hill country on land so dry, no one in
South Africa bothered to farm it. They were followed by
the two local security police, Biko's "minders," and as they
sped up the dusty hill road that led to the clinic, Woods
glanced in the rearview mirror at the police car eating their
dust and creating a second cloud of its own.

"They follow you everywhere?" Woods asked.

Biko glanced in the side mirror. "They think they do."
He smiled, as he stuck his arm out the window and waved
back at them. Woods wasn't too pleased with the implication of that, but he decided to keep his mouth shut and his
eyes open. He'd already had one surprise. The clinic occu-
pied the top of a hill, and its most prominent building was
a chapel. As a building, it had the uneven look of volunteer
labor, but its squat shape and the cross towering above it
had that stark African quality that Woods had grown up

with and Picasso had introduced to the world. So the rebel Biko is a Christian, Woods thought. Well, Vorster and Kruger and the rest of them were, too, so it didn't prove anything, but it was a surprise nonetheless.

Woods turned the car into a little parking space just below the clinic compound. The police car had stopped at its usual spot, farther back on the road. Woods and Biko got out, Woods lingering by the door to view the whole complex. There were three buildings—long, single-storied, of wood, looking a little like a military barracks—then the church and a large outhouse. There was a line of blacks waiting outside the building nearest them, pregnant women, women with small babies, children, old men.

"So that's it?" Woods said.

"That's it," Biko replied. "Not very grand, but a clinic *for* black people, *staffed* by black people—and *run* by a black doctor."

Mamphela had come out of the center door to select some patients from the waiting line. She was in her white clinical coat, a stethoscope around her neck, some files in her hands. She paused on seeing Woods and Biko together, staring off at them. Even with her hair drawn back and her figure straightened by the loose coat, she was a remarkable sight. For a moment she watched them, expressionless, then she gave a short nod to Woods, glanced at Biko, and turned back to her patients.

Woods looked across the top of the car. "Was this place *her* idea—or yours?" he asked Biko challengingly. Having met her, he suspected she had more than a little to do with it.

"It was a collective idea," Biko replied, answering the challenge in Woods' voice with a bit of steel in his own.

Then he glanced up at Mamphela again. "But we were lucky to find *her*," he added.

Woods weighed it all, her intelligence, Biko's reputation. Well, it didn't make any difference; the clinic was a kind of miracle, whoever had pulled it off. He turned to Biko again, the challenge still in his voice but some of the unpleasantness gone. "And a white liberal doctor doing the same thing wouldn't serve your purpose?" he queried ironically.

Biko's voice took on a solemnity Woods hadn't yet heard. "When I was a student, trying to qualify for the jobs you people let us have," he began, "I suddenly realized that it wasn't just the jobs that were white; the *history* we read was *made* by white men, *written* by white men . . . medicines, cars"—he hit the roof of the Mercedes—"television, airplanes, all invented by white men, even football . . ." He paused for a moment, reflecting on it broodingly. And Woods was as struck by his somber reaction as by the thought itself. "In a world like that," Biko went on, "it's hard not to believe that there's something inferior about being born black."

He let it hang in the air for a moment, then he glanced back at the two policemen watching him from the shadows of the police car. "I came to think that *that* feeling was even a bigger problem for us than what the Afrikaners and the System were doing to us." Slowly he turned back to Woods. "I felt that first, the black man had to believe he had as much capacity to *be* a doctor—a leader—as a white man." He paused, and Woods made his first concession, nodding his understanding of that thought, impressed by it, and at last impressed by the man who had reached it.

Biko looked off at the clinic. "So we tried to set this

place up," he said. "My own mistake was to put some of those ideas on paper."

"And the government banned you."

Biko nodded and glanced across at him. "And the fighting liberal editor, Donald Woods, started attacking me."

"I attacked you for being *racist*," Woods replied.

Biko smiled. "How old are you, Mr. Woods?"

Woods hesitated, a little irritated at the tone of that question. "Forty-two," he answered, "if that makes any difference."

Biko leaned on the top of the car, staring at him. "A white South African," he said musingly, "a newspaperman. And forty-two years old. Have you ever really spent any time in a black township?"

Woods squirmed a little. He'd passed through a few townships, but as for "spending any time" in one, it wasn't something one did. "I've—I've been to many a—" He was stammering, and Biko's smile broadened.

"Don't be embarrassed," he said. "Except for the police, I don't suppose one South African in ten thousand has." But Woods *was* a little embarrassed, and Biko stopped grinning at his discomfiture. His voice grew personal, as though he were speaking to an old friend. "You see, we know how *you* live," he said quietly. "We cut your lawns, cook your food, clean your rubbish. How would you like to see how *we* live, the ninety percent of your countrymen who have to get off your white streets at six o'clock at night?"

It wasn't an empty challenge. He meant it.

Late that afternoon, Woods had what he hoped would be a cooling dip in his swimming pool. But four of his five kids were home, so it wasn't exactly relaxing. Duncan and

Dillon were nine and ten respectively, and just big enough to give Woods a real workout when they ganged up on him, which they did at every chance. Gavin, who was seven, usually joined in, but he often put himself on Woods' side, and that meant Woods had to protect him, as well as himself. The "baby," five-year-old Mary, fortunately preferred to teach her dolls to swim in the shallow end, or to help their black maid, Evalina, with the house-cleaning.

Woods finally gave up, dunked the two bigger boys, and swam to the side, bolting for the shower and dressing room that was attached to the playroom bordering the pool. Even then, their big English sheepdog, Charlie, barked and chased him the whole way, trying to get in on the game. "I'm going to write Dr. Evans and insist he give you blokes more homework!" Woods shouted as he turned on the shower. There was a chorus of boos and a couple of splashes from the pool, but he was allowed to shower in peace.

He had a view of the big garden and lawn as he did so, because the latticed shower door only came shoulder-high, and he saw Wendy and Jane come in the driveway up near the house. Wendy was driving her VW, and the back was stuffed with grocery bags. After his day at the clinic, Woods had to admit to himself that the whites of South Africa lived pretty well. He knew that in most countries, having a maid and a gardener was considered a luxury, but there were few white South Africans who didn't have at least a maid. And the land and houses too. He'd heard foreigners marvel that someone who had a very routine job would have a home with two or three acres of lawn, a tennis court, and a swimming pool. It was a rich country, there was no doubt—blessed by God with rich soil, incredible mineral wealth, a climate that made you want to sing with the joy of life. And yet there were the blacks—what to do about the blacks?

Wendy left the groceries in the car—Evalina would get them later—and she and Jane came bounding down to the pool. Wendy was about four years younger than Donald and, like him, had kept both physically and mentally alert. She was a marvelous pianist, better than Donald, and many thought Donald should have turned professional. And to look at her slender, vital body, you would never think that she had borne five children. Jane was their eldest, fourteen, her mother's buddy and her dad's favorite.

"Well, what was he like?" Wendy shouted as she fought off the affectionate attentions of Charlie.

Woods turned off the shower, slipped on a terry robe, and came out drying his hair.

"Dillon!" Wendy shouted. Dillon was barraging Duncan with water. He didn't look at his mother, just ducked underwater and swam off to some other diversion. Mary came running to her mother's side, eager to show her how she'd dressed her doll. Wendy hugged her and "oohed" at the doll but glanced up at Woods with impatience. "Come on, Donald. Stop holding out! What was he like?" And she flopped on a deck chair, expecting an answer.

Woods sat on the edge of the table near her. "Well, like the pictures," he answered. "He's young, twenty-eight to thirty, I'd say, handsome, tall—compelling eyes."

"I'm not intending to date him, Donald! I mean, what was he *like,* what kind of person is he?" Though she was far more liberal politically than Woods, her response to Black Consciousness was much the same as his. She would not have been surprised if he had described Biko as a budding Hitler.

"I'm not sure," Woods said pensively. "But they've built a damn clinic up there. Everything is black. She's the doctor. You should see it; people come from miles."

Wendy stared across at him doubtfully. "What did they use for money?"

"A little black money apparently, a lot of church money from overseas—and even the mining companies put a few pennies in."

"*South African* mining companies?" Wendy asked incredulously.

"That's right," Woods answered. "Apparently someone important heard him make a speech that impressed them. And I have to tell you, he can be impressive."

Evalina had brought a tall glass of orange juice down from the house for Wendy. She placed it down, bent to admire Mary's little doll, then started up for the VW to empty the bags. Wendy thanked her offhandedly, but her mind was on the conversation with Woods. "He hasn't talked *you* into Black Consciousness, has he?" she demanded tartly.

"No," Woods replied with less than complete conviction, "but I *have* agreed to let him take me through a black township."

Wendy was floored again. Her husband was not that easy to maneuver, especially by some young black. And then she had a further thought. "But he's banned. How can he take you anywhere?"

Woods shook his head. "I'm not sure," he said. "But I intend to find out." He put on his glasses, leaned forward, and kissed her on the cheek, smiling at her bafflement, though in truth he felt more than a little baffled by it all himself.

# vi

THE DAY SET for Woods' educational journey to the township came some three weeks after their first meeting. Biko intended to take him to a township area outside East London. It meant going out of his banning area, but he'd done that before, and he thought it might really have an impact on Woods if he saw what was in his own backyard. He and Mamphela had been working in his office on a speech she was to give when the time came for him to get ready for the encounter with Woods. He put on some scruffy shoes and an old sweater, with some patched holes and some unpatched. Mamphela handed him the old brown army coat he'd put on the floor. It was a war-surplus *dlamini,* the long, nondescript coat worn by all black laborers. Biko slipped it on, and Mamphela handed him a workingman's cloth cap.

As inappropriate as the cap looked, she watched him put it on without any hint of amusement. "Do you really think this is worth the risk?" she asked reprovingly.

Biko grinned. "The education of a white liberal? It's a duty."

She tossed him a ragged scarf, fiercely. She clearly wasn't amused. "If you get caught out of your banning area, *you* go to jail. All that would happen to Mr. Woods is that he might have to write a letter of explanation to his Board of Directors."

"That's what we call justice in South Africa, didn't you know?" Biko replied dryly.

Mamphela had to smile at that, but she turned away and sat back down at the typewriter. He looked over at her in his most winning way, but her foreboding was not that easy to dispel. "I don't want them to get you in a jail," she said darkly.

And Biko honored her concern with a serious response: "We won't get caught," he said soberly.

Ntsiki suddenly appeared in the open door with a bill in her hand. "I've got to pay for the electric sockets," she said. "The man's waiting."

Mamphela got up automatically from the typewriter but continued the exchange with Biko as she stepped outside the door. "You won't get caught," she said, "if some paid informer doesn't run to the police."

Once Mamphela was standing outside the shed, Ntsiki was free to go in, and she moved right to a small strongbox on the floor opposite Biko's desk. She looked at his outfit and gave him a mocking smile. "We'll make a workingman of you yet, Steve Biko." Biko grinned at her and did a little workingman's shuffle.

Ntsiki got the money for the bill, then paused before she left. "How do you want to do this?" she asked. She meant how he intended to sneak off.

Biko started to pull the curtain over the little window.

"You tell Thabo to come over here," he told Ntsiki. "Only tell him to stay behind the tree until I come out. I'll turn on the desk light. Then Mamphela will go and occupy the System for a couple of minutes. I'll slip out, and Thabo will slip in and sit in my chair. All he's got to do is pretend to read until I get back." Ntsiki was staring at him, half smiling, shaking her head. "I'm glad I wasn't your mother," she said, and headed back toward the church.

Woods had put on some old clothes for the rendezvous, too, but compared to those worn by Biko, he looked like an ad in a men's magazine. The plan called for him to park his car on a country lane about three miles out of town. When John Qumza, who was driving for the expedition, was sure the way was clear, he'd pull alongside and Woods would hop in. Then they'd move to another point to pick up Biko.

Technically no unauthorized white was allowed in the township areas. It was, however, just a minor proscription in the profusion of racial separation laws, and the likelihood of a white who was only there to look being prosecuted was small. But there was a danger to any blacks who took part in an illegal visit. And that was especially so on this trip, because a white in a group of blacks would certainly draw the attention of the blackjacks—the black township police—and once questions were asked, Biko's breaking of his ban could lead to real trouble. So the whole operation was planned like a military exercise.

As poorly as Woods thought he was dressed, John Qumza shuddered at the sight of him when they drove up beside his car. "Jesus," he said aloud, "maybe we should run over this guy a few times to dirty him up!"

John was a friend of Biko's from his days at the university, one of the founding members of the black student

organization, SASO, that Biko had headed. He was used to
Biko doing the unorthodox in black-white relations, but
perhaps this time he'd gone too far. John had himself
trained for the ministry and, like a lot of educated blacks,
had received his early education in white missionary
schools. He was both at ease with whites and convinced
from experience that an integrated society was both possible and desirable. He also had a patience for white intran-
sigence that many others around Biko—especially
Mapetla—did not have.

When their car skidded up before Woods, Mapetla
jumped out the back, holding the door open. "Goddamn,
get in, man," he barked. And he half pushed Woods into
the center of the backseat. It wasn't easy because there
were already three people in it. Woods kept saying "Excuse
me" as he tried to find a place for his legs and his backside,
but Mapetla shoved in behind him, lurching Woods onto
the lap of a thickset black who laughed and said, "I'm
pleased to meet ya. I'm Meja." Woods tried to nod acknowledgment.

"You said you were going to wear *old* clothes," Mapetla
chided angrily.

"I did!" Woods protested.

John had already pulled the car away at speed, and he
glanced in the rearview mirror anxiously. "Stop arguing
and get him down in the middle! We don't want him sitting
up there where no one can miss him!"

Woods started to shift around, but was pulled down for-
cibly by Mapetla and another passenger Woods soon
learned was named Dye, so that he was crushed into the
middle of the backseat with Dye half seated on one of his
legs and Mapetla on the other.

"Give him your hat, Dye," Mapetla ordered. Dye removed the dirty knit stocking cap from his sweating head, and Mapetla shoved it onto Woods' white hair. Woods couldn't get his arms free to adjust it.

"Pull it all the way down in back," John yelled from the driver's seat after another glance in the mirror.

"You could lift it a little higher on my forehead too," Woods added in a martyred tone. His tone brought a laugh from all of them. It made Woods feel a little more comfortable. "And you might just brush that hunk of hair out of my eyes too," he added as Mapetla studiously pulled the hat down to the back of his neck and pushed up his coat collar. Mapetla smiled and adjusted the hair. It was the first sign that Mapetla might accept him, after all.

The car they were driving was a taxi—a *black* taxi. There were laws about that too. Some taxis were for whites only, some for blacks. The black ones, which spent a lot of time on the township roads, were always in a chronic state of disrepair. This particular one didn't look or ride any worse than most of them, but it was pretty bad. After they'd hit a couple of bumps that Woods thought were going to rearrange his anatomy altogether, he uttered a mild question. "Are we this crowded so that you can cover me up, is that the idea?"

It produced another laugh. "Hey, we're going into the township at the end of the working day, Mr. Woods," John answered drolly. "Our people have to travel back and forth to work, Monday through Saturday, and there's no one I know who makes enough money to do all that in their own personal taxi."

"I seen some *preachers* who had enough money for taxis!" one of them teased at John.

"Considering what they have to do to save *some* souls, it's only right, Zeke," John retaliated. Their whole mood was one of rollicking adventure. "Our taxis get *loaded,*" John continued. "People aren't used to seeing them any other way. Most of the time we have at least six in the backseat, sometimes seven! We decided to let you travel in luxury so you could get a good look at things as we went along."

"That was thoughtful of you," Woods muttered dryly. It drew another laugh and further helped to ease his way into their confidence.

After a few more turns and some wicked bumps in the road, they pulled into a farmyard on a tractor path. Biko was standing in some bushes. He came out and pushed into the front seat. Tully, the youngest in the group, hunched up and then straddled across Biko's knees and the other front-seat passenger. There were four in the front and five in the back. John had already started backing the car out into the road again when Biko turned around and glanced at Woods. He burst into a huge smile. "You comfortable enough?" he asked solicitously. The others laughed.

"Hell, he's got the best seat," Mapetla declared.

They lurched onto the road, and John gunned the car away, Woods being leaned upon and crunched at every pitch and roll of the car. Biko was still grinning at him.

"Listen," Woods said defensively, "I was raised in a black homeland—I'm not half as uncomfortable as you think!"

"I know," Biko said gravely, "you only drive that white Mercedes because of the *neighbors*. As a liberal, if you had *your* way, you'd be riding around in buses and taxis just like us."

The others smirked at Woods and he had to smile, but he wasn't beaten. "Well, despite all the evidence *to the contrary*, you keep telling me my days of white privilege are *numbered,* so I'm just enjoying them while I can." The ironic allusion to their own pretensions brought another touch of laughter.

"Listen, we may not have all the *transportation* problems of the revolution licked," John rejoined, "but don't think that just because we're sneaking around like this, we haven't got the System over the barrel." There were a few amens.

"Oh, ho," Woods said mockingly at that bit of bravado.

"No, you listen to him, man! Listen to him!" Mapetla demanded cheerfully.

When they reached the township, the mood inside the taxi was still sportive, but they were soon caught in a long, dusty line of taxis and buses. In the deepening twilight, everything seemed to turn gray: the buildings clustered together near the rutted road; the red and black taxis, so covered in dust that they looked like moving parts of the earth; the faces of the people jammed into taxis, hanging from the sides of buses, waiting by the roadside for a friend or a father or a husband or a wife.

And the mood inside the taxi turned gray too. The thing that struck Woods most was not the mass of people all crowded and moving together—a sight absolutely unfamiliar in white South Africa where one of the glories of life was the sheer size and roominess of the country—but the all-pervasive weariness in the faces. Young girls of fourteen, muscular young men in their twenties, and of course, the old and middle-aged who had been ending the long working day in the same way year after year. There was a gray numbness in all their faces, broken now and again by a smile at some friend or acquaintance, but returning almost instantly with a heaviness and torpor that stunned Woods. He'd seen plenty of tired blacks before, sweating, laboring at jobs of all kinds. But always there were smiles and jokes, an acceptance and vivacity that he had often envied. But that was during the day. It had never struck him till now that to get to town in the early morning, these blacks would have had to get in lines like those outside the car now long before dawn, and every night they would have returned long after the sun had gone down. Day after day, year after year. He had lived among blacks all his life, but here he was, an hour from his home, and he was looking into eyes he had never seen before.

They crept through the township's main streets. Only a few of the streets were used by the taxis and buses. People walked down the little side streets, trudging to the flat matchbox houses in streams. There were little outdoor shops and some canteenlike stores on the roads with traffic, and customers crowded around them like bees at a hive, buying vegetables and fruit and bread. Oil lamps hung on posts made little yellow pockets of light in the growing darkness. And the sober black faces gathered under them suddenly seemed mysterious and even threatening to Woods. There was a sullenness to them that again was new to him. Long ago he had noted how people could have one personality at work, and a totally different and surprising one at home or at play. But this was different. It was as if the whole black world, which he felt he knew so well, had a life he was totally unaware of. And he didn't mean the externals—the dirt roads, the crowded buses and taxis— he meant the faces, the fatigue, the sullen apathy in those large, dark eyes.

They circled in the taxi, saying nothing, until most of the roads were empty, the great evening rush was over, and people had found their way to their homes. A few stragglers hurried along the dark paths, but the great, teeming mass of people that had so surprised Woods in the twilight had now melted away in the darkness.

From their silence and the way they avoided his eyes, Woods knew the others in the car sensed some of his reaction to it all. Biko had never looked back at him. He just sat with his chin in his hand, staring out the window, absorbing it, it seemed, like someone who has experienced it many times but who was affected by it each time anew.

"Let's stretch our legs," Biko said at last. John pulled the car over to the side of the road, and they all got out. It was something they needed, and their groans and stretches lightened the mood of solemnity that had fallen on them.

"Next time we'll bring your Mercedes," Dye joked as he danced up and down to get the kinks out of his legs.

"They won't let you ride in a Mercedes even when you get to *heaven*," Mapetla scoffed. "You haven't got the class."

"Little do you know, son," Dye retorted. "Give me a cigar and one of those fine suits, and even the angels will be salutin' me."

"My, my, and you haven't even had a drink," Mapetla mocked.

Biko had put his hands on the front fender and bent his lithe body up and down, first crouching, then stiff-legged. Finally he stood and looked at Woods. It was their first direct contact since they'd come to the township, and Biko's eyes were searching. He seemed to find what he was looking for, and he smiled tightly. "Let's take a walk," he said quietly.

He took Woods off the central street and back into the little side paths. John and Mapetla walked a little behind them, keeping guard. They moved along between the houses, some with electricity, some with kerosene lamps.

A pall of smoke, from small fires set up outside the houses and from wood stoves inside the houses, was beginning to settle over the whole area. They caught glimpses of meals being cooked in overcrowded rooms, a man bathing in a small metal tub, a couple of prostitutes at the side of a house talking to a man in dirty overalls. Several old men were cooking in soup cans that they placed over fires built on bricks in the little areas beside the houses. Here and there the body of an old jalopy was being used as a shelter. Twice they caught glimpses of roving gangs of youths: *tsotsis*—the black gangs that fed on their fellow blacks, tolerated by the police because they kept the townships in turmoil. Woods had never knowingly met one, but he knew of their existence, knew of their method of enforcement: a bicycle spoke in the spine that crippled you for life.

In the doorways of some of the houses, young—and middle-aged—toughs leaned against the door frames, idly watching the street, their gaze following a dog skulking from yard to yard, a cart being unloaded, and especially Woods and Biko as they moved along.

Woods took it all in, much as he had the unloading of the buses and taxis. It was a new world to him. As blacks were not allowed in the white residential areas after sundown, so, too, was there no reason for a white—other than the police—to ever visit a black township after dark. What amazed him as much as anything were the well-dressed blacks. Clerks, he imagined, office workers of some kind—male and female. He realized that when he had seen them at work in their sometimes frayed, but always neat dark suits and dresses, when he heard their crisp English, their fluent Afrikaans, he had always assumed they lived in neat little houses—poor, perhaps, but like their clothes and languages, suitable reflections of white life. Yet as he glimpsed into the houses without running water, many with no electricity, all with crude outhouses and tiny rooms crowded with people and activity, there they were, part of this strange, unknown community, just like the laborers and toughs and straggly children.

They turned a corner just in time to see a little boy peek out of one of the houses. The kid cautiously checked the street—for gangs, for danger—eyeing Woods and Biko, then running off as fast as he could for another house farther on.

Biko spoke for the first time. "Run, son, run," he said quietly as they watched the boy go. He turned, looking at the shadowed life all around them. "It's a miracle a kid survives here at all," he said, embittered. "Most of the women who have work permits are domestic maids, so they only get to see their kids a couple of hours on Sundays. The place is full of—of drunks and thuggery, people so desperate for anything that they'd beat a kid bloody if they thought he had five rand."

Woods turned from the dark, forbidding street and stared at Biko for a moment. "Was that kid you a few years ago?" he asked.

"Yeah." Biko smiled. "Except I was probably *more* scared."

"Were you raised in a township?"

"Mostly. My father died when I was still pretty young. I was taken into a mission school run by German and Swiss priests." That explained a good deal to Woods. He was going to question him about it, but Biko went on, his voice personal and introspective.

"But if a kid does run fast enough, if you do survive, you grow up in these streets, these houses—your parents try, but in the end you only get the education the white man will give you . . . then you go to *their* city to work or to shop, and you see *their* houses, *their* streets, *their* cars. And you begin to feel there's something 'not quite right' about you, about your humanity. Something to do with your blackness . . . because no matter how dumb or how smart a white child is, he's born into *that* world. But you, the black child, smart or dumb, are born into this and, smart or dumb, you'll die in it. . . ."

His eyes turned to meet Woods'. Woods could not mask the impact of those words, nor did he try.

They walked on silently for a bit, then Biko spoke again. "And even to get to stay in a legal township like this one," he continued mordantly, "the white boss has got to sign your pass every month or you lose it, *and* the right to stay here. But if he's kind enough to do that, the government still tells you which house you'll live in, how many will live with you, and what the rent is. You can never own land yourself, or pass anything on to your children. The land belongs to the white man . . . and you, all you've got to bequeath your kids is this." He gently squeezed a bit of the dark skin of his cheek.

Woods, for all his imaginative powers, had never before truly understood the emptiness, the hopeless insecurity of the black community. But Biko's words made him feel it that night—all around him . . . like something living.

# vii

THEY WALKED FOR several minutes more. Biko was clearly taking him somewhere specific. And they finally came to a house on the outside exactly like the others, but a lot of light shone from around its curtains, and as they drew nearer, they could hear the emphatic beat of African pop music. Some black men—talking, laughing among themselves—entered the house just before Biko and Woods arrived at the door. Woods glanced around and noticed four or five jalopies parked nearby. In one of them he could see some men drinking from a bottle.

"Ever been to a shebeen?" Biko asked.

"Not a black one," Woods responded.

"If they aren't black, they aren't shebeens," Biko asserted with a grin. He ran lightly up to the door and held it open for Woods. "Welcome to the real thing."

Inside Woods was introduced off-handedly to the Shebeen Queen, and she acted like she had white visitors all the time. In fact, except for an initial glance of surprise,

Woods was ignored by the whole crowded room. Peter and Mapetla got a little table in a corner, and Biko brought beer in big liter bottles, then he went off to dance with the Shebeen Queen.

Woods was amazed at the number of people who were squeezed into the little room. And the place was littered. Every corner was stacked with possessions of some kind, piled up one on another, to leave some room for business. The record player that was pounding out the music sat on a stack of blankets, cardboard suitcases, pots, pans, winter coats, summer hats, and that was the *smallest* pile.

The clientele was male. Besides the Shebeen Queen, there were only two young girls in the room. One, a seven-year-old who was dancing immaturely with someone who looked like her grandfather; the other a slightly older girl whom Woods was told was the Shebeen Queen's niece. And *she* served beer.

Several men were dancing—either by themselves or in loose but happy communion with some other guy. A small group was in a corner smoking pot by drawing it through the top of a broken bottle—a device that Mapetla told Woods enhanced the impact. Woods knew that pot had been around for years in the black community, but again, this was the first time he'd actually seen it being used.

After what he'd seen on the outside, the most distinctive impression he got from this place was the joy in it. The men drank and laughed, talked and laughed, danced and laughed, smoked and laughed. And it didn't appear to be neurotic release from the fatigue and numbness he'd seen earlier. Their pleasure seemed real and even wholesome.

And Biko was changed too. He danced with the plump but vivacious Shebeen Queen with abandon and joy. He was a lithe, natural dancer and clearly reveled in the music and the masculine showing-off that went with it. His partner was in some kind of heaven too. Despite her size, she was surprisingly supple and danced with a flare that managed to be erotic despite her amplitude.

Woods leaned across to shout at Mapetla over the din. "I had heard all Shebeen Queens were informers."

"They are," Mapetla yelled. "The police would close them down if they weren't." Woods frowned, not understanding why they were being so carefree about their own position. "Some things she informs on," Mapetla explained, "some things she . . ." And he gave a shrug and a wise smile. "Besides, she fancies Steve—he's got that way with women."

Woods looked across at Biko again. He could see the truth in that statement. "He's very articulate," he yelled at John. "How long was he with the Swiss priests?"

"He was never *in*articulate"—John laughed—"but he was with the Swiss priests about two years. His father died when he'd just turned seventeen, and they took him in then."

Woods nodded—he could see the bright young boy just at the age when he might have turned to violent rebellion, having his energies and imagination stretched by the priests in a way that wouldn't allow him easy answers, but perhaps twisting him to something that might be worse.

The Shebeen Queen's niece suddenly moved from the table where she was serving beer to a door to the only other room in the little building. It was just behind where Woods sat, and when she went in, the door was left open. Woods peered in. He caught a glimpse of stacked beer cases and more litter—clothes, wood for the stove, a cluttered dresser—but most of the room was taken up by a rickety metal bedstead. In the center of its rolling mattress an old grandmother lay with her head propped up on pillows. Her eyes were wide open, staring at Woods. On each side of her a little kid was sleeping. The woman didn't take her eyes off Woods until the niece came out again, toting another case of beer.

Woods poked Mapetla before she pulled the door closed, signaling off to the bedroom and then to the Shebeen Queen. "Do those belong to her?" he asked.

Mapetla shrugged. "I suppose. Hers or relatives'."

"*I*'d hate to try to sleep through this every night!"

"They get used to it," John assured him. "The great thing about humans, the *bad* thing about humans, is that they get used to almost anything. . . ."

Woods nodded agreement to that bit of wisdom. The number ended, and after a carefree, flattering squeeze of the Shebeen Queen, Biko sauntered to the table, picked up a bottle, and took a long swig. Still holding the bottle and breathing a little heavily from the exertion, he looked down at Woods. "I ordered champagne," he declared, "but she said they got through it all by teatime." The multiple irony in all that produced a run of sparkling laughter from John. Woods had to grin too.

"Well, nobody seems too unhappy about it," he said.

"No," Biko replied, "that's one of our gifts. We do manage to enjoy life once in a while." Still holding the bottle, he glanced back around the crowded room. "Most of these guys you see in here tonight," he said, "are living in a bed out there on their own. No work permit, no residence permit, so a man and wife who can't find work in the same white town can't live in the same black township. They've got to risk living in an illegal township or live apart. You've managed to do what even American slavery didn't do—you've split up black families so that for thousands of husbands and wives, if they see each other once a year, they're lucky."

"That's the Afrikaner government," Woods asserted defensively. "Don't blame *all* whites for apartheid."

John glanced at Biko, then turned back to Woods. "We *don't* blame you all," he said lightheartedly, "but it's left us short of women. How many live-in maids do *you* have, Mr. Woods?" The tone of the last was prurient.

Woods responded virtuously. "Only one, John."

"She married?" John asked.

"Sorry," Woods replied, nodding affirmatively.

"And how many days does she have off?" John inquired innocently, but Woods was beginning to suspect the trap. He glanced up at Biko and knew he'd been lured into one.

"A half day on Sundays, like all the other maids, right?" John continued.

Wood stammered. "Well—she—"

And John closed the trap. "If she was your wife, Mr. Woods, and you and your black kids had to be out of that white town by six o'clock at night, even on the Sunday you *could* visit, would you be mad at the Afrikaners, or the people she was working for?"

Woods wanted to make a decent reply to that, but before he could think of one, Biko interjected, "Don't pick on him, John, he's here to have a good time." He glanced down at Woods. "Come on, drink up. I'm taking you to eat with a black family you didn't break up."

The little township house Woods was taken to had been divided into four small rooms, so the central room—the one where cooking and washing and eating took place—was much smaller than the shebeen room. It was the home of Tenjy's relatives, and she was there to greet them. After

53

the introductions to the big, extended family that called the place home—the elderly father and mother, a son, the mother's sister and *her* husband and their three kids, two teenage cousins, and the niece and nephew of the old man —Woods was placed at the end of the table that had been expanded by boards and boxes to seat everyone. Mapetla was on one side of him, but Biko and John were at the far end of the table that actually had been pushed into one of the tiny bedrooms. Again Woods was struck by that clutter that no storage space apparently made necessary. Bedding, winter clothes, shoes, some old paperbacks, frying pans, pots, wooden bowls, all the stuff of living for thirteen people was piled along the walls of each of the rooms.

The meal itself was a stew served on big plates with bread and rice. There was no electricity in the house, so they ate by the light of two kerosene lamps—one hanging from the kitchen ceiling, one on the far end of the table near Biko. Despite the difficulty in moving, Biko was up and down all the time, serving people, opening beer, beguiling Tenjy's aunt with smiles and hugs every time she resisted his help. It was all very noisy and convivial. They were hungry and glad to be eating and, in the perverse way of the world, honored that a white man would be eating with them.

John had said grace before they began and his "Lord, we thank you for this food" had a meaning and impact Woods had never felt before. He had been raised in what was open country, and as far as he knew, hunger had never been a problem among the blacks, but here, he sensed the effort, the rough struggle it was just to place food on the table. When John's "Amen" was echoed quietly around the table, Woods' voice was there. Then he lifted his head and spoke directly to Tenjy's aunt and uncle. "You know, this feels like home," he said. "My father was a store-keeper in a homeland. We were often the only white family for miles."

He had felt the impulse to impress them with his liberal credentials—and it was true, of course—but what he could not bring himself to say was that never in that time had he or his father broken bread at a native's table. The closest he had ever come to that kind of experience was on summer evenings when his father would close the store and take a chair out onto the lawn and smoke his pipe and drink from a large brandy flask. He always had one glass he used for his own drinking, and one for the native men who would filter in from the darkness to form a half circle on the ground around him. As a young boy, Woods would stand behind his father's chair and listen to the men tell stories. At the time his father was considered very liberal for sharing those evenings.

Tenjy's aunt smiled at Woods. "I've never been to a homeland," she said.

"They aren't home, and the land is rotten. That's why the government is trying to get us to take it," Mapetla declared. "But the idea would be fine if they just turned it around and gave us nine tenths of the land, and left the homelands to the whites."

John and Tenjy's uncle pounded with their knives in buoyant approval of that idea. But the teenage nephew looked at them in surprise. "The Boers won all the wars against us. That's why they have all the land," he said, as though stating the obvious.

Biko turned to him in a flash of anger, but then he squeezed his way along the table, carrying a big bowl of stew. "That's what they teach you at school, is it, Tom?"

"Sure, but it's true. We *did* lose all the wars," the boy replied.

Biko dumped a large spoonful of stew on his plate. "In those history lessons, did you ever hear that the Germans and the Japanese lost the last war?"

"Course. And I read it in the comic books."

"Well," Biko said, smiling, "what more proof do you want? But they haven't put the Germans and the Japanese up on some mountaintop or out in a desert and told them that was *their* homeland, now have they?"

The boy shook his head, and Biko tousled it. "Homelands are just another way they're trying to divide us, Tom. Telling us we're not South African, we're Zulus and Xhosas and Sothos. Well, you remember, the whites are Boers and English and Welsh and German—if they want homelands, let *them* each have a homeland. You can go be a storekeeper in Mr. Woods' homeland."

The young Tom smiled.

"That's okay by me," Woods asserted. "I know I'd get a lot more credit from 'honest Tom,' here, than I ever would from Steve."

*"That* you could count on," Biko confirmed emphatically.

In the conviviality of it all, the uncle made a suggestion. "Maybe we ought to invite Mr. Woods to our football match." It produced silence and embarrassed glances all around the table. Biko finally eased it.

"Oh, I don't think Mr. Woods would betray a trust," he said. But that was the last word on the subject that day, and Woods was left to guess what it meant. As he searched the faces at the table for some hint, Biko put another dollop of stew on his plate. "Come on, eat up," he said, "it's going to be a long night for you."

After dinner the men sprawled out, John and the father in chairs, the rest of them on the floor. They drank beer and talked some more about liberals, like Woods. The women worked during it—first doing the dishes, then washing their work clothes, which were hung near the stove to dry for the morning—but they listened and interjected whenever they felt like it. Woods noted that they had to use an outside pump to get water and had to heat it on the stove. It seemed crude and tiring, but like a lot of communal work rituals the world over, the women seemed to enjoy it ... though he felt perhaps this was especially so this night when he—the visiting white—was the target for an assault by the whole group.

Mapetla began it with a marvelous description of the white man's coming to Africa. "First," he said, "this white guy comes and says, 'Do you mind if I pass through here?' And we say, 'Hell, no, man—the land belongs to God.' Then he comes back and says, 'Do you mind if I bring my wife and kids along?' and we say, 'Of course not, there's lots of land, we'll just go hunt over the hill there for a couple of days—may God help you on your journey.' Then the white man finds a spot and builds a fence around it and says, 'I'm going to settle here and farm this land.' And we shrug our shoulders and say, 'Okay. We'll just move around you, friend.' Then the white man extends his fences and says, 'Look here, every time you go by, it disturbs my cattle. Would you mind not coming this way?' And we shrug and move a little off, and then the white man gets his gun and says, 'Listen, we can't have people wandering all over the place like this. You're going to have to have a pass, so we can keep track of who's coming and going.' And all the time his ministers are preaching to us about brotherly love. So in the end, what we've got is brotherly love, and they've got all the land!"

Woods had to smile at the truth in that, just as the others did, but it only reinforced his own position. "Come on, I'm not defending the past, or even what's going on here now, but you have to recognize the value of change, of what an industrial society produces."

"For *us?*" Mapetla said incredulously.

"Okay, not for you *now*," Woods answered, and pointed to Biko, who was sprawled on the floor whittling on a piece of hardwood. "But if you'd stop listening to Steve Biko and let us liberals integrate you into *our* society, then—"

Tenjy was hauling in a bucket of water with the nephew. Like the other women, she had slipped into a somewhat frayed robe while her good dress went in the wash. She had heard Woods' last remark and bristled. "Yeah," she said, cutting in, "you want to give us a *slightly* better education so we can get *slightly* better jobs—"

"At *first*, maybe," Woods interjected, "but only at first. In the long—"

John interrupted now. "First or last. What you're saying is your society is better than ours, so you liberals are generously going to teach us how to do it your way."

Woods was flummoxed a bit by that; he believed it true, but how could he rebut it without offending? He glanced down at Biko, and Biko was wearing that penetrating, slightly amused grin he'd seen before.

"We don't want to be 'put' into your society," he said. His smile became less amused, more challenging. "I am going to be me—as I am—and you can jail me or even kill me, but I'm not going to be what *you* want me to be."

And by now there was no smile at all, and Woods could feel the frisson of tension that had built up between them.

"It's not what we *want* you to be," he replied, trying to defuse the hostility. "But you have to admit there are some advantages in our *kind* of society, like fewer white babies die in infancy than black babies, and we have more—"

"Guns and bombs and ulcers and suicides," Biko interrupted. "As well as your swimming pools and Mercedes. Your priorities have produced a world where you can blow up the whole planet if one guy makes a mistake."

"Okay," Woods conceded, "so some bad, but a lot of good, and—"

"Ours is *only* bad?" Biko cut in sharply.

"No, I'm not saying that," Woods asserted.

"When I was studying under those Swiss priests," Biko continued, ignoring Woods' protest, "I read a definition of culture. It said, 'Culture is simply a way of saying "this is how a group of people try to answer the problems of life."' Would you agree to that?"

Woods produced an ambiguous smile. "What I'd agree to is that those Swiss priests have a lot to answer for. But beyond that, yes, I'd agree."

"In your white society," Biko went on, his tone making only a small concession to Woods' effort to keep the exchange lighthearted, "when you knock on someone's door, if he's nice, he'll say, 'What can I do for you?' It assumes that people are there for what you get from them, or what they give to you. But we don't think that way. We just say, 'Come on in!' We *like* people. We don't look at having to live together in the world as some great celestial mishap that has disastrously plunged us into endless competition and rivalry."

Woods laughed—that was one way to look at the

"white" mentality. His taking it humorously also brought the smile to Biko's face that he had been looking for.

"You say you were raised among blacks," John said, taking up the argument. "Haven't you ever noticed that all our songs are *group* songs—not someone keening to the moon about being all alone and lonely in a forbidding world?"

Again Woods laughed, but he nodded quickly, saying, "Yes, yes," because it was a valid observation about African songs. He wasn't sure how much significance there was in it, but it was certainly true, and he loved John's image of whites "keening to the moon all alone and lonely."

Tenjy intervened again. With the other women, she was stringing their good clothes out to dry on a line suspended above the stove. "We know the great white powers have done wonders in giving the world industry and arms and medicines," she said, "but maybe our culture has something to give in teaching people how to live together. We don't want to lose that, just to be absorbed in your clothes, your attitudes—"

"She's right," her uncle broke in. "This is an *African* country. First let us have our place, in our way, then we will come together with our white brothers and sisters and find a way to live in peace. It cannot be just their way."

"That sounds fair," Woods answered, "but it can't be done in a vacuum, either. You can't go back; the twentieth century is marching on for all of us."

"But it doesn't have to march only to *your* time," Mapetla declared. "The best you want for us is to be allowed to *sit* at your table, with *your* silver and china, and if we can learn to do it like you do it, you'll kindly let us stay.

We want to wipe the table clean. It's an *African* table. We'll sit at it in our *own* right."

The assertiveness of Mapetla's words revealed layers of bitterness Woods had never felt before. He stared silently at him, trying to come to grips with it in his own head, when John, sensing the impact all this was having on him, touched his hand. *"You*'ll sit at that table too," he said. "We know this is your home, as it is our home. But you will sit, not as master of the house but as one of the family."

"I'm relieved you're planning to allow us to sit at all!" Woods sighed, making the most of the concession. It brought the first unreserved smiles since the conversation had started.

Tenjy's uncle poured more beer into Woods' glass. "You must remember," he said good-naturedly, "before you arrived many generations ago, we had our own culture. We had many, many villages—small, everyone known to everyone. You understand our language, you know the word we use for *nephew* is 'my brother's son.' Tenjy calls my wife not *aunt,* but 'Mother's sister.' We have no separate words for members of the family—all begin with 'brother' and 'sister.' And we took care of each other."

That thought really caught Woods. He had known this about the African tongues as long as he had spoken them, and that was since he was a young boy. When he grew old enough even to think of such things, he accepted it as an evidence of the poverty of their language, but he realized now that it was perhaps something more profound, a way of keeping the family links close, of forging that ultimate extended family that was another facet of black life he had observed from his first awareness that there were blacks and whites.

"You see those villages we lived in as primitive," Mapetla added, "but there weren't rich men and starving men in those villages. The land belonged to *all* the tribe. There were no homeless sleeping in the streets, or children living in orphanages."

And that registered with Woods too. Tenjy was removing a sweater from her father to put in the next wash, but her eyes were on Woods, and she saw that they were getting through to him. "We got a lot of things right," she said, "that your society has never solved."

Woods smiled at her. "You *did* have tribal wars, you know—in this idyllic land of yours."

"What do *you* call World War I and World War II?" Biko asked. There was a moment of silence, and then they all burst into laughter.

Woods glanced down at Biko. Behind him, in the tiny bedroom, he saw the three little ones asleep on a mattress on the floor. There was a homeyness to it that jarred with his early image of a black bigot. Biko held out the figure he had been carving. "Here," he said. "For your kids. 'African art.' I learned it when your society generously bestowed a hundred days' solitary confinement on me."

Woods took the little figure, a man with a spear at his side. "Thank you," he said. Then he glanced from Biko to the others. "You all put the words together well, but there's something about it that scares me."

"Of course there is," Mapetla responded. "In your world, everything white is normal—the way the world is supposed to be—and everything black is wrong, or some kind of mistake."

The others chorused agreement.

"And your real genius," Biko added, "is that for decades you've managed to convince most of *us* of that too."

Woods grinned, but he felt the comment wasn't the whole truth. "You're being unfair to a lot of people who—"

But Biko didn't let him finish. "In fact, our case is very simple," he said quietly. "We believe in an *intelligent* God. We believe He knew what he was doing when He made the black man . . . just as He did when he made the white man."

He held Woods' gaze, and the profundity and godlike neutrality underlying those words affected Woods more than anything he had seen that whole eventful day.

# viii

IT WAS SIX weeks before the next board meeting at the newspaper. In that time Woods had taken Wendy to the Zanempilo Clinic. The first trip was like a test of his own feelings. Would she see what he'd seen, or would she, with her rational, no-nonsense mentality, make him feel like a gullible romantic? He should have known better. She had an almost instant rapport with Mamphela and Ntsiki. She was slower to accept Biko. He was so obviously appealing physically, and he seemed master of a special relationship with both the beautiful Mamphela and his comely wife. Wendy instinctively resented the situation but was reluctant to probe into its inner workings.

When the conversation turned to Black Consciousness, Biko was always the last to speak, but his insights, his quiet confidence, and the originality of his thought swamped whatever reservations Wendy first held. She knew the world would never go back to living in villages, but she responded to the essence of what he was saying about the black approach to community life. She saw the need for grounding black dignity in black action and black thought.

And there was something else. With her piercing feminine intuition she also saw that beneath Steve's eloquence and humor lay a man deeply touched with a sense of tragedy. Whether it was for his own life, or his people's, or South Africa's, she wasn't sure, but she felt it, deep and certain. And once she'd expressed it, Woods saw it too. And, of course, it strengthened the bond growing between them.

They had a fair bit of fun learning Steve's ways of dodging the scrutiny of his "minders." At the clinic there was always someone watching the two police, so that if there was the slightest danger of their breaking in on a gathering, Steve was always forewarned and would retreat to a room on his own. When they went for a walk, either Wendy or Donald would linger about ten paces behind, so that though they were technically keeping within the regulations of his ban, they could still have a three-sided conversation. But when he was openly in view of the police, Steve always scrupulously obeyed every detail of the ban. He would not be seen with a pen on his person. He would not even take a drink of water or a cup of coffee if it meant he was with more than one person, if only for a few seconds. His principle was that if he religiously conformed to the ban in their presence, they were less likely to suspect that he was defying it in major ways when he was out of their sight.

It was during one of the Woodses' visits that Biko first suggested to Donald he should hire a black reporter. It was such an unconventional idea that at first Woods thought he was joking. Wendy did not. She not only thought he should hire a black but that it should be a black *woman*.

By the time Woods met with the board, he had convinced himself that he needed both: a woman and a man.

The board was harder to convince. What the hell would they report on? And who would care? Woods argued that they'd get new readers in the black community, and Ted Heizel, the accountant, countered that they would probably lose one white advertiser for every new black reader they got. Woods argued that the blacks constituted a big market, and advertisers would welcome a chance to influence them. Not everyone agreed with him. In a vote, Woods felt it might go against him, even though the heavyweights were now supporting him. For the others, he didn't know which angered him most: the lack of faith in him, or the smugness of their belief that black news couldn't matter unless it involved a riot or more action by the government. He let them move onto the next bit of business. When it was over, he suggested that anything less than a unanimous decision on the new staff would undermine the effort. He felt they should vote on it, but with the clear understanding that he regarded the issue as one of principle, and even a single vote against it would force his resignation.

The next day he came to the office late. The staff were all briskly at work when he entered, with Tenjy and Mapetla on his heels. They both acted as resolute as he did, but he knew that both of them were tense with fear and expectation as they followed him into this all-white citadel of power and influence.

People stopped to stare at them in mid-sentence, midword. Julie Davenport, his society editor, spilled coffee all over her desktop and didn't even notice it till long after the little procession had entered Woods' office.

Ken Robertson was perched on the edge of Woods' desk, reading some copy, when Woods pushed in the door. Ken lifted his head to speak but stopped with his mouth open.

"Ken," Woods said crisply as he hung his jacket on the back of his chair, "this is Tenjy Mtintso and Mapetla Mohapi. They're from King William's Town, where we met a few weeks ago, and I'm glad to say the board has approved their appointment to the staff."

Ken looked at Woods blankly. He stared at Tenjy and Mapetla. They were both dressed in their best clothes, but there was no doubt, they were black. Like everyone else, he'd heard there had been fireworks at the last board meeting, but no one had guessed this!

Woods grabbed the phone while watching Ken's awkward greeting to Tenjy and Mapetla. "Ann," he said, "I want you to call Bob and tell him I'm sending two new employees up for payroll registration, and then would you come in and show these people to his office?" He hung up and turned to Ken. "I want you to brief them on our copy rules," he said. Ken had still not recovered, but he numbly nodded compliance. Ann came in. "Ann, these are our two new reporters, Tenjy and Mapetla. Show them around, please, after they're finished in personnel."

"Of course," Ann murmured, looking at him for some sort of further explanation.

It wasn't forthcoming. Woods simply turned back to Ken. "When they've had a look around, I'd like you and Bob to teach them how to use our press cameras." Tenjy and Mapetla were being ushered out of the office by Ann, and Tenjy turned back to say thank you. Woods waved his hand dismissively, like no thanks were needed. He went to his desk and started checking his mail and telexes. Ken lingered. Woods looked up at him. "I'll put something on the assignment sheet for both of them tomorrow," he said.

Ken stared at him a moment. "Okay," he muttered absently, then moved closer. "Ah, excuse me, boss, but—ah —*where* will they be working?"

Woods looked up at him matter-of-factly and gestured to the large area outside the glass walls of his office. "In the newsroom."

Ken nodded. "The newsroom. Of course. Who would have thought anything else?" Woods smiled. Ken shook his head. "Tell me," he asked, "does this Biko practice black magic as well?"

This time Woods' smile was more tentative, and his answer came more slowly. "I'm not certain," he said reflectively. "But I think this is worth a try. They're going to cover black news. Things we've never covered before— weddings, music, sports, crime. There's nothing illegal in that, and we'll pick up a lot of new readers."

"Oh, I'm sure the white readership will be delighted! And when they start writing about Black Consciousness . . ." He opened his hands to the heavens. "Whoopee!"

Woods grinned. "Don't worry," he said. "Just remember that my blue pencil still determines what goes in this paper."

Ken was on his way out the door. "Of course it does— *baas,* sir." He bowed from the waist and started to shuffle his way into the newsroom.

"Ken!" Woods called. Ken stuck his head back in the door. "You like football, don't you?" Woods asked. Ken nodded, a little baffled by both the question and the big grin on his boss's face.

* * *

It was two weeks after Mapetla and Tenjy had started working on the paper before Ken discovered the real meaning behind that question. Woods had told him not to make plans on Sunday, then had him come to a rendezvous point off a side road way out in the country. When he arrived, Woods signaled him to pull his car off the road, next to his. Five minutes later a black taxi arrived. Mapetla and Dye were in it. They squeezed Woods and Ken into the backseat between them. Ken was baffled and a little bit apprehensive.

"Where the hell are we going?" he demanded. "Should I have let my next of kin know that I might not be back?"

"You're going to a native football game," Mapetla answered. "The only danger you'll be in is losing your faith that the whites play the best soccer in this country." His whole manner with Ken showed that their relationship had come a long way in the two weeks since Ken had first laid eyes on him.

Ken looked at Woods. "If you'd told me, I'd have worn my East London Pirates' scarf."

"Oh, if you did that, I'm not sure I could guarantee your safety," Mapetla chimed in. "Our boys are pretty loyal."

Both Ken and Woods knew there was a whole world of black sport in South Africa and that loyalties ran high. Though you would never read about it in the papers or see it on television, they had their own football leagues, cricket leagues, and rugby leagues, but because the pass and residency laws stifled the easy movement of blacks to any part of the country, there were no great national black teams. A star might evolve in one area and even gain enough fame for whites to have heard about him, but because there was no way for a black sportsman to get training time or first-rate coaching, their sports remained very much "amateur." The sides were always local, and everyone in the black crowds knew the players as members of the community, so there was fierce loyalty and lots of fun at the matches . . . as well as occasional fights.

Mapetla had timed it so they got to the grounds after most of the fans were already in the stands. The stadium was not large, but it had been built in a natural bowl that allowed for about ten rows of spectators on each side of the field. People stood at both ends and sprawled on the embankment.

Mapetla paid for the taxi and then hurried Woods and Ken along with the other stragglers heading for the entrance. They got a few questioning looks from people, and then three tough-looking men stepped in front of them, their legs spread, clearly ready to keep them from going in. One of the men put up his hand. "Excus: me, *baas*. Can I help ya?" he asked.

Mapetla moved forward with Dye. "It's all right," Mapetla said, "they're friends of Steve Biko."

The tough looked at him with narrowing eyes. "Biko?" he said coldly. "He's in King William's Town, he's got nothin' to do with this game." Some more toughs were gathering. There seemed to be a ring of them around the stadium, acting as stewards.

"Listen, man," Mapetla protested, "you're not to worry. These whites, they—" And he stopped because John Qumza was running over to them from the entryway.

"G. P.! G. P.!" he shouted, and the tough turned to him. "They're okay," John called. "Steve asked them to come!"

G. P. turned back to Woods and Ken, but he remained skeptical. John drew alongside. "Hi, Mr. Woods," he said, then appealed again to G. P. "Come on. If they were informers, they wouldn't be wearing white skin. And if they were the System, they wouldn't be waiting for anyone's permission."

G. P. still didn't seem totally convinced. He reached out and grabbed Ken's camera. *"They* may be all right," he said, "but *this* ain't!"

For a moment John was at a loss. He did think it was stupid of Woods to have allowed Ken to bring a camera, but then, they didn't really know what was happening. "Mapetla," he said, "run the camera over to my car. He's right, it's not a good idea." He tossed Mapetla his car keys and pointed off to where it stood. That seemed to satisfy everyone, and G. P. and his two colleagues stepped aside to let Woods and Ken pass, though they still eyed them with distrust.

They could hear someone talking on a loudspeaker as they neared the entryway. John hurried them on. "A native football game is one place where you normally would never catch a white," he explained. "So if somebody can take care of the blackjacks one way or another, you can have a pretty large private meeting!"

They'd entered the grounds, and Woods and Ken could hear the speaker clearly now: ". . . and sure, sure as hell, he's paying some of our people to stir up trouble between us!" Woods didn't recognize the man as he stood in a flowing gold-and-brown robe on a platform right in the middle of the crowded stands, but he would have recognized his name if he'd seen it written. For this was Mzimbi, a black leader sought for by the Security Police because he was an open advocate of violent revolution.

The two teams were already on the field, warming up as he spoke, and some of the crowd was watching them, but they were all listening.

"And why does the white man pay them?" Mzimbi continued. "Because when we fight among ourselves, when we get one tribe going for another, he can say, 'See! They aren't fit to run their own lives!'" There were some cheers. John was leading Woods and Ken up the steps of the stands to a place near the top. With Mzimbi across the stadium, and the teams out on the field, their movement only caught the eyes of a few, but those few looked at them with alarm and suspicion.

"And once he gets us fighting among ourselves and our friends overseas see it," Mzimbi went on, "why, then, he can convince them that he should go right on telling us *where* to live and *how* to live!" Again there was a kind of angry assent in the round of applause. Woods and Ken took the seats John had saved for them and tried to look as inconspicuous as possible.

"He can go on keeping us out of the best jobs," Mzimbi continued. "He can go on paying us less for doing the same job as a white man. And he can go on passing his laws without listening to *one word* we say!"

Again the angry applause. Ken glanced at Woods; his expression seemed to say, "What the hell have you got me into!" Woods smiled. He was listening attentively.

"And you remember," Mzimbi demanded, "that they killed over four hundred black students last year!" Now it was not applause but a roar of anger that greeted his words. "So we've got to stick together!" he shouted. "As one people, we've got to make the white man know his free ride on the back of black labor is over!"

People were standing in the stadium now to applaud him. Ken glanced at Woods again and shook his head in wonder.

Mzimbi kept the cadence of his speech going right over

the applause. "And if the only way we can get the message to him is to make him know he can never sleep in his big white bed in his big white house and know he's safe—*then so be it!*"

It was his climax, and the crowd roared. Mzimbi took the applause, raising his hands in triumph. Woods looked around him—he knew that Biko advocated nonviolent change—and he wondered how he would deal with this crowd, inflamed as they were. Finally Mzimbi signaled the crowd to silence, and people began to sit back down. "Now, we've got a surprise for you," he said. "He's a little modest—but you listen to what he has to say!" Then, with one wave of farewell, he turned and disappeared into the crowd, protected by a phalanx of guards.

For a moment there was silence, then a disembodied voice came over the loudspeaker. "This is the biggest illegal gathering I have ever seen!" the voice pronounced. It drew a surge of approval and laughter. Woods recognized Biko's voice immediately, but he couldn't find him in the crowd. Everyone was peering around, trying to see where the voice was, and a few were muttering, "It's Biko, it's Steve Biko."

"I heard what the last speaker had to say, and I agree—we're *going to change* South Africa!" There was a shout of approval.

Mzimbi was being spirited away from the grounds in an old Renault, four of his aides with him. He heard the shout of the crowd and felt assured that Biko wasn't going to kill the impact he, himself, had made.

In the stadium, Biko's voice carried on, "All we've got to decide is the best way to do that! Believe me, the white man is not invincible!"

The words drew another roar of approval. Woods and

Ken were still looking for him, but Ken was listening too. "I'm sure glad you brought me," he muttered under his breath. Knowing Biko's beliefs, Woods was not worried. He saw that with humor and an appeal to the new South Africa, Biko had skillfully taken over the crowd—and, given the power of Mzimbi's speech, that was no easy thing to do.

"One thing we can do," the loudspeaker blared, "is attack him where he's strong. We can do that—it is in our power, and he knows it."

"There!" Ken exclaimed, pointing off to a section of the stands to the right. And Woods saw him, Biko on the very top step, John Qumza and Mapetla on either side of him, others crowded around.

"But as angry as we have the right to be," Biko continued, "let's remember we're in this struggle not to kill *someone* but to kill the *idea* that one kind of man is superior to another kind of man!" His genuineness, his personal, one-to-one tone of delivery had sobered the crowd altogether. Even the players on the field were beginning to stop their warm-up and were sitting or standing, some sprawled on the ground, listening.

"And killing that *idea* is not dependent on the white man. We've got to stop looking to him to *give* us anything." There was a ripple of applause. The crowd was with him, but they really didn't know yet where he was taking them.

"We've got to fill the black community with our *own* pride," Biko went on. "Not something he *gives* us but something we make out of our own lives!" Woods glanced at Ken now, forcing an acknowledgment that he was getting something other than what he expected. Ken shrugged noncommittally.

But if he didn't have Ken, Biko had the rest of the crowd. He wasn't speaking in the old shibboleths that could get an automatic response, he wasn't appealing to vengeance or bitterness; he was saying something they hadn't heard before, and they were listening in a way that let Biko leave large silences between each thought, letting them sink in.

"We've got to teach our children *black* history," he continued, "tell them of our *black* heroes, our *black* culture, so they don't face the white man *believing* they're inferior."

And now the crowd did react, applause ringing around the stadium. Not cheers and shouts but steady, purposeful affirmation.

"*Then,*" Biko declared forcefully, "*then* we will stand up to him in any way he chooses. Conflict if he likes . . . but an open hand, too—to say that we can both build a South Africa worth living in. A South Africa for equal men—black or white. A South Africa as beautiful as this land is, as beautiful as *we are!*"

There was a second of silence and then an overwhelming response, cheering, applause, whistles, a stamping of feet that would not stop. Woods was standing and applauding with everyone else. Ken stared at him in amazement but finally stood and, with a perfunctory hand clap, put himself with the rest of the crowd.

# ix

THE SAYING AMONG the black revolutionaries in South
Africa is that if you get any three blacks together, one of
them will be an informer for the government. That is an
exaggeration that reflects a somber truth. There are so
many ways to bribe informants in South Africa, not just the
negative threat of arbitrary arrest and imprisonment, or the
threat of losing your job, but positive inducements, like a
work permit for a son or daughter, or a residency permit
for your wife, or the promise of a better job.

It was small wonder, then, that the meeting at the football grounds became known to the Security Police. It took
them a little longer to identify the principal participants,
but within days Biko's minders were told to bring him in to
the King William's Town police station.

The informant's great fear is discovery and subsequent
revenge. So the police had developed a crude but effective
way of masking the identity of those whose information
they used. When Biko was brought into Captain De Wet's

office, he was held in a chair that faced a six-foot-tall cardboard box, the kind used for refrigerators. There was a single slit in it, and through that slit Biko could just make out a pair of eyes set in black skin.

"That's him," a voice said from within the box. "That's the one who made the speech."

De Wet stepped in front of Biko, and the informant moved out of the box from the rear and disappeared in an interior corridor. When the door slammed to mark his departure, De Wet smiled slowly down at Biko, then crossed his office and closed the outer door. Biko knew this was probably the prelude to a very "physical" interview. He spoke quietly, but his tone was as minatory as the presence of the two detectives at his shoulders. "You know I don't advocate violence, De Wet, but don't make the mistake of treating me without respect."

De Wet walked back to face him again, the smile on his face going very sour. "Don't you tell me what to do, *kaffir*," he said slowly. "Out of your banning area, talking to a crowd . . . you won't be a *witness* at that trial, you'll be up there on the stand *with* your friends. Inciting racial hatred."

Biko scoffed. "On whose word? What's his name?" He nodded toward the cardboard box. It took some of the menace out of De Wet's expression, who suddenly seemed a little unsure. "Captain De Wet," Biko went on with a dangerous familiarity, "you aren't going to send me to a Pretoria court on the 'evidence' of a paid informer in a cardboard box, are you?" De Wet didn't speak and Biko smiled. "Everyone knows that kind would say whatever you wanted them to say."

De Wet paused, absorbing that, then he bent his head so he was almost at eye level with Biko. "You're a bit of poison, Biko," he drawled. "And I'm going to see you're put away."

Biko's smile was almost friendly, but there was a recognizable touch of disdain in it. "Not on that kind of testimony," he said. "Hell, we don't want you looking like a fool."

De Wet's rage was piqued. He swung his fist right for the center of Biko's face. But Biko shook free of the hands on his shoulders and caught the blow with the speed and force of the natural athlete he was. *"Don't,"* he said with a controlled fury equal to De Wet's.

The two detectives grabbed his arms and pulled him back, tight against the chair. Biko didn't resist, but his eyes remained fixed on De Wet's, and the anger in them was either a challenge or a threat, depending on where you thought the power lay. De Wet felt it lay with him. He glanced at the two detectives, and they held Biko more firmly. De Wet backhanded Biko across the face with a blow that snapped his head to one side and brought a flush of blood to his mouth.

Biko pulled his head back, letting a trickle of blood ooze down his chin, but his eyes still held De Wet's, though now with a look of stoic resignation. De Wet was finally satisfied that Biko understood who was boss in this building. He signaled the two detectives to stand easy, and they relaxed their hold on Biko's arms.

At that instant, Biko sprang up and backhanded De Wet as viciously as he had been backhanded. De Wet was flung across the room, saved from a fall only by the cardboard box, which crumpled as he lurched into it. The two detectives were on Biko immediately, wrestling him back across the room, one of them pulling a blackjack.

"No! Wait! No, man, don't beat him!" De Wet shouted

in Afrikaans. It stopped the detectives. De Wet's nose was bleeding; he took a handkerchief out, pressing it against his nose, tipping his head back, trying to stanch the flow. Slowly he moved back across the room. "He has to go to that trial," he said between daubs to his nose. "We don't want it to look like anything happened to him." He finally came face-to-face with Biko, his head still held awry. He studied Biko with cold hatred. "You're lucky, Biko— lucky," he said.

Biko was still being held forcefully by the two detectives. "I just expect to be treated like you expect to be treated," he asserted, without responding to the hatred in De Wet's voice.

"Treated like a white? You and your bigheaded ideas," De Wet responded.

Biko grinned. "If you're afraid of ideas, you'd better quit now," he said.

"We'll never quit," De Wet growled.

The detectives were holding Biko tighter and tighter, but he remained smiling and struggled to speak. "Come on," he said, "don't be afraid. Once you try, you'll see there's nothing to fear. We are just as weak—and human —as you are."

For a second De Wet didn't understand, but then the "inverted" idea struck home. He turned back, his enraged face moving closer to Biko's. "We're going to catch you red-handed some day," he threatened. "Then we'll see how 'human' you are."

He wanted the depth of hatred underscoring that threat to be clearly understood by Biko. He wanted him to live with it, live with that promise of revenge every day and night of his life. When he felt that Biko clearly understood, he signaled scornfully to the detectives. "Throw him out," he said. Biko was dragged through the station and pitched forcefully out the side door into the alley.

It was an entirely different Steve Biko who took the stand two weeks later at the court in Pretoria. The trial had been a long time in preparation. Two years earlier, two organizations Biko had been instrumental in founding, SASO (the South African Students' Organization) and BPC (the Black People's Convention), had organized a rally in support of the new government in Mozambique. The South African government had recognized that new government and accepted that the time of Portuguese rule in Mozambique was over, but they banned the rally and arrested a group of Black Consciousness leaders who were associated with organizing it. For a long time they were held in detention without charge, but finally a group of charges was drawn up against nine of them that rested primarily on the allegation that they were inciting racial hatred. It became clear from the beginning, however, that it was Black Consciousness that was on trial. Biko was called as the leading witness for the defense.

When he took the stand, he was dressed in a conservative suit, a tie, and an immaculate shirt. As he was sworn in, his presence and bearing put him on a physical level with anyone in the courtroom. His mental stature was to be tested by the state prosecutor and by Judge Regter. The prosecutor began his cross-examination by quoting from the charter of SASO, the student organization Steve had founded. "I quote: 'I believe that South Africa is a country in which both black and white shall live together.' Those are your words. What do they mean?"

Biko's response was without hesitation. "It means that I, and those gentlemen in the dock, believe that South

Africa is a plural society with contributions to be made by all segments of the community." There was a little stir of response in the gallery of the courtroom at the fluency and content of his reply. Wendy, seated in the white section, glanced across to the black section, where Ntsiki and Mamphela were sitting. They exchanged a smile. The prosecutor would soon find he had a "native" on his hands whose mental agility would stretch the best of barristers.

The prosecutor was a little surprised, himself, but he had been warned about Biko and he was supremely confident that he would be able to best him in any prolonged encounter. "I see," he replied dryly. "Are you familiar with the language in some of these documents the accused have discussed with black groups?"

"Yes, since some of the documents were drawn up by me."

"Ah, by *you*," the prosecutor said, seizing the opportunity. He lifted one of the pamphlets. "The one 'noting with concern and disgust the naked terrorism of the government'?"

"Correct."

The bald directness of that seemingly self-incriminating answer took the prosecutor by surprise and drew a kind of collective intake of breath in the courtroom. Wendy and Ntsiki both felt a quiver of apprehension. When he recovered, the prosecutor chose to press the point. "You say, 'naked terrorism'? Do you honestly think that is a valid statement?"

"I think it is far more valid than the charge against these men."

*"Really?"*

"Yes, *really*," Biko answered. His mocking of the prosecutor's patrician hauteur brought a flash of fire from the latter's eyes, but having made the point that he wasn't to be toyed with verbally, Steve answered the question for the court. "I am not talking about *words,*" he continued, "I am talking about the violence in which people are baton-charged by police, beaten up. I am talking about the police firing on unarmed people. I am talking about the *indirect* violence you get through starvation in the townships. I am talking about the desolation and hopelessness of the transit camps. I think that, all put together, that constitutes more terrorism than the words these men have spoken. But *they* stand charged, and white society is not charged." Again the answer brought a hushed response from the whole court-room.

But the prosecutor was more prepared. "So your answer to this so-called 'naked violence' is to provoke an answering violence in the black community?"

"No. Our movement seeks to avoid violence."

And the prosecutor was convinced he had him trapped. "You write here that your 'true leaders have all been imprisoned in Robben Island or banished in exile'?"

"Yes."

"Who do you mean by your 'true leaders'?"

"I mean men like Nelson Mandela, Sobukwe, Govan Mbeki."

"Is it not true," the prosecutor said triumphantly, "that what each of those men have in common is a call for black *violence!*"

"What each of those men have in common is a willing-ness to struggle and fight against our plight as *black people!*" Biko responded. There was a chorus of support from the black gallery, but Judge Regter cut it off with a sharp rap of his gavel.

"So you agree with all of these men?" the prosecutor persisted.

"I agree that their concern, their sacrifices, for the support of black people have gained them the natural support of all of us. We may disagree with some things they did, but we know that they spoke the language of the people and will always have a place of honor in our minds." There was a murmur of assent from the black section, which Judge Regter cut short with a frown.

"And you say you disagree with their call for violence?" he asked.

"We believe that there is a way of getting where we want to go through peaceful means. There are alternatives, but we have accepted that we are going to take this particular course."

The prosecutor seized another pamphlet and held it high. "But your *own words* call for direct confrontation."

"That's right. We will not accept society as it exists in South Africa. We *demand* confrontation."

The prosecutor stared at him; he was giving him his case. "In short, you 'demand' violence?"

"No," Biko replied calmly. "You and I are now in confrontation, but I see no violence." There was a titter of laughter. The prosecutor was nonplussed for a moment.

In the hiatus, Judge Regter leaned forward. "But nowhere in these documents do you say that the white government is doing anything good."

Biko turned to him respectfully. His attitude to Regter, who clearly seemed intent on conducting a fair trial, was much less defiant. "It does so little good, my Lord, that it is not worth commenting on."

There was laughter. Regter glanced up at the courtroom with severity. Wendy was one of many who was trying to keep the smile from her face. Regter turned back to Biko, not with the prosecutor's attitude of attack but with genuine perplexity. "But despite that belief, you still think it is a government you can influence nonviolently?"

"Yes, sir. I believe that inevitably this government will listen to black opinion. In my view, it is buying time. Mr. Vorster can postpone some problems and say—well, the colored issues will be solved by the next generation. But I believe that as the voice that says no grows, he is going to listen; he is going to accommodate the feelings of black people—"

"In short, when that happens, you will then confront Mr. Vorster with a decision of war or peace?" the prosecutor said, cutting in.

Biko turned back to him. "Yes. But we are not interested in armed struggle. In fact, the whole process of bargaining is then damaged. We believe we have interpreted history correctly, that the white man is going to eventually accept the inevitable."

Again the prosecutor seemed at a loss, but Judge Regter was still seeking to understand. "But surely an approach that accuses the government of 'naked terrorism' inflames racial hatred and anti-whiteism?"

For the first time Biko hesitated a little before answering. He wanted Regter—and the court and the press—to understand, to really understand. "My Lord," he began, "blacks are not unaware of the hardships they endure. They don't need us to tell them what the government is doing to them."

There was a titter of laughter, and Biko smiled, but his face and voice quickly regained their solemnity. "What we want to do is to tell them to stop *accepting* those hardships, to confront them. I think our central theme about black society is that it has elements of a defeated society. A society that has lost hope in its ability to shape its own destiny.

But we believe people must not just give in to that. They must find ways, even in this environment, to develop hope."

The whole courtroom had turned silent. As Biko continued, he was, he knew, speaking to more than just Judge Regter. "Hope for themselves . . . hope for this country. That is the point of Black Consciousness. Without any reference to the whites, to try to build within ourselves the sense of our own humanity . . . our legitimate place in the world. . . ."

His own humanity, his own dignity, filled the silent courtroom. What began as an attack on Black Consciousness had become a platform for its most articulate spokesman. The next day, papers all across the country carried excerpts of the exchange. Woods printed the whole of Biko's testimony.

# X

THE NEXT BOARD meeting was not easy for Woods. A number of advertisers had been lost, but Woods was able to point to a big increase in the readership and an income thirty percent higher than the previous year's. But Biko was a banned person, and it was against the law to quote him at all. In the case of the trial, Woods argued, the situation was ambiguous because it *was* legal to quote from court testimony. Since so many papers had done it, he was certain the government would not go through the embarrassment of attacking any particular one. But despite his arguments, the board felt his policy was endangering the very life of the paper. The chairman summed it up when they closed: "I think you sense the mood of this meeting," he said. "Our responsibility is to the paper, not to some private crusade—however sympathetic we might be. The paper is thriving now, but if you slip on that score, you'd better recognize that your bank of goodwill with this board has already been used."

John Briley

Woods was angry at the pressure but determined to take it philosophically. It was, after all, the usual thing. If he succeeded in an attack on the government, they were "damned proud" of the paper. If he failed—well, they had warned him. But what he *had* done without their really recognizing it was establish a regular role for Mapetla and Tenjy, and a place for black news that was accepted by the staff and the readership.

Tenjy did one article on the community center they were putting together in King William's Town. It brought a flood of gifts from blacks and whites. Steve called Woods to thank him and to say they didn't know what they were going to do with all the stuff. "Well, find some place for it," Woods joked, "because Wendy's on her way over with another carful right now."

"Don't worry, we'll find a home for it," Biko assured him, "but it's amazing what a little positive thinking can do."

"Be careful, you'll be talking like a liberal soon."

"Oh, no," Biko replied. "It's going to take more than a few pots and pans and a secondhand refrigerator to do that to me."

That night, Dilima, the elderly man who was acting as nightwatchman in the old church in King William's Town, was disturbed by noises outside in the yard.

He had been sleeping on a truckle bed in the room used for sewing classes. He sat up and listened closely. He was certain. Someone was trying to jimmy the front door. Kids, he bet, who had heard about all the new gifts. He swung out of the bed and slipped on his trousers, shoes, and a shirt.

There was a sudden loud crash, and the front door of the

church was pushed open. Dilima started to utter a shout of warning but held back when he saw three hooded men push in. They carried crowbars and looked frighteningly big. Dilima pulled back into the shadows. Another hooded man joined the first three. He issued an order in Afrikaans, then joined the others in smashing everything in sight.

Terrified, Dilima inched his way to the side door. The hooded men were going for everything, windows, the partitioned walls, typewriters, dolls, the pottery furnace. It looked like they were trying to reduce the place to rubble.

Dilima picked his moment and slid out the door, closing it softly behind him. He was shaking with fear and didn't know what to do. His first thought was for the telephone in Steve's office shed, but as he moved toward it, he saw that three men were smashing the shed up too. One of them came out and started for the side door of the church. Dilima ran softly into the fronds of the massive old tree, then stealthily pulled himself up into the first fork.

He could see a hooded man in Steve's office pull the telephone from the wall and smash it against the toppled desk. The man who came out first stopped almost below Dilima. He was breathing heavily from exertion. When the other two men came out to join him, he pulled his stocking hood from his sweating face. Dilima recognized him immediately. It was Captain De Wet of the Security Police!

When the other men came to him, De Wet spoke in Afrikaans, sending them in to help the others in the church, then he walked toward the road, where Dilima could see two cars standing at the curb.

The next day, Donald and Wendy were summoned by Steve. He was not at the church when they arrived, but Mamphela and Ntsiki were, along with Father Kani, a black priest who had become one of Biko's most ardent supporters. The church itself was a shambles. People were trying to sort through the wreckage to find anything that was not beyond repair. But the hooded men had done a thorough job. Anything of real value had been smashed to bits.

Woods was numbed by it, but Wendy was furious. She was helping to clean up, but she could see that once they got it clean, it would just be an empty shell again. "Who do you go to when the police attack you?" Ntsiki said glumly to nobody in particular. Wendy stopped and looked across to Donald. He was leaning against a shorn partition pillar, staring angrily into nothingness.

"Donald," Wendy said forcefully, "go to Kruger. He's the Minister of Police, and he's told you personally that he'd fight police illegality. Well, take him up on it!"

Mamphela was trying to make some order out of file papers that had been tossed in all directions. She laughed at that suggestion. "Kruger? He'd probably give them a medal!"

Woods shoved off from the pillar, doing what he always did in moments of indecision, lighting a cigarette. "Come on, Mamphela, cabinet ministers may have their prejudices, but they don't condone this sort of thing."

"Don't they?" Mamphela said scornfully. "I'll bet you he'd find an excuse for it if you did take it to him."

Father Kani, who was as discouraged as the others, turned once more to Dilima. "You're positive it was Captain De Wet?" he asked. Dilima looked a little uncertain, and Father Kani rephrased it in Xhosa, and now Dilima responded positively, nodding his head up and down. *"Ndimbonile!"* he asserted. "I'm *positive.*"

Woods puffed out smoke disconsolately. "Where's

Steve?" he asked irritably. At least he might have some ideas.

"He went to the clinic," Mamphela answered. "He wanted to draw off the Security Police. He didn't want anyone seeing Dilima talking to you."

"Well, that was probably smart," Woods conceded. "But I can't print what happened on the allegations of someone who can't testify."

"You mention Dilima's name," Ntsiki said, "and he will never make it to court."

"I'd be surprised if he made it to the end of the week," Mamphela added.

Wendy had heard enough. "Donald, fly to Pretoria! If you go to the police here, they will only laugh at you. But you can't just let this happen without doing something."

Woods stared at her uncertainly.

"Do it. *Go!*" she said.

Woods didn't even take an overnight bag. He'd called Kruger's office, and Kruger agreed to meet him at his home on Saturday.

It was a little past noon when the taxi pulled up to the gates of Kruger's home. It was some way outside Pretoria, and the grounds were huge. Woods expected a guard or two to be posted at the gate, but he walked in unchallenged. He wandered up the long, winding drive, taking in the lawn and gardens of the spacious estate. When he neared the house, he looked back and could see nothing but rolling hills on all sides. There wasn't a sign of other human habitation. He knew there must be housing for blacks tucked away behind one hill or other, because some of the land was being farmed, but from the house all you could see was an endless vista of beautiful South African countryside.

He turned back and approached the door to knock, when suddenly a voice disturbed the quiet of the hills. "Ah, Mr. Woods, you found your way." Woods turned, and Kruger was standing on the pillared porch that jutted from one wing of the house. He was in slacks, an open shirt, and carpet slippers, holding a drink. Two little dogs had appeared with him, and they bounded across the lawn, yapping for attention from the stranger. Woods bent down, allowed them to sniff his hand, and petted them a little.

He looked back up at Kruger. Kruger was heavyset, but in his relaxed, informal attire he appeared comfortable rather than frightening. "The Minister of Police," Woods said, "and I walk right into your grounds—and not a soul in sight." He gestured to the empty grounds.

"Oh, perhaps not in sight, but if you weren't expected . . ." He lifted his eyebrows; the gesture was jovial enough, but it suggested something dire nonetheless. "Come in, come in," he added convivially. "I was just having a drink. Will you join me?"

He led Woods into his study. It was a large, comfortable room decorated with a number of sports trophies and one or two autographed Springbok pennants. The books that were in the two bookcases lining the far wall had the battered exteriors of books that are read rather than merely displayed. Kruger walked over to a large drinks trolley.

"Well, what will it be?" he asked.

"What are *you* drinking?"

"I'm on whiskey myself."

"That'll be fine," Woods replied. "I want to thank you for seeing me at the weekend."

"Ach, it's nothing, man. I always like to help the press

CRY FREEDOM

if I can. What is it you wanted to see me about?" He handed Woods his drink. *"Gesundheit,"* he toasted.

*"Gesundheit,"* Woods returned. They each took a sip, and Kruger gestured Woods to a chair as he plumped into his own generous armchair.

"It's a matter concerning Steve Biko," Woods began.

"Biko?" Kruger exclaimed. He put his glass down in comic consternation, crossed his legs, covered his face with both hands, and lifted his feet off the ground, rocking back and forth. *"Mein Gott,* man, I know all *about* Steve Biko!"

Woods smiled politely at the routine, but he persisted. "Why is he banned?" he asked. "He's committed to non-violence and you need a black leader you can talk to—and, I can tell you, he *is* such a leader."

"Look, Mr. Woods, I know you mean well, but I promise you, we have *reason* to ban Mr. Steve Biko."

"If you have, then why not charge him in open court?"

Kruger looked at him, assessing his seriousness, his purpose, then he leaned forward confidentially. "Listen, I don't need to tell *you,"* he said, "that this country has a special kind of problem, and we have to do certain things we don't like to do. Shit, man, do you think I like banning and detaining people without trial? I'm a lawyer—these things go against the grain." A sudden idea took hold of him, and he touched Woods' arm, "Come, come . . . I want to show you something, Mr. Woods."

He stood up and led Woods into the hallway at the far side of the room. One wall of the hall was decorated with framed photographs—a family history. The oldest pictures were on the left, and they progressed chronologically along the hall toward the main entrance. Woods was led to the first group, an old picture of a family gathered around a

Conestoga wagon, probably taken in the 1860s or 1870s, then a homestead farmhouse, three quarters completed, a group of men working on it, posed among its beams and sidings, and three women holding milk buckets nearer the camera.

"We Afrikaners came here in 1652," Kruger began, "two hundred years before there was such a thing as a camera, and yet look at this"—he pointed to the old photo of the Conestoga wagon—"the trek across the wilderness, the homesteading"—and he moved along the hall—"the concentration camps the English put our wives and children in during the Boer War." Woods had seen such pictures before. They looked exactly like the pictures of concentration camps in World War II—starving children and women, skeletons with a cover of waxen skin. One of the hardest things about being of English descent in South Africa were those reminders of the concentration camps and the thousands who had died in them. That was how the Boer War was won. The English never defeated the Boer guerrillas, but the men could not keep on fighting with their families dying in the camps.

Kruger had moved on past some photos of the Boer guerrillas to some shots of a small town, muddy streets, a man and two boys standing proudly before a hardware store. "The working of the land, the building of the cities," Kruger said as his hand passed swiftly on to pictures of a farm in the 1920s, then a huge orchard with a '33 Ford touring car in the foreground, holding two men and three girls who were seated on the folded top. The pictures went on to a youngish man in a rugby uniform, who was standing, holding a ball, the rest of the team gathered around him. Woods could recognize the young Kruger, though, in fact, there were uncanny family resemblances in the whole long sequence of photographs.

Kruger waited as Woods glanced at the last few pictures, one of which was of the house they were now in. "Remarkable," Woods said. "A treasure for any family to have."

"Let me assure you," Kruger responded, "*any* Afrikaner family could show you the same thing. We didn't colonize this country, Mr. Woods. We *built* it." He held Woods' gaze, letting it sink in, then he tapped a picture on a table in the main entrance hall. "Grandfather Johannes," he said, "a formidable drinker." He went on to the main entrance, but when he reached the door, he turned and faced Woods. There was no aggression in his manner or his voice, just a profound sincerity.

"Do you think we're going to give all that up?" he asked, gesturing back to the pictures. "That's what Mr. Biko wants. This is a black country, he says. *Gott!* What's here was made as much by Afrikaner blood and toil as it ever was by the blacks—who came to *us* for work. Remember that. We didn't force anyone to labor."

Woods had always known the Afrikaner argument, but never before had it been put to him so sympathetically— and by, of all people, the Minister of Police. "No," he said with an understanding smile, "you didn't force anyone to labor, but the blacks had very little alternative, since you'd taken over most of the land. And wouldn't you say their cheap labor has had something to do with the success of our economy?"

Kruger huffed, but it was not derision; it just implied it was an argument he had heard before. He opened the main doors, revealing again the spectacular grounds and vista. From this angle one could see that the house overlooked a large lake that filled one valley on the horizon. Kruger led Woods out on to the lawn. "I know what you're saying," he conceded, "and don't think I don't understand their argument. I do." He gestured toward a garden table with a number of chairs around it. "Here, let's go sit in the shade."

"We know there has to be a way to work together," he said, "and live together, and we're trying to find one. Maybe a little too slow to suit some of them, but it's no good your Mr. Biko filling them with false expectations. We're not just going to roll over and give all this away."

In one sense, the setting made it hard to deny the strength of his position. But in another sense the almost regal splendor of it, when juxtaposed to life in the townships, made the threat of revolution seem more real to Woods than ever. The contrast with his own house was bad enough, but this!

Kruger leaned forward again, confidentially; it was obviously one of his mannerisms. "Listen," he said in a hushed voice, "trust me, I know a lot more about Mr. Steve Biko than you do, Mr. Woods. Now, is that what you wanted to see me about?"

"No, sir," Woods started, but Kruger never let him finish. He sat back, petting one of the dogs who'd followed them out, and went right on talking.

"But if that's your recommendation," he said, "if you really think it's worth it, I will certainly consider it."

"Thank you, Minister," Woods answered dryly. "I do think you would find it worth your time. But I've really come about an incident at a sort of community center Biko was trying to put together. It was smashed up the other night and—"

Again Kruger cut him off. *"Ja,* I know about that, my police are investigating it."

"Your police are the ones who *did* it!"

Kruger was in the act of raising his glass to his lips. For a second he froze, not looking at Woods, not seeming to react at all, then he took a sip of his drink and turned to Woods very calmly. "What makes you say that?"

Woods was a little thrown by his reaction. Did he know? Did he not believe it true? "An eyewitness saw a local police captain and some of his men smashing the place up."

"Will he testify?" Kruger asked coldly.

"He's afraid to," Woods answered, "and I felt it would be more effective if *you* took some action internally. You've always stated you were against any illegality by your officers."

And Kruger's attitude shifted back to his former friendliness. "Ach, and by God I am!" he declared. "And I appreciate your most helpful attitude, Mr. Woods. I assure you I'll pursue this. I want no thugs in my department."

Now it was Woods who was surprised. The vehemence and resolve in Kruger's response truly impressed him. "Well, I—that's it," he stammered, feeling it was all a little too easy and rather anticlimactic after his long trip to Pretoria. "I thank you," he continued, "and I won't take up any more of your weekend." He finished his drink and stood.

"Ach, thank *you,* for the way you've handled this unpleasant business," Kruger responded. As they moved toward the center of the lawn, Kruger's fifteen-year-old son came around the house, wearing tennis gear and carrying an armful of tennis rackets. He looked at Woods and nodded politely, then turned to his father. "Will you still be able to play tennis, Papa?"

"*Ja*, of course," Kruger replied amiably. "Johan, this is the editor of the *Daily Dispatch*, Mr. Donald Woods."

"I'm happy to meet you," the boy said courteously.

"Did you come by car, Donald?" Kruger asked.

Woods was surprised by the sudden use of his first name. "No, sir, by taxi."

"Ah, I'll drive you back to the city."

"No—no," Woods protested. "You have your game of tennis. If you'll just call me a taxi, I'll—"

Kruger would have none of it. "It's no trouble, man. We have all afternoon for tennis; besides, the dogs want a ride." He had taken his car keys out and rattled them, and the dogs instantly started jumping at his legs. Woods was amused. It made a nice picture, the relaxed patriarch, the polite son, the spoiled, affectionate dogs.

"This is very kind of you," Woods said as they moved on toward the drive in the rear.

"Ach, Mr. Woods, we're not really the monsters we're sometimes made out to be." And at that moment Woods believed that assessment was probably right.

Sunday afternoon, Wendy was resetting some flowers in the little patio off the kitchen and Woods was reading in the living room when the knocker on the door was banged forcefully. Charlie started barking and raced for the door. "It's all right, Evelyn," Wendy called. "I've got it. Charlie, get back here!" she scolded. When she opened the side door from the patio, two men who were standing at the front door turned to her. Their clothes and manner made Wendy think they were salesmen. "Yes," she said, "can I help you?"

"Mr. Donald Woods—is he available?"

At that moment Woods opened the front door. He was carrying a part of the paper, his glasses down on his nose, and he was a little annoyed at being disturbed. "I'm Donald Woods," he said curtly.

"You made a complaint to the Minister of Police?" the senior of the men, Fred Lemick, half declared, half questioned.

And Woods smiled. They were from the police. "It's all right, Wendy," he said. Wendy took Charlie by the collar and pulled him back into the patio. "That was *prompt*," Woods said. "I only saw him yesterday. I didn't—"

"You had a witness to the alleged crime," Lemick cut in.

"Yes. I explained to Mr. Kruger that I couldn't name him, but there was definitely a—"

Again Lemick cut him off. "You reported a crime, Mr. Woods, and the law states you must name the witness."

Woods, who'd been pleased at the minister's promptness, suddenly realized he was going to have to deal with some literal local policeman who was going to require half the afternoon in just getting the basic facts straight. "I said that I told—"

"You must *name* the witness—or you'll go to prison," Lemick insisted with impolite abruptness. "That is the law."

It was too much for Woods. Local buffoon or not, this man was offensively pushy. "I'd hate to go back to Kruger," he said angrily, "simply to report that you—"

Lemick smiled and cut him off again. "Report to whoever you like," he said smugly. "Our orders, Mr. Woods, come from the very top."

For a moment Woods just stared at him. What did he

99

mean, "the very top"? Then it began to dawn on him. "Kruger?" he muttered dumbfoundedly.

Lemick smiled. He was now in charge. He glanced back at the other detective for confirmation. "I didn't say 'Mr. Kruger,' I said, 'from the top.' " He turned back to Woods, and from his smirking confidence Woods knew who the order had come from and was furious at the cold-blooded betrayal it implied. He glared at Lemick and started to close the door. "The next time he sends you," Woods declared bitterly, "you'd better have a warrant!"

Lemick was unmoved. "The law is on our side," he said confidently.

"Yes, well justice is on *mine,*" Woods retorted. "We'll see how we make out in court!" He started to slam the door but caught himself and turned back to Lemick. "Oh, and tell Mr. Kruger he must come to *my* house for a whiskey someday!" He glared at Lemick again and *then* slammed the door.

Nothing happened for several weeks and Woods assumed the minister had decided that prosecuting would make him look less than honorable and had abandoned the idea. Woods printed a long article by Tenjy and Mapetla on the damage done to the church by "vandals." It produced another flood of gifts even larger than the first response. There were some gifts of money as well, and gradually the partitioning was replaced, along with the pottery oven and a few sewing machines.

Woods made time on Thursday afternoon to go out and see how they were doing. As he left the paper, a process server was waiting and handed him the envelope from the court.

That afternoon was a scratch rugby day for a bunch of

blacks. Most were unemployed, but a few had been let off from work for the match. There were no spectators—until the very end of the match when a sole white figure on the hillside overlooking the field watched the final play. It started with a scrum, the front lines of the two teams locked, shoulder to shoulder, in heaving competition. Their uniforms were a mishmash of personally owned gear, but even with them muddied and sweaty as they were now, you could make out that one side wore shirts with hoops of some kind, the other side a vertical stripe, though the color and the width of the hoops and stripes varied wildly.

The ball was finally heeled back from the scrum by the hooped scrum halfback. He fed it to the center, and the defense began to spread across the field. The center drew a tackler and then fed out to the flanker. No amount of dirt and sweat could disguise that the flanker was Biko. His face bore a grin that combined pleasure, deviltry, and determination. He faked off a tackler who was almost on him when he took the ball, then ran at the defense, breaking one tackle, swinging loose from another. He had speed, strength, and cunning, and he reveled in the chance to display it all. He dodged between two safety men, changed pace to leave the fullback standing, darted toward the sidelines to give his own backs a chance to get in position. He twisted free of another tackle and raced on but was hit hard as he neared the touchline. He held the ball till the last second, then passed off to a winger. The striped tackler who brought him down rose quickly to give chase, but Biko grabbed his leg and pulled him back down again. The tackler twisted and kicked out at Biko. "God damn you, Biko," he shouted as he kicked again, "they ought to keep one referee on the field just to watch *you!*" Biko laughed and let him free—much too late. But the hooped winger had been brought down short of the touchline, and the whistle blew for the end of play.

The two teams broke up with some friendly pushing and some handshakes, but as they started for the sidelines, one or two spotted the witness to their play and gave a hushed warning. "Steve! It's the System!"

They all saw the figure in silhouette against the skyline now. Another voice gave a command. "Get around him, get in the middle, Steve—put your arms around his shoulder." Another player, farthest from the white man who was looking down at them, said, "Just keep in a bunch till we reach the truck, then Steve, you slip away."

"I'll go talk to him, keep him busy," another voice offered.

But as they moved along, Steve felt certain he recognized that silhouette. Finally the figure started to move along the edge of the rise. The way it moved convinced him he was right. "It's okay," he said quietly. Then, with even more certainty, he repeated it loudly. "It's okay!" He broke the loose grip they had on him and advanced toward the hillock.

As he came forward the figure called out, "You're a dirty player, Biko!" As Steve expected, it was Woods' voice.

"I was taught by a Catholic priest," Biko called back. "What do you expect?" As he came closer to the rise he could see the top of Woods' car. "Are you alone?" he asked.

"All alone," Woods answered.

The others had been looking around warily, but this convinced them. They straggled on toward a bread van parked a little off the field, where a young boy was taking water and beer out of the back.

"Who told you I was here?" Biko queried.

"Your wife," Woods answered. "She didn't say where the *police* thought you were."

Biko poured some water over his head and grabbed a bottle of beer. "We planted a phone call saying I was going to spend the afternoon going over the books at the clinic, then I sneaked off in the bread van." Smiling, Woods just shook his head at it. "Want a beer?" Biko asked. "Sure," Woods replied, and Biko tossed him one. Woods had come down the hillock, almost to where the players were gathered.

"I got my summons today," he said weightedly. "They're actually going to prosecute."

Biko looked at him in amazement. Woods smiled. "I think they're trying to break up our friendship."

Biko got one of those wise grins on his face as he studied Donald. "I don't know," he said dryly. "A few months in jail might be just what you need to prove your credibility as a budding activist." Some of the players laughed, but Biko lost his grin, and his look challenged Woods. It seemed to say, "If it came to prison, would you really stick by us?"

Woods sensed the challenge in that expression and tried to state his feelings, first logically, then personally. "Don't worry," he said. "My old law professor, Harold Levy, is going to defend me. He'll outwit anyone they've got." This was already a concession because Biko knew that Woods usually defended himself against charges brought by the government. Then he added soberly, "I'm not going to name Dilima—whatever they do." For a moment he let his conviction speak for itself, then he raised the beer bottle to Biko. "But Kruger obviously means business," he said, and took a long drink.

"Hell, he's always meant business against *us*," one of the players chimed in.

"Someday *we'll* be the damn System in this country," another player snarled. "Then watch out!"

Biko smiled and sprawled on the grass near to where Woods had found a spot to sit. He took a drink of beer, then glanced at the man who spoke last. "A lot of us are going to die for nothing, Tom, if our System turns out to be nothing but a black version of theirs."

"I could live with that," the player who had tackled Steve on the last play said. There was a mutter of agreement and a few amens. Biko grinned and stared out across the field. So often he found that blacks only wanted to be where the whites were, and then they'd do exactly what the whites were doing.

"A bent policeman is a bent policeman, Soga," he said quietly. "He breaks the same heads for the same reasons. To substitute a black one for a white one isn't worth the price of one child. . . ." It hung in the air for a moment, then he leaned up on one arm and nodded toward Donald. "Never mind six months in jail for Mr. Woods!"

The irony drew smiles all around, but the change in mood left no doubt that he'd made his point.

Biko's living quarters were in the township area of King William's Town. It was the standard size, but since the government wanted to keep an eye on him, he, Ntsiki, and the children had the tiny house all to themselves. One night, about a week after Woods had received his summons and a court date was set, Biko was working late on an article for the SASO Newsletter. It would be printed under the byline "Frank Talk." Peter Jones would smuggle it out once he'd finished it.

In the midst of it, Ntsiki whispered a sudden warning. Steve stopped his writing. They both listened tensely. "There's someone out there with a flashlight," she said quietly as she went to the window and carefully peeped out. Almost the instant she did, there was a loud rapping on the door. Steve hurriedly gathered up the papers he had been working on. Ntsiki took away the ink and pen. According to the ban, he was not permitted to write anything, not even a letter. There was another impatient rap on the door. "Get that article by Mapetla," Steve whispered, then pulled his shirt out of his pants and mussed up his hair. The rap became a heavy pounding and stirred up half the dogs in the township, setting them all off barking.

Steve opened the door slowly, looking very sleepy-eyed and drowsy. He left the latch on. What he saw was not reassuring. Lemick, the worst of the local detectives, was facing him. Behind Lemick were Steve's two regular minders. "Yes?" Steve grumbled, licking his lips as though his mouth were dry from sleep.

"We have reason to believe you are in possession of subversive documents," Lemick said briskly. "We have orders to search these premises."

Biko looked at him coolly, nodding his head at it all, then he lifted his eyes and smiled at the two regular Security Police. "They're keeping you boys up late," he said sympathetically.

Lemick was annoyed at the seeming familiarity between them. "Just *open the door!*" he ordered.

Biko stifled a yawn. "Do you have a warrant?" he asked. Lemick was annoyed at his cheek, but knowing Biko's reputation, he had taken the precaution of getting a warrant. He smiled acidly and pulled the double-sheeted document from his breast pocket; he held it up, waving it beneath Biko's nose. "Good," Biko said in the same sleepy manner. "Well, just bring it to the window over there and I'll read it." And he shut and bolted the door.

For a moment Lemick stared at the flat door in silent dudgeon. He didn't want to seem impotent in front of the two security men, but he decided he'd just look foolish if he told them to break the door down. Sighing heavily, he walked to the side window.

In the house, Biko made a quick search, found another paper, and gave it to Ntsiki, who now had their youngest son in her arms. Biko went quickly to the window, but when he opened it, his face bore that same sleepy air. It was a latched window, where the top pane swung out. Biko had to stand on tiptoes to put his head in it. Lemick was standing impatiently on the uneven ground below the window. "I'll need your flashlight," Biko said to one of his minders.

The man stepped forward awkwardly and threw his flashlight onto the warrant. "Okay," Biko yawned, "will you hold it up?" Lemick grunted, but he held the warrant up. Biko glanced over at the minder with the flashlight. "Just a little closer," he said. The man moved in, throwing the light on the paper. Biko scowled in the effort to read and pushed his head a little forward, apparently studying each word.

Behind his back, Ntsiki had put a rough diaper on their bed, putting the papers flat on it. Then she rolled the sleeping Samora over. He already had a diaper on. Ntsiki lifted him gently onto the papers in the "extra" diaper. Samora moaned in his sleep but didn't awaken.

At the window, Biko's head was still moving back and forth across the lines, apparently reading each word carefully and slowly. He reached the bottom of the first page and looked up at Lemick. "Fine," he said. "Just turn the page, please."

Lemick glared at him. He was suffering from the sheer physical discomfort of holding the warrant up, but he flipped over the page. "Could you read a little faster?" he said sarcastically. Biko glanced at him, then bent again to the paper, his head moving across the page one word at a time but appearing to do so at the greatest speed possible.

Behind him, Ntsiki cleared her throat in signal that she had finished. She picked up Samora with his double diaper and held him against her shoulder.

Biko finally nodded his head and sighed. He'd finished it. "Well, it's all in order," he said, "but you won't find any such papers in my house."

Lemick folded the warrant and stuffed it back in his pocket. "We'll see," he said caustically.

Steve started to close the window. "All right," he said. "As soon as my wife's properly dressed, I'll let you in." And he closed the window.

Lemick was furious. He glared at the two regulars and stormed for the door. He circled before it impatiently for a few seconds, then pounded on it vehemently.

Biko opened the door slowly, his finger to his mouth. "Ssssssh," he said. "Don't wake the boys." Lemick reacted like most people do to that caution, and though he glowered at Biko, he stepped into the room quietly. The two minders practically tiptoed in.

Quietly, irritably, Lemick fanned the two regulars out to search. There was not much to investigate. There was only one kerosene lamp burning, so they used their flashlights to search a wooden bookcase, the cooking utensils, a wood stove, the beds. They even pulled the covers off the sleeping Nkosinathi, ran their hands under his mattress. He hardly stirred, but Lemick was beginning to smell defeat, and he threw the covers back over the boy in pique. Ntsiki bent down stoically, still holding Samora, and pulled the covers from Nkosinathi's face. Lemick looked around angrily, trying to reason where the papers might be hidden.

"I told you you wouldn't find anything," Biko said with a bit of steel in his voice.

Lemick stared at him, his frustration sitting darkly on his countenance. He turned his eyes to Ntsiki and the boys, and Biko sensed he was thinking of doing something gratuitously vicious; he immediately tried to disarm his anger.

"It's a crime they send you people out on these wasted missions. It's bad for morale," he said sympathetically.

Lemick turned back to him, not knowing if that was sarcasm or not. But Steve sounded sincere, and he was acting like someone who was forced to suffer through this with them.

Lemick sighed irritably, and signaled the two regulars out. He followed them but stopped in the doorway to issue one last threat. "We'll be *back*," he said firmly. His eyes swept the two rooms again, then he started to slam the door, but Steve nodded to the sleeping Samora in Ntsiki's arms and put his finger to his lips. "Sssssssssh . . ." Lemick stopped himself and closed the door quietly.

Steve turned. Ntsiki was weaving with laughter she could hardly suppress. Steve grinned at her. Suddenly her expression changed and she looked down at Samora. She patted his diaper. "I think we'd better rescue these," she whispered. And they both had to fight to contain their laughter.

\* \* \*

At the paper during these weeks, Mapetla and Tenjy had proved themselves both as reporters and people. With one or two exceptions, the whole staff had come to like them, and they had moved in some instances from covering solely black subjects to general news. Mapetla, for instance, now attended the City Council meetings with a white reporter, and often the final account was solely from his typewriter. Tenjy was great at feature articles. She did pieces on schools and children and local history that crossed right over the racial barriers.

So when Mapetla suddenly came into his office and told Woods he had something he wanted him to see, Donald was willing to give up the half day Mapetla said it would take. At Mapetla's suggestion they brought Ken along, Mapetla feeling that Ken's work with the camera was always superior to his own.

They picked a Thursday afternoon. Ken drove, and they went several miles north before Mapetla had Ken turn off on a dusty side road. They had driven along it about forty minutes more when Mapetla leaned forward and tapped Ken's shoulder. "It's just ahead," he said.

Woods and Ken both strained to see. They could make out a mass of some kind on the right side of the road. But the terrain was very dry, and the buildings, or whatever they were, were so covered in dust, they looked like part of the landscape.

"Slow down," Woods commanded, and Ken gradually let up on the gas. Mapetla had asked them not to question him about the place until they saw it. Woods now felt they should know what the hell they were doing. "What is it, Mapetla, tell us," he demanded. They could now make out that the "buildings" were tents, and that a tall barbed-wire fence surrounded the whole settlement.

"Well," Mapetla began, "you know that when the System picks up people without work permits, they say they are shipped to a homeland. Usually it's a homeland they've never seen before, but anyway, that's where they're going. On the way they're put in 'transit camps.' I'd never seen one, and I figured you probably hadn't, either."

They had now reached the gate area. A black soldier was the only one on duty, but there was one large tent where some other soldiers were lounging. Beyond that, the camp spread out for acres. There wasn't a tree in the whole area. Everything was covered with dust, the tents, the people, even the barbed-wire fence that surrounded them. "How did you find it?" Woods asked.

"A friend told me about it," Mapetla answered. "I didn't really believe him. Then, when I saw this one, I found there were two others within about fifty miles."

"Will they let us in?" Ken asked.

"Sure," Mapetla stated ironically. "They're not ashamed of it."

Ken pulled the car into the gate and stopped. The soldier on duty approached the car on his side. "We're just here to look around, is that all right?" Ken said.

"Yes, sir," the soldier replied. "You just park over there by the sentry's tent and I'll call Lieutenant Heyman to say you're here."

Mapetla rolled down his window. "We don't have to wait for him to arrive, do we? The last time—"

"Oh, yeah," the soldier cut in. "You was here the other day, I remember you. No, you don't need to wait, just take a look around. The lieutenant, he may come and talk to you if he feels like it. You still workin' for a newspaper?"

"That's why I got a white chauffeur," Mapetla responded, and the soldier laughed like it was the best joke he'd heard in years. He waved the car on, and Ken pulled into the shade of the sentry's tent.

They walked slowly through the camp. After his first look into one of the tents, Woods seemed numbed by it. His gait was slow enough for a funeral procession. The tents were simple and small. They sometimes contained six cots—all covered in dust. People stretched out on them, or sat on them, their little pile of possessions collected in a dusty heap beneath the cots.

What affected Woods was not so much the conditions as the look on the people's faces. There was almost total lethargy and despair. Even the children sat and stared—at them, or at nothing, as the blistering sun shone down. Even one person moving along the dirt paths between the tents sent up a little cloud of dust.

Though they saw several mothers cradling sickly children, there was no evidence of starvation, and at one spot there was a soup line where people waited without tension or anxiety as the line moved forward. No one seemed worried about getting to the big cans before they were empty, but the hollow-eyed men and women exuded a sense of despair such as Woods had never seen.

"This is what they do with 'surplus' blacks," Mapetla stated. "The homelands are too poor to take them in, so these transit camps were set up. Some of these people have been here so long, they don't think they'll ever see a homeland or a city again. Their only hope is that maybe the white man will need them for some job and they can go back to a township."

Ken was taking pictures as they moved along. Even here kids made little "cars" out of twisted bits of wire and pushed them back and forth between the tents. He shot a picture of one. The two kids playing with it stood up, throwing their shoulders back, to have their pictures taken. Ken yelled, "Smile!" and they both broke into huge grins. They were the only smiles they saw in the whole camp.

About every three tents, there was a latrine that smelled in the heat and buzzed with flies, but there were buckets of lime near them, and Woods could see that basic sanitation was taken care of. What one did about the flies was another matter.

One answer was provided at the end of the camp. It was a large field, and as they approached it, they could see some toys on little mounds of earth. On the path, peering between the tents, it looked like half a dozen small toys, one of them a twisted metal "car." "What is it?" Woods asked Mapetla.

"It's a graveyard," he responded. As they drew nearer, they could see that some of the mounds contained little feeding bottles, some just a nipple covered in dust. When they got past the tents, they could see that there was row after row of the little mounds, each with some carved "toy" or some other memento of a child's life. As the three of them stood there, dumbstruck at the sheer number of them, Mapetla spoke.

"There was a nurse here, giving shots, the first day I came," he recounted. "She said they do all the right stuff medically, but the infant death rate in these transit camps is about the highest in the world. Some say it's lack of proper food"—he paused, looking over the rows of little dusty mounds—"and some say it's because the parents have given up." He turned to look at Woods. "Take your choice."

Woods' face was taut. Water had seeped into the eyes of the imperturbable Ken.

Before they left, Lieutenant Heyman appeared. He was a crisp, young Afrikaner, filled with figures about the numbers he had to care for, the daily cost of food, the lorries required to bring water. All in all, he thought they were doing a damn fine job. Woods could see he had never once in the smallest degree questioned the propriety of what he was doing. He had an assignment, a few men, a tight budget. He was fulfilling his duty as well as any man could be expected to. He and his wife lived in a small town nearby, and even that was a sacrifice because there was very little there for a young couple socially. Asking him what a young, old, or middle-aged black couple could do "socially" in his transit camp would have been like speaking Greek to him. Ken did ask him if his men were rotated, and he answered, "Frequently. The duty is so boring, and the heat is quite a problem."

Woods thanked him, and they piled into the hot car and started back for East London. No one spoke for a time. Then Mapetla said quietly, "I'd like to do an article on it. Would that be all right?"

"Yes," Woods said somberly. "That will be all right. You do your article," he continued rigidly, "and we'll use Ken's pictures to make a four-page section of it." For the rest of the long journey home they hardly spoke again.

# xi

THE FEATURE ON the transit camp had one effect that
Woods could see. Lieutenant Heyman was removed from
his post. Not in order to reform the camps, of course, but
to teach young lieutenants that talking to the press was not
within their province. Woods thought there might be another summons for him, but it didn't materialize. What did
please him were the number of letters he got from whites,
Afrikaners as well as others, deploring the fact that such
places could exist. The most telling bit of the piece was a
low shot Ken had made across the rows of little graves
with their mementos stuck in the dusty soil. Letter after
letter attested to people "crying for those little children." It
confirmed Woods' belief that few whites outside the government had any idea of what life was like for the blacks.
As Biko had said, "Forty-two years old, a newspaperman,"
and what had *he* known six months ago? Woods was convinced that if the ordinary whites did know, things would
change. Not miraculously, but for the better.

One saving grace were the courts. Woods' trial came up, and he was faced with a prison sentence of six months for not naming Dilima. If at the end of the six months he still refused to name him, he would get another six months, and so on until the end of time or the end of Donald Woods, whichever came first.

He would not deny having some trepidation, but his confidence in Harold Levy was almost total. Harold had looked at the situation and felt they could make a grand philosophical argument and perhaps come up winners, but the more certain way was to treat it purely legalistically. Which is what he did. And the outcome raised even Donald's opinion of him.

The Woods and the Levys were going for a celebratory dinner, and Woods was already dressed when the trouble began. He was in the living room mixing himself a drink and telling the two middle children, Duncan and Gavin, about his day in Court. Jane and Dillon were playing cards in the den, but listening, too, with a little less credulity than their little brothers. Donald *was* dramatizing a bit.

"So at that moment," he said theatrically, "the prosecution finished their case, and the whole courtroom thought I was as good as in jail."

"Does that mean you're going to prison, Dad?" Gavin said excitedly. Duncan poked him.

Woods was about to conclude the triumphant story, but Charlie's sudden growling at the back door distracted him. He took a step into the kitchen but couldn't see anything, so he simply said, "Shut up, Charlie," and went back into the living room. "Well," he said, "that's what *they* thought, I was going to prison. But then Uncle Harold began his cross-examination. He started on the charge itself. It wasn't the proper wordage, the dates were all wrong..."

He moved to the kitchen door again because Charlie's growling had grown more fierce.

Wendy was still upstairs in the bedroom, finishing her makeup. She could hear Charlie's growling and went to the window to see what it was all about. Some stray cat or something, she suspected. But when she got to the window, she could see two flashlights moving around on the path near Evalina's room. The room was set apart from the house, as most black servant quarters were. There were steps down to it from Woods' patio, and it could also be reached by a path to the garage. That's where the flashlights were. They moved right to Evalina's door. There was a pounding, and her light came on. Evalina opened the door, and in the light Wendy could see two policemen.

Downstairs, Woods had given up on Charlie and was continuing his story. ". . . and besides the dates being wrong, all the precedents they'd cited, one after another, he showed applied to totally different situations. In twenty minutes not a word of the charge was left—"

He stopped when he heard Wendy's high-heeled footsteps clambering down the stairs. "Donald!" she shouted. "It's the police! They're after Evelyn!"

Woods put down his drink and raced to the hallway. "It's the police!" Wendy repeated. "They're at her door!" Jane had come rushing out into the hall too. Woods grabbed her by the shoulders and turned her to the stairs. "Go up to Mary—quickly!" Dillon followed, and Woods pointed his finger back to the living room. "You keep those two in there. Go on, I'll handle this."

Woods went to a cupboard, reached up, and opened a top drawer. Charlie was now barking madly, absorbing tension from Woods and Wendy. Wendy screamed at him, "Charlie, be quiet!" But her voice grew even more panicked when she saw that Donald had taken a gun from the drawer. "Donald, what are you doing?"

Woods ignored her and headed for the back door. Wendy grabbed at his arm, Charlie circling the two of them, barking furiously. Woods turned and freed her grip. "Go in to the boys!" he commanded. "And take Charlie!" She almost grabbed him again, but he pulled free. She got Charlie by the collar and made one more pleading effort. "Donald!" she cried. But he was out the door.

When Woods came storming across the patio, the two policemen turned up to him with gloating pleasure. They'd heard the dog, heard the voices shouting. They knew they'd upset him and the household. When Woods saw that expression, it was like another goad to him. "What the hell are you doing here?" he yelled, and closed the distance between them, standing right at the top of the stairs to Evalina's room, pointing his pistol at the senior policeman. Officer Nel was not about to be bullied, either.

Evalina, terrified, pleaded desperately to Donald, "It's all right, Master. It's all right."

"We want to see her passbook," Nel said belligerently. "Our right, Mr. Woods."

"At this time of night?" Woods demanded.

"It's all right, Master, I'll get it," Evalina interjected.

Nel was still facing off with Woods. "This time of night is when they have their boyfriends in," he said suggestively.

Woods shook the gun at him. "You're talking to a *married* woman, you bastard, and I resent—"

"*Master,* I *find* it!" Evalina screamed hysterically.

Woods just looked at Nel. The gun was still pointed at Nel's face, and in Woods' eyes was all the anger that had been seething in him since he'd first turned his focus from what South Africa was to a white man to what it was to a black man. "I suggest you *leave!*" he demanded, snarling at Nel.

Evalina had started frantically looking around her little room for her passbook, hoping to bring an end to this madness. As usual, when she was frightened, her asthmatic wheeze almost stopped her breathing.

Nel was losing some of his confidence in the face of Woods' fierce aggression, but he knew he was in the right, and he had been given very explicit instructions about the Woods household. "We have asked this female Bantu—" he began defiantly. But he got no further.

*"Woman!"* Woods shouted. "She's a *woman*, not a female Bantu! You think you're talking to an animal?"

Nel stepped back from the pistol that was pointed at him, but he and his younger partner were beginning to get angry themselves. They knew how much power they had. The younger man, thick-armed, thick-necked, started tapping his nightstick against his leg, his hand clenching and unclenching the handle in his eagerness to act. Woods turned to him, looking from the nightstick to his face and back again. "You've seen too much television," Woods said scornfully. "You tap that stick one more time and I swear I'll—"

The young man leaned forward and was about to reply, but Woods clicked off the safety catch on the pistol and turned it on him. The anger in Woods' face seemed insane, and the young policeman looked at him as you would an armed madman. He took a step backward.

Evalina had found her passbook and she came to the door but just stared, wheezing at the sight before her. Nel sensed that the moment of greater danger had passed, and he tried to reassert his authority. "We are allowed to ques-

119

tion Bantu *anytime,"* he declared. "It's our job. There may be an illegal male in—"

Woods' gun swung to him again. "You're on my property!" he said with enough rage in his voice to convince Nel that he was wrong, the danger wasn't over.

"You think you're a big editor who can get away with—"

Woods cut him off. "I think I'm a man who's found two intruders in *my* backyard!" He took another step down toward Nel, and Nel decided Woods was too irrational to deal with in this way.

"Come on, Kobus," he said to the younger man. "We'll see about this!" He took the path out toward the garage. He turned back to say something to Woods, but Woods was half following them. "Go on, piss off!" he taunted, waving the gun again, but now the aggression had gone out of it.

He turned back to Evalina, who was just standing in her doorway, staring at him in astonishment. "And I want you to tell Sipo to bring the children here whenever he can!" he said firmly.

"Yes, Master," Evalina mumbled quickly. She was still dumbfounded by a side of him she'd never seen.

Woods walked up the steps toward the house, and Wendy came running out the kitchen door. She put her arm around him. "You're crazy, Donald Woods," she said wonderingly. "A crazy, insane man!"

"I'm also shaking like a leaf," he said, putting an arm around her waist to steady himself. "And if you let go of me, I think I'll fall flat on my face." Wendy laughed and kissed his cheek. "They're trying to intimidate us," he said. "We can't let them do it." Wendy hugged him tighter and opened the kitchen door, where Charlie was waiting, his tail wagging excitedly.

* * *

The next day, the police took their revenge. Ken saw it all, even got pictures of it. It was mid-morning break time. He had bought some ice cream for himself and Doreen, the prettiest girl in the typing pool. They were walking along the street leading to the *Dispatch* building. Ken had turned to scoop some of the ice cream from her cup onto his plastic spoon. "Come on," she scolded flirtatiously, "if you wanted strawberry, why didn't you get it?"

"Ah, but if *I* got strawberry, you wouldn't get a chance to taste *my* chocolate," Ken returned. He was walking half backward, so that he faced her. "I'm just being considerate," he said with a smile that responded to the flirtation he saw in hers. "I'll take a little bit of yours, and you—"

He stopped. Over her shoulder he saw an unmarked police car—they were always black Chrysler Valiants—swerve in toward the curb, just in front of Mapetla. Three plainclothesmen jumped from the car. Two of them grabbed Mapetla, and the third held off the two blacks who had been walking with him. Ken had tossed away his ice cream, taken his camera from where it hung on his belt, and raced into the street to get pictures of the abduction. Mapetla, too startled to react, had been slammed into the backseat of the car before he realized what was happening to him. One of the policemen pointed an admonishing finger at Ken, and a driver who had almost run into him honked his horn furiously, but Ken kept right on taking pictures until the police car had sped away and turned at the first corner.

Woods debated with himself a long time before deciding not to run the pictures. The police were well within the law. They had the right to arrest any black for questioning. But more importantly, he had to weigh what the move meant in terms of his own conflict with them. He had just had two "victories" over them, one in court, one in his backyard. If he splashed Ken's photos all over the front page—and they were dramatic enough to justify that—it might lead them to be much harder on Mapetla. An issue of pride was at stake, and he felt it was best to let them have this "victory" and save his fire for a time when they were attacking someone or something less vulnerable than Mapetla.

Later that night, after Jane and Dillon had gone to bed, he related the whole incident to Wendy. They, too, were getting ready to go up. Woods had fixed himself a nightcap, and Wendy was turning out the downstairs lights. "What do you think they'll do to him?" she asked.

"Oh, I suppose they may beat him up to scare him off the paper and let it go at that," Woods replied. "But it's more pressure they're putting on, and I'm afraid they may try to make an example of him, so no other black will dare come near me." Wendy was already halfway up the stairs, and Woods was following. Both of them were startled by a loud knocking on the door. Charlie came bounding out of the boys' room and charged past them, barking furiously.

"For God's sake, shut up, Charlie!" Woods exclaimed. He could see the silhouette of someone standing at the door. He glanced up at Wendy—another move by the police? He went back down, put his drink on the table in the hall, and walked slowly to the door. As he got nearer, he suddenly recognized the silhouette and opened the door hurriedly. "Steve!" he whispered. Biko went quickly past him, and Woods glanced around outside, saw only one car, then closed the door. "What the hell are you doing?"

Steve had bent to pet Charlie but turned now to face Woods. "I want to know about Mapetla," he said gravely.

Woods nodded his understanding but signaled him nervously into the living room.

"God . . ." Woods sighed. "Steve, I don't know—traveling into a white area at night . . ." He shook his head.

"This is *my* country," Biko replied. "I go where I like." It was not bravura, just the statement of a man who will not bend on certain principles. Woods admired it but was appalled by it too.

Wendy had come down now, and she just stood in the entrance of the living room, staring incredulously at Steve. When Biko saw her—and her expression—he just smiled. "Hello, Wendy," he said calmly.

"You're insane!"

Woods was mixing Steve a drink. "He's heard about Mapetla," Donald explained. He gave the drink to Steve. "I've put Harold Levy on it," Woods told him, "but they wouldn't tell him anything, and legally they don't have to."

Steve weighed it soberly, then started to sip his drink. Wendy cautioned him. "You sure you should do that?" Biko nodded. "Peter's driving," he said. He turned back to Woods. "All being well, I'm going to Capetown in a few days," he said. "When I come through, I'll drop off something I want to write about the arrest. Maybe you'll publish it."

"Capetown?" Wendy protested.

"Steve, you must be out of your mind," Woods added.

Biko looked at the two of them and sagged back in his chair. He took a long drink. When he spoke, all the fire and energy he had when he came to the house seemed to have drained from him. "It's a meeting of black students," he explained. "An important one . . . and before they make a stand, I want them to hear what *I*'ve got to say." The importance of it to him was in no doubt, but for once he sounded almost tragically tired.

For two days nothing happened. Woods did not print the news of Mapetla's arrest, and the police refused to give Harold Levy any new information whatsoever. Woods felt it was a sign that the police were retaliating, and he hoped that in a few days their anger would dissipate and they would release him.

But he was badly mistaken. At twelve o'clock, when the streets around the *Dispatch* building were most crowded, a police car and a barred police van pulled up right in front. Three officers marched crisply into the building. They took the stairs up to the newsroom and went directly to Tenjy's desk. She had been typing an article but, like everyone else in the room, had looked up and stared at the entrance of the three policemen. When they turned toward her, she knew what was going to happen.

"I have a warrant for Tenjy Mtintso," the senior officer said. "Are you Tenjy Mtintso?" She nodded. "Please come with us," the officer said curtly. Tenjy bit her lip and glanced around the silent newsroom. Everyone was staring, but there was clearly nothing anyone could do. Julie Davenport had tears in her eyes.

Woods was in the print room when Ken scrambled down to tell him what had happened. The two of them ran to the front door, but it was too late. The police were already closing the back door of the van on Tenjy. A crowd had gathered, and Woods pushed through them. Tenjy peered at him through the metal wires of the little window at the back of the van. Woods rushed to the police car and took the arm of the senior officer.

"I would like to know what charges are in that warrant," he said. The policeman freed his arm from Woods with a look that was as chilling and menacing as the man could make it. "There are no charges," he said severely. "There don't *have* to be charges!" He got in the backseat of the police car, slammed the door, and ordered the driver to pull away.

Ken snapped his picture. The van followed, and Ken snapped that too. There were two street policemen keeping the crowd on the sidewalk. Woods glared at them. In a voice loud enough for the whole crowd to hear, he said, "Well, we'll print the news of her arrest—and it'll go on the *front* page!" He turned and strode through the crowd to the front door of the paper. Ken snapped the two policemen, and then he followed.

Woods kept the promise. He now felt it had been a mistake not to print the pictures of Mapetla's arrest. It didn't assuage the police, it had merely confirmed them in their power to do whatever they wanted. He was not going to make that mistake again. So he did a front-page feature on both arrests. The pictures of Mapetla's arrest were the more dramatic, and he used them without an explanation of why they hadn't appeared at the time.

The story produced some reaction from readers, and two of Ken's pictures were picked up by papers across the country, but they heard nothing from the police, and Harold Levy was still meeting a stone wall in his requests to speak to his client or have information about him.

A week later, Tony Morris, the makeup man, was preparing to go home when his buzzer sounded. He took his coat back off. He knew what that meant: Woods had pored over the page proofs and had come up with some new idea for a layout. He'd be late for dinner again.

There were only a couple of people in the newsroom when he went through, but he could see Woods in his office, staring out the window at the darkening sky. Maybe he was weighing whether the change of format was worth getting home after dark, Tony Morris speculated optimistically.

He stuck his head in the door of the office. "What's up?" he said.

Woods turned to his desk slowly, and Morris knew that something serious had happened.

"We're going to remake the front page." He looked up at Tony. "Mapetla is dead," he announced numbly. "They claim he hanged himself in his cell." For a moment Tony stared at him in stunned disbelief.

"Mapetla wouldn't—" Morris began, but he knew it was something that didn't need saying. So the two of them stood there in the growing darkness feeling ravaged by a truth they could not print.

Biko heard of Mapetla's death almost as soon as Woods did. Devastated as he was by it, he immediately did what he felt absolutely necessary. With Ntsiki and Mamphela, he did his best to console Mapetla's young widow, Nohle. But, as delicately as he could, he pointed out that if they were ever to prove what really happened, they would have to get an autopsy on Mapetla. If Nohle had the strength to go to the mortuary, Mamphela would go with her, and as next of kin she had the right to demand the autopsy.

Nohle knew Mapetla never would have hanged himself. Her grief was mixed with bitterness toward the police— enough, she felt, to see her through the ordeal of going to the mortuary.

Steve thought their case would be strengthened if another doctor performed the autopsy with Mamphela, so she contacted a friend from her days at the medical school who agreed to come.

As Biko had suspected, the autopsy raised enough questions to demand an inquest. He called Woods to see if Harold Levy could act for them at the inquest, but Levy was in Pretoria and had to remain there for several days. At his suggestion, Woods contacted Wilfrid Cooper, who did agree to represent them.

The star witness at the inquest proved to be Tenjy. She was so tiny, and the policeman escorting her so large, she looked fragile and helpless. She wore a severe prison uniform, her hair had been cut and drawn back, and though still pretty, she looked drawn and enfeebled.

The clerk swore her in, and it was Cooper who began to interrogate her. First her name, then her occupation. Tenjy answered, "I was a reporter on the *Daily Dispatch*. I am now a prisoner."

"Charges?" Cooper asked.

"None," Tenjy answered defiantly.

"This inquest," Cooper explained, "is to determine the cause of the death of another reporter, Mapetla Mohapi . . . who was found hanged in his prison cell." Tenjy turned and looked in angry bitterness at Security Officer Captain Schoeman, who was seated just behind the counsel for the State.

Cooper pressed on. "Medical examination," he continued, "has revealed bruises on the *side* of the deceased's neck, rather than *under* it. These are inconsistent with the theory that he hanged himself. Can you offer an explanation of how they might have been produced?"

"Yes," Tenjy answered forcefully. "There is a method of interrogation used by the Security Police that—"

Cooper interrupted her gently, "Is this *hearsay?*"

"No," she answered firmly. "I was interrogated personally in this manner by Captain Schoeman and his subordinates." She turned her gaze from Cooper directly to Schoeman. "First," she continued, "they dragged me around the room by my hair, then beat me to the floor and kicked me." Her voice choked with emotion, but she went on. "When this was insufficient to make me swear to something I had not done, they tied me to a chair and placed a towel around my neck. This was twisted tighter and tighter until I lost consciousness." She kept her gaze for a moment on Schoeman, then turned back to Cooper. "It was repeated several times . . . and produced *these* bruises." She pulled down her collar, revealing large black bruises on the *side* of her neck.

Wendy was crying. She reached over and took Donald's hand. "We must get her out of there," she whispered. Woods nodded, though he knew no easy way to accomplish it.

Tenjy had turned back to Schoeman. "It is widely known in prison," she began, but the State's barrister rose to object.

"Hearsay, Your Honor. I object."

"Sustained," the judge intoned.

"And I really do find this story of a towel around one's neck rather like the articles Miss Mtintso produced for the *Dispatch,*" the barrister continued, "overblown fiction by a political hysteric." He remained standing, evidently hoping the judge would comment on the testimony, too, but Cooper intervened.

"If Your Honor pleases," he stated, and turned to his

junior counsel. The junior counsel and Cooper had been briefed by Biko, and the junior produced a towel from his bag. Glancing at the State's barrister, Cooper crossed to the witness stand and handed it to Tenjy. "Perhaps, Miss Mtintso, you could demonstrate for us."

There was a stir in the courtroom, and Tenjy herself was taken a little off-balance. Then she took the towel and, with a chilling promptness and familiarity, rolled the towel, then threw it over her face from behind and tightened it around her throat . . . pulling the ends taut until she gagged. She swallowed a couple of times, recovering, then she looked at Schoeman coldly, accusingly. She did not take her eyes from him, but tears began to flow down her cheeks.

The judge was in his chambers only fifteen minutes when the court was gaveled back to order and he read his conclusion. "The inquest finds," he said flatly, "that Mapetla Mohapi died of strangulation. Blame can be affixed to no one. The inquest is closed."

Woods stared at Wendy in utter disbelief. He turned, and Mamphela was looking at him. She bore a bitter smile. *You see?* it said. *What did I tell you!*

Later that night, Biko phoned Donald. He made the call from Mamphela's room where he had been writing. She was typing the pages as he spoke.

Woods was in his office. He had finished his piece on the inquest and was sitting in the room on his own. Only his desk light was on, and out in the newsroom, only the light at the sports desk was still burning. The place seemed as melancholy as Woods felt. When his private line rang, he picked it up languidly. "Yes. Donald Woods speaking," he said.

"Donald. Steve." Woods sat up at the sound of Biko's

voice. "A piece of news," Biko went on. "The day *before* he died, the police showed another prisoner a puppet of Mapetla hanging from a string."

Woods sank back in his chair, shattered by the malice and crudity of it. "Shit . . ." He sighed desolately. "Steve . . . I just don't know what to say."

Biko was more touched by that than by anything Woods might have said, and he himself suddenly felt a wave of despair for the whites and blacks of South Africa. "Just say," he replied, "that someday justice will be done. And let's hope it won't be visited on the innocent." He paused, then lowered the phone to its cradle.

Mamphela had stopped typing during the call. She didn't look at Steve, but she had caught the emotion in his voice. "You shouldn't make that trip to Capetown," she said. "It's too dangerous."

Biko looked across at her. Her back was to him, but she turned and stared at him. "It's a dangerous country," Biko replied stoically.

# xii

THE ROADBLOCK WAS put up at ten P.M. The police always tried to change the place and times of roadblocks because word traveled so fast on the "black drums," as they called the network that somehow passed news from one black community to another throughout the whole country.

They didn't keep the blocks in place long, either, because they found that truckers very swiftly carried the news of one down the particular road they were on, and once that happened, no one was ever caught who was worth catching.

So if you fell foul of a roadblock, there was always a bit of bad luck in it. On this night only two cars had been stopped before Peter Jones, one of Steve's closest friends, drove round the bend and saw the flashing police lights of a roadblock ahead. There were two police cars and a Land Rover. There was no chance of making a U-turn, and certainly none of running through it.

Peter slowed the car. "They'll probably only ask for my

pass," he said nervously. Biko was riding next to him in the front seat. They were on their way back from Capetown.

"Have you got anything in the back?" Steve asked.

"No . . . all the posters were given out in Capetown. I've only got a spare tire back there."

The car ahead of them was sent on by the police. One of them used his flashlight, signaling Peter forward. Peter slowly moved the car forward and stopped. A policeman threw the beam from his flashlight onto Peter's face. "Keys and papers, hey," he commanded. A second policeman went to the trunk.

Peter passed him his passbook and the keys to the car. The policeman tossed them to his confrere, then threw his flashlight on Peter's passbook.

The policeman at the truck fiddled with the lock; he was having trouble opening it. Biko glanced sideways at Peter. Peter shrugged, but neither of them dared say a word.

The policeman at the window handed Peter back his passbook, satisfied, and threw his light around the backseat. He stepped back, prepared to let them go, but the policeman at the back was still tinkering with the key to the trunk. "I can't get the blarry thing open," he said.

The policeman at Peter's window was instantly suspicious.

"What's in there?" he demanded harshly.

"Nothing," Peter answered with desperate honesty.

One of the policemen at the roadblock itself started back toward them. He was on Biko's side of the car. "What's the matter?" he asked officiously.

"I think they got something in here," the policeman at the trunk answered. Another policeman from the roadblock joined them, and they both pounded on the trunk and struggled with the key.

"Can I try?" Peter asked, opening the door to get out. The policeman on his side just signaled him to the back.

But the policeman on Biko's side of the car stopped at the window. He tapped it. "Out!" he ordered.

Biko hesitated for a moment, but he had no option. He pushed open the door and got out. He stood a head taller than his officious adversary, and he just kept his eyes straight ahead at the blackness beyond the roadblock.

"Papers," the policeman demanded.

Again Biko hesitated. Then he reached into his coat and handed the man his passbook. Perfunctorily the policeman flipped open the cover and shone his flashlight from Biko's face to the face in the passbook. Suddenly he stiffened. His light went back to Biko's face—then once again to the passbook. "What's your name, *kaffir?*" he said, astounded.

"It's there in the book," Biko answered.

"*Say* it! *Say* your name!" the man bellowed. The other policemen all turned to look. What the hell was the matter? There was another silent pause, then Biko answered. "Bantu Stephen Biko," he said levelly. The other policemen stared in stupefaction.

It was a catch beyond the local police's wildest dreams. They radioed the news into the regional headquarters at the Walmer Police Station in Port Elizabeth. There, the news that Steve Biko had been caught several miles outside his banning area was considered of sufficient importance to warrant the waking of the station's senior officer. He ordered that Biko be held where he was until a force of six detectives could be sent to bring him directly to the station.

It was still the dead dark of night when Biko was taken

into the station. He had been handcuffed with his hands behind him, and there were no formalities or paperwork. Flanked by the six detectives, he was taken up the dimly lit stairs to the cells reserved for hardened cases. As they moved down the shadowed corridor, Biko could hear the weakened sobs of someone recovering from deep pain.

It was among the last sounds he was ever to hear.

Six days later—again in the dead stillness of night—a lone police car drove toward the grim mass of the Walmer Police Station. The perimeters of the police yard were lit by harsh lights, and when the car paused by the gated fence, it was greeted by the deep growl of watchdogs.

That car carried a doctor and the station's senior officer.

Fifteen minutes later they were being led by a police sergeant down a long corridor. The sergeant opened one barred door for them, then another forty feet on, and another, and finally led them to a far cell at the end of the corridor. It was September 11, 1977, a day that the three men would come to remember well.

As the sergeant opened the cell door the doctor could see a naked figure on the bare cement floor. His hands were handcuffed behind him, and one leg was manacled to irons attached to the bars of the cell. His breathing was heavy but very erratic. In the shadows he could tell no more.

When the sergeant had the door open, the senior officer directed the doctor in. He could now see that the figure on the floor was covered with bruises. More critically, he could see injuries to the forehead and eyes that seemed to have dislocated portions of the frontal cranium. He bent down on one knee and lifted the prisoner Biko's eyelid. The eye was glassy, unfocused. He was obviously in a coma. But the doctor had to be sure.

As he took his pulse, he examined the body cursorily. There were bruises and untreated sores on his legs from the manacles; bruises on the wrists from some twisting of the handcuffs; abrasions on his chest; a swollen upper lip, crossed by a deep, untreated cut; and a deep contusion and possible dislocation above the left eye.

The pulse was very weak but steady. He raised one of the prisoner's arms. It was limp, lifeless. The breathing was alternately feeble and heavy, in both cases accompanied by a liquid wheeze that suggested bleeding inside the mouth. It was not his business to make a judgment about what had happened to the prisoner, but he wished medical attention had been called for much earlier.

He turned to his bag and took out a patella hammer. He traced it along the left foot. No reaction. He tapped the foot once, twice. As he feared, the toe went upright. He rested the hammer on the floor for a moment, his own breathing having become rather heavy too. He knew what he must recommend, but he knew, too, that the prisoner Biko was very important to the police.

He stood. The senior officer was looking at him coldly. He was a prominent man in the community, and one from whom the doctor received many fees. He had to make his case as strong as he could.

He opened the medical file on the prisoner. His eyes went down it tensely, and he saw what he dreaded he would see. The decision should have been made earlier; now the burden of it had been put on him. He looked up at the senior officer. "I—I think he should see a specialist," he said, fighting the dryness in his mouth.

"Could he be shamming?" the senior officer asked sternly.

My God, the doctor thought, how could you sham a

crushed forehead, or eyes that protruded from the pressure
of the blood behind them? Even a layman could answer
that question. But he deferred to the harsh gaze of the senior officer. "The extensor plantar reflex," he began feebly,
"indicates a—a possible lesion on the brain."

"*Could* he be shamming?" the senior officer demanded
fiercely.

"You—you can't 'sham' a reflex, sir," the doctor replied. He could not meet the inquisitorial eyes of the senior
officer. He looked down at the file. "And—and the lumbar
puncture Dr. Hersch took revealed an excess of red blood
cells in the spinal fluid," he went on defensively. "That
also points to—it's a—possible sign of serious brain damage."

"But why has he collapsed now?" the senior officer insisted. He had seen a lot of men in Biko's state who had
managed to survive quite well.

The doctor could not truly answer that, since he could
only surmise what had happened to the prisoner in the last
few hours. But he knew he must find some answer that
would satisfy the senior officer and at the same time not
offend him. He looked over at the sergeant. "Has he—has
he eaten, gone to the toilet?"

The sergeant glanced at the senior officer before answering. There was the minutest nod, and the sergeant
turned back to the doctor and answered, "No—not today."

The doctor faced the senior officer; even he must recognize now that the brain was malfunctioning, that some deep
injury was threatening the life of the prisoner Biko. "He
must be seen by a specialist," he said with fear, but with as
much certainty as he could muster.

The senior officer weighed it, glancing from the ashen
face of the doctor to the bruised and inert figure on the

floor. "We'll take him to the police hospital in Pretoria," he said at last.

The doctor stared at him, agape. "But that's—that's seven hundred miles," he stammered. There was a hospital three miles away, in Port Elizabeth.

"He might escape from the hospital here," the senior officer stated firmly, as though in answer to the doctor's unspoken thought. "I want him in a *police* hospital," he continued.

The doctor looked down at the comatose prisoner. It would be lucky if he could walk or talk within weeks, but escape? Whatever had happened to Biko, it was clear that the senior officer did not want civilian doctors to see him. He knew that by the Hippocratic Oath he should insist that the prisoner be taken to the nearest hospital—without delay. And he was determined to demand it. He looked up into the stern, glowering eyes of the senior officer . . . and said nothing.

Half an hour later the doctor stood by as the prisoner Biko was brought to the loading dock of the prison garage. The prisoner was still naked. He was being carried by four police officers, all in heavy jackets against the cold. Another officer threw a blanket onto the floor of the Land Rover, and the prisoner Biko was put on it.

A police captain gave the four-man team who were to take him their final orders. "I want you to go Seymour way. Stay off the main roads. And when you take a break, one man stays in the vehicle at all times." The doctor thought they would cover Biko or put a mat under his head, but two officers simply piled in the back with the prisoner, and the other two went to the cab in front.

Again the doctor turned to the senior officer at his side. He wanted to say something, but the senior officer had his

eyes fixed on the Land Rover as its engine turned over and
it drove out into the night.

Biko's head bounced on the floor as the Land Rover
sped over the uneven dirt road leading from the prison
loading dock to the main road to Port Elizabeth. His face
was already badly bruised, with bits of blood encrusted on
the nose and ears. His mouth flopped open, and occasionally his semiconscious eyes would half open as the Land
Rover took another bump. He had seven hundred miles of
country roads yet to survive.

Woods received an anonymous phone call. It might have
been from one of the black prison officers, or perhaps one
of the black attendants at the police hospital. At first he
didn't believe it. Biko was too big a name, he was too
prominently associated with nonviolence. After all, he'd
been arrested before and they'd put him in solitary, but he
had come out unscathed. Then he received another call
from his night editor. A government order had come in
over the wires. Any article about police activities had to be
cleared with police headquarters in Pretoria.

Woods dressed and went down to the paper. During the
whole drive he tried to convince himself it was not true.
The government couldn't afford the scandal; they needed
black leaders to negotiate with. Beyond that, it was incon-
ceivable that someone as vital and alive as Steve was suddenly no more.

By the time he got to the paper, there was a message for
him to call John Qumza. John had heard it from the black
underground. There was no doubting it.

Woods called in all his key staff, and they spent the
remaining hours of the night preparing a special morning
edition. He framed the front page in black, and in letter

sizes that are normally reserved for announcing war or peace, he filled the page with the headline: BIKO DIES IN CUSTODY!

He dared not guess at how he died. He could only give the date of his arrest and the fact that he died in a police hospital in Pretoria.

But it was enough. With the government proscription already broken, the news was taken up by every paper in the country. Woods spent hours on the phone calling friends and acquaintances he had among the press outside South Africa to be sure it would receive worldwide coverage. In some key cities where he knew no one—Bonn, Tokyo—he called leading editors, anyway. Every news service carried the story, and it was printed in almost every country in the world.

There was no danger that the *Dispatch* would be fined or punished for ignoring the government proscription. Even this government knew *that* much about public relations. Besides, the government was busy handling the reactions to the news.

There were riots and protests in black townships up and down the country. Police stations were attacked with bricks and stones and, in a few instances, Molotov cocktails. In Crossroads, there was a huge, disordered procession with drums and wild, plaintive music. Thousands marched through one whole day and into the night, with the police only standing by, knowing that an incident now could unleash a fury that in sheer numbers alone could endanger their power.

For Ntsiki the news was too painful to share with anyone. She stayed in their little township house, holding the baby, Samora, cradling the mystified Nkosinathi, sobbing

for Steve . . . and for herself and the boys. And they, not
knowing what was the matter, cried with her.

A crushed Father Kani took the news to Tenjy in her
prison cell. In a few short weeks she had lost Mapetla, and
now Steve. Where was God? Yet what she wanted to do
most was pray to Him for their souls, and for herself and
for Africa. The elderly Father Kani cradled her sobbing
body for over an hour before they made him leave.

No one saw Mamphela cry. When John first phoned the
news, she, unlike Woods, knew it was true. She told the
other staff at the clinic, then walked slowly off across the
barren countryside. No one saw her return. The next day,
soft, solemn music came from her room, but no one saw
her. The next day, she made her rounds in the clinic but did
not speak to any of the staff. She ate alone, without reading. It went on like that for several days.

Wendy was another one who did not cry. She couldn't
say why, but even when tears filled Donald's eyes when
talking about Steve or when there were sudden silences in
the house, she felt a kind of knife-twisting desolation, but
the tears would not come. She spent hours walking around
the side of the pool, and Jane and Dillon saw that no one
disturbed those melancholy walks.

By the second day, there were huge bonfires in many of
the townships, and people stood around them, just staring
into the flames. Those fires burned every night until the
funeral.

Initially all but the most right-wing Afrikaner papers
attacked the police. But the police had a wise and cunning
voice working on their behalf: Donald's old "friend," the
Minister of Police, J. T. Kruger. First he denied any police
responsibility for Biko's death. It was true the man had
been discovered several miles out of his banning area, and

he had quite properly been arrested for it. But the police had been meticulous in their treatment of him. When all the facts were known, some of the hysterical voices in the press would soon feel as foolish as they ought to.

As luck would have it, there was a major rally of the Afrikaner Nationalist Party Kruger was scheduled to address. When he stood up, the applause was tepid. But in five minutes he had won the crowd over. Yes, Mr. Biko had been arrested. Yes, this man who was going to take over South Africa on behalf of the blacks and to hell with four hundred years of Afrikaner sweat and toil and tears! Yes, that man had been arrested! That man who was going to drive you and your children from this land that your father and his father and his father before him had labored over was treated *politely* and *properly* by the police authorities.

Why did he die in a hospital? Because he had gone on a hunger strike. Every effort was made to induce him to eat. But Mr. Steve Biko was not willing to unless the government would lift his ban and allow him to carry his message the length and breadth of this land. On the minister's *own* orders, he was informed that that would never happen!

The crowded hall erupted in applause. His condition had become worse, the minister continued with a smile. He could not personally attest to how Mr. Biko lived his life or why his health was so fragile. There were sniggers and laughter. But when he seemed in extreme danger, he was transported to the police hospital in Pretoria, and he died there. Of his own mouth, you might say.

The crowd cheered, laughed, applauded. Kruger lifted a hand to still them. "So Biko's death leaves me cold!" he bellowed. He received another huge round of applause. "He died after a *hunger strike!*" More applause, but this time one of the delegates had risen and was clamoring for attention. Kruger nodded to him, urging him to speak. When the crowd had quieted, the man shouted out, "I commend the minister for being so democratic that he gives prisoners the democratic right to starve themselves!" There was a ripple of laughter and many shouts of "Hear! Hear!"

"*Ja*, that *is* very democratic," Kruger continued. "I suppose," he said with more sobriety, "one feels sorry for any death. . . . I suppose I would feel sorry about my *own* death." He smiled, raised his hand, and shrugged, meaning, "What do you expect?" The delegates made his little joke into something hilariously funny—by laughing, whistling, and cheering.

That rally was televised, and it drove Woods from the torpor into which he had sunk in the aftermath of Steve's death.

The next day, he and Ken drove north and at one o'clock were parked beside a road sign that read, KING WILLIAM'S TOWN. It was a small road, going to a small town, but beneath the sign hung the usual Rotary, Round Table, and Rapportryers emblems to suggest that life in this town was normal.

When the bus stopped across the way, a living proof that life was not "normal" stepped off the bus into the road. It was Ntsiki, Steve's wife. Woods had called to have her meet him, and she had come. It was the first time they'd seen each other since Steve's death. Ntsiki stood at the side of the road, waiting until the bus pulled off again. Then, when the road was clear, she started to cross. Woods moved to greet her.

There was no traffic, and when Woods neared her,

Ntsiki just stopped. He paused too. They looked at each other for a moment—a moment dense with a sense of memory and loss, of tragedy and sympathy. So much had happened between them since their first meeting less than two years ago. Then Woods moved forward and embraced her. "He was a giant, Ntsiki," he said softly. "A man the world will always remember. I hope what you had together will make your grief more bearable."

Ntsiki returned his embrace with a rigidity that was a measure of the control she was exercising. Tears formed in her eyes, but when Woods released her, she walked on to the car with the same stoic mien she had first displayed when she got off the bus.

Woods had not dared tell her what he had in mind when he phoned her for the rendezvous. He felt certain that the public phones in the township were tapped, and he suspected his own was too. But he knew, and she knew, that Steve had not died of a hunger strike. The question was: How had he died? By the time they had reached the mortuary for non-whites, Woods had explained what he wanted to do. It was a move he had learned from Steve, but it required her agreement. She didn't say yes or no, she simply nodded her head, though Woods could see that the part of her that wanted to see Steve's body had to fight terribly with the side of her that was afraid to.

When they got out of the car to go into the little building, she asked Woods how he had gotten permission.

"I didn't," Woods answered. "I knew if I asked, it would tip them off and they might move him." The building hadn't been painted in years, and it looked as grim and unwelcoming as its function. "I've checked the law," Woods told her, "which is why I needed you here. I don't think they'll dare stop us."

A short middle-aged Pakistani opened the door. He was a little alarmed at Woods' request, but he led the three of them—Woods, Ntsiki, and Ken—into the office of the head mortician.

Woods said they wanted to see Biko's body. For her own peace of mind his wife wanted to identify it and to pay her last respects.

The mortician was clearly panicked by the request. "I'm afraid that's not possible," he said stiffly. "This is a special case. There's been no inquest and—"

"It's not special *at all*," Woods cut in. "The law is quite simple and clear: The next of kin has the right to see the deceased." The mortician steeled himself to make an answer to that, but Woods read his reaction and moved first. "Mr. Biko's death," he said coldly, "has caused enough uproar in the press already. If you'd like to create another issue for me to put on the front page, I'll be very happy to comply."

The anger and force of it was enough to terrify the mortician. He could see trouble either way, but looking into Woods' face, he knew if he resisted now, one kind of trouble was certain. Reluctantly he rose and led them into the morgue.

There were three pairs of feet sticking from the large drawers of the holding bay. A tag was tied to a toe of each. The mortician moved to the top row and twisted a tag. It read, "Biko." He signaled to the Pakistani assistant, and the man operated the crude hand winch that drew the slabs out and lowered them. The body was covered with a white sheet. When the slab was about hip-high, the Pakistani stopped the winch. The mortician looked at them all severely, then left the room. Woods knew he would be on the phone immediately. He stepped forward and gently pulled the top of the sheet off Biko's face.

He had not known what to expect, but the sight chilled him. The body had been treated a bit by the mortician, but there was a huge contusion on the forehead, one cheekbone was out of position, his lips had been stitched but were swollen and misshapen. The eyes that once had been so compelling and complex were now puffed and bruised. Even if he was alive, one wondered if he could have opened them.

Ntsiki had moved to the side of the slab. Slowly she worked her way up the covered sheet, touching it like it was some precious but terrifying shroud, until she came to his face and she could hold her grief no more. She bent over the body, suddenly sobbing, putting her arm over Steve's chest, her head to his. "Oh, Steve . . . Steve," she sobbed. "What have they done to you?"

Woods was too touched to move for a moment. Ken grimaced in the background, stifling his own reaction. But finally Woods put his arm around Ntsiki, prying her gently free. "We must hurry, Ntsiki, before he notifies the police." She slowly relinquished her hold on Steve, and Woods turned her toward the door. The Pakistani assistant, who had stayed at the winch, moved forward to help. He put one arm around Ntsiki and started to walk her from the room. At the door he turned back. "Don't let them frighten you, Mr. Woods." It was a heartfelt appeal by a man who obviously lived in fear.

Woods closed the door, and Ken took a small Nikon with a flash attachment out of his jacket. "From every angle," Woods commanded. Ken moved around the body quickly, getting shots of the head, straight on and from the side. Woods pulled the sheet down so that the whole of

Biko's bruised body was exposed. Steve had not been playing rugby regularly and had put on some weight. "Died of a hunger strike," Woods repeated bitterly. For a moment he stood over the familiar features of the hate-free man who'd last inhabited this battered body, and cried as he never had as a grown man.

When they returned to the car Ntsiki was sitting in the front seat, just staring ahead. None of them spoke. Ken got in the backseat, and Woods started the car. Before he pulled away, Ntsiki broke the silence. "You and Wendy will come to the funeral, won't you?" she asked quietly.

Woods was a little taken aback by the question. Considering what had happened to Steve, he wondered about others' reactions to a white man. "W-well," he stumbled, "would his other friends—would we be welcome?"

Ntsiki's eyes were still staring off in space. "Yes, Donald," she answered, "you and Wendy are our brother and sister."

She still hadn't looked at him. "We will be there," he promised, and he pulled the car away from the mortuary.

The funeral was held two days later. Woods had never been to a black funeral before. He knew they were often occasions for huge displays of grief or political statement. He and Wendy had gone to the stadium where Biko's funeral ceremony was to be held very early. But even so, there were thousands of people there when they arrived. Many of them carried placards with a blowup of Steve's face. Everywhere they turned, the sight of him brought difficult memories to them both.

There were police roadblocks operating on the main roads, but even so, the stadium kept filling. The mood of the crowd did not surprise him. It was a combination of grief and anger. He and Wendy took a place in the middle of the field. They saw no one they recognized from the clinic or the community center, but no animosity was shown to them. They were just ignored, as though they weren't there at all.

About an hour after they arrived, a group of people went out onto a big platform that had been erected on one side of the field. Woods turned Wendy around so she could see. Several dignitaries appeared first. They recognized the British ambassador and his wife, the American and his wife, the Swede and his wife. Then Helen Suzman took a seat and there was a mutter of welcome from the crowd, guttural and deep, but a welcome it was. Some church officials, black and white, followed. They only recognized Bishop Tutu. And finally John Qumza came in with Father Kani and Mamphela. The last to come on the platform were Ntsiki and the two boys. Then that deep, guttural sound swelled in the crowd till it filled the stadium. It was like the wounded welcome of a great animal who is dying, Woods felt. Half frightening, half tragic.

The stadium was packed now. There were hundreds of placards of Steve. Out in the grounds, Woods could see white faces here and there, and he said to Wendy, "When I despair, remind me of this someday. . . . There are whites in South Africa who've been thinking a long time before we started to."

Suddenly a great chant could be distantly heard. As it drew nearer, they could see the crowd beginning to part, and then it came, the vanguard of the cortege procession. Woods knew that Steve's fame had spread all over South Africa, that he was known to those who were politically active and politically concerned, but it truly amazed him to see the organization and numbers who had created this moment. More people were still filing into the stadium as the procession started across the field, parting the thousands who were gathered on it. It was led by Malusi and Steve's brother, both of whom they had met at the clinic. But unlike the atmosphere at the clinic, there was a powerful belligerence in this ceremony. A group of young men in matching jackets led the chant, which had a forceful beat and was pounded out with their feet as well as with their voices. And at each beat they thrust their fists into the air in unison.

Some of the crowd began singing the chant with them and stamping their feet to its beat. It filled the stadium with a sense of power.

A line of clergymen followed the uniformed young men. Again Woods was amazed. He had talked religion with Steve, and he knew Steve thought the church had been used as an instrument to colonize and, in cases, to destroy African culture, and yet he knew that Steve was still deeply affected by his faith and that he held a number of clergymen among his closest friends. But whatever he thought of the church, this procession of clergymen indicated what the church thought of *him*.

The casket itself followed the clergymen. It was on a flatbed trailer drawn by two scrubbed oxen that were decorated like the trailer in the colors of Azania, the word Steve's followers used for the land we now call South Africa. The casket itself was made of beautiful dark mahogany, and bore in gold script the words: "One Azania . . . One Nation." As it proceeded through the crowd, hands reached out everywhere to touch it.

A mass of schoolboys made up the end of the procession. They were evidence of Steve's influence on the young and represented, Woods felt, the impact he would have on generations to come.

When the cortege reached the main platform, the casket was raised onto a catafalque draped in flowers. The defiant chant lost its dramatic beat and came to a lingering, elegiac end.

For a moment there was silence, then a young black speaker in a gold-and-brown robe stepped to the microphone at the front of the platform. He held up his hand, stilling the murmuring rumble of the crowd.

He clutched the microphone. "We are here to mourn one of the great men of Africa!" he said, and his voice echoed around the stadium and produced a huge roar from the crowd; not a cheer but an almost angry acclamation.

"I loved Steve Biko," the speaker continued. "But I *hate* the System that killed him!"

And now there were bellows of assent. Feet were stamped, fists were raised, and the fury underlying this gathering was given its head.

Woods reacted tensely to the bitter, continuing howl that spread around the grounds. Where was this crowd being taken? He put a protective arm around Wendy. "God," he whispered against the enraged thunder of the crowd, "I had hoped this wouldn't happen."

Finally the speaker held up his arms, and gradually the crowd quieted again. "Even today," he began, "the day of Steve Biko's funeral, in their white arrogance, they have turned back thousands who sought to come here simply to pay their respects to him!" There were shouts and a protesting rumble, but he continued over them. "The buses from Soweto, Durban, and Capetown have all been turned away!" Again it seemed the crowd would explode, but he raised his voice again and kept it going, not letting them react. "And roadblocks have been set up to prevent others from *every part* of the country from entering this area!"

And now he spread his arms and let the crowd give vent to its anger. It exploded around the whole stadium. The placards with Steve's picture were held high and waved back and forth.

At last the speaker's hand went up again to still them. When it was quiet, he thundered, *"But—we—are—here!"*

The crowd roared with triumph as well as with anger. They beat the ground with their feet and found a rhythm with their shouting that echoed through the stadium.

The speaker stalked back and forth on the platform, letting their anger and pride have its full vent, encouraging it . . . until he stepped back to the microphone. Again he stilled them. "I hate the System," he said quietly, "but I welcome *all* South Africans who join with us today in mourning the man who gave us faith in the kind of country South Africa *could* be—the kind of country South Africa *will* be—when all men are judged as human beings, as equal members of God's family."

The applause began again. Softer, warmer, with many shouts of "Amen!" Woods glanced around at the other whites he could see. There were many students, here and there a middle-aged couple, one giant of a blond with his wife, carrying a towheaded child on his shoulders.

"And toward that day," the speaker continued, "when the isolation that creates hostility becomes the closeness that permits friendship, let us join in the Song of Africa that Steve Biko cherished, as we do." As he began the song, the massed thousands gradually took it up while they held their placards of Biko aloft.

# CRY FREEDOM

*Nkosi Sikelel' i Afrika*
*Maluphanyisw' upondo lwayo . . .*

There were three white students near Woods, a girl and two boys. When they saw Woods singing with the throng, the girl pushed through to his side. "Do you understand the words?" she asked.

Woods nodded and half sang, half spoke a translation as he worked it through in his head.

> God bless Africa,
> Raise up her name . . .
> Hear our prayers
> And bless us . . .
>
> Bless the leaders,
> Bless also the young
> That they may carry the land
>     with patience,
> In their youth, bless them.
>
> Bless our efforts
> To unite and lift ourselves
> Through learning and understanding,
> And bless us.
>
> *Woza Moya! Yilha Moya!*
> Come, Spirit! Descend, Spirit!
> *Woza Moya Oyingewele!*
> Come, Holy Spirit!

Woods, Wendy, and the students stood caught in the solemn stillness of the crowd, as the echoing sound of the beautiful anthem, the moving impact of the massed, emotional voices died on the wind. . . .

On the platform by the catafalque, all had stood for the singing. Ntsiki was holding Samora, and tears were running down her cheeks. This time Mamphela's tears were joined with hers as they watched the thousands of placards with Biko's face still waving to the rhythm of the song. . . .

# xiii

WOODS HAD GONE to Pretoria for a national meeting of editors two days after the funeral. He hoped to get their cooperation in demanding an inquest on Biko's death. Wendy knew what a task he had, because the government was still sticking to the story that Steve had died as the result of a hunger strike. They also threatened to shut down any paper that used the Biko issue to, as they said, stir up trouble in the black townships. They stated that the situation was already dangerous, and if law and order were to be maintained, inflammatory material in the press had to be prohibited.

Woods had held on to the pictures. In this case, he felt the government really would close down the paper if he used them, and he had a fundamental responsibility to the staff and the owners. He also believed that if he had published them before the funeral, there would have been riots and bloodshed up and down the country, that wounds would have been created on both sides that would take

years to heal. He was tempted to reveal them to some of
the editors in Pretoria but feared that any leak would lead
to the police seizing them before *anyone* could print them.
An idea was forming in his head, but he wasn't willing to
share it yet.

The first night Woods was gone, Wendy was reading in
bed and half listening to the television news when the subject of Biko's death was raised. The announcer said they
had taped an earlier interview with the Minister of Police,
J. T. Kruger. Wendy put down her book. The minister was
seen at a table on his front lawn. He was asked if there was
any doubt about how Steve Biko died while in police custody. "No," the minister answered convincingly. "The fact
is," he said, "Biko had gone on a hunger strike." He gestured vaguely to his arm. "We tried to feed him by intrave-
nous drip, with a tube in his arm." He made another
gesture, to Wendy, a theatrically vague one. "I don't know
about these things," he continued, "I'm not a doctor." The
phone rang. Wendy turned down the volume on the television and wished she could blot Mr. Kruger off the face of
the earth with the same ease. She picked up the telephone.
"Yes, hello, is that you, Donal—"

A voice with a thick Afrikaans accent cut her off. "All
right, you traitor! You black-loving bitch! We know you're
alone—and we're coming to get you!"

Wendy went to speak, but the caller slammed off, and
she heard only the buzz of an empty line. Slowly she put
the phone down and glanced toward the window. Even her
own shadowed bedroom suddenly looked frightening.
There was a startling knock on the door, and Wendy turned
in terror. The door pushed open. It was Jane.

"I can't sleep," she said. "Was that Daddy?"

Wendy sighed in relief. "No," she said. "Not Daddy."
Jane could see her tension.

"More threats?" Wendy nodded. She kept few things
from Jane, and in what they were going through now she
felt she needed her as an ally and confidante. Jane had
been precociously mature from the time Gavin was born,
and Wendy knew she could deal with reality as well as she,
herself, could.

"The police?" Jane asked.

Wendy shrugged. "They're the only ones we *know* are
doing it."

Jane shook her head wearily. "When Daddy gets home,"
she said, "we ought to put a recording machine on the
phone, then print what they say in the paper."

Wendy smiled. "They'd have to use a lot of asterisks
and dashes."

Jane grinned at the thought. "Well," she sighed. "I think
I'll go downstairs and make some hot chocolate."

"No! Don't go downstairs!"

Jane looked at her quizzically, but before Wendy could
explain, they heard the sound of a car pulling up outside.
Wendy quickly turned out her bedside light. She got out of
bed and started for the window. She clicked off the television as she went by, and now the room was dark, except
for a bit of light spilling in from the hallway.

She peered around the edge of the curtain. Jane came to
her side. They could see a car pulled in at an angle across
the road. Its lights had been turned off, and as they
watched, two figures ran from it toward the wall of their
garden.

"Who can we call?" Jane whispered as she pulled away
from the window. She was as frightened as Wendy now.

Wendy had already started for the door. "You just stay

here!" she insisted fearfully. She went out into the hall.
The light that Jane had turned on was still lit. Wendy hesitated. Should she turn it off, or would that only reveal
where she was? She left it on and started slowly down the
stairs.

Despite her mother's admonition, Jane came out in the
hallway, standing by the railing, as Wendy crept down.
Wendy could see some of the living room and some of the
playroom from the stairs. She lowered her head to peer into
them—and suddenly a shot rang out. And another. And
another. Wendy froze. Jane screamed. There were two
more shots, one producing a crashing of glass.

Charlie came barking out of the boys' room, but Jane
lifted her hand threateningly to him. "Be quiet, Charlie!"
she whispered. Whimpering, Charlie came to her feet and
lay down, his tail wagging ingratiatingly.

Wendy and Jane were still listening breathlessly for
whatever was going on outside. There was a shout in Afrikaans, and they could hear footsteps running in the road,
and finally the car being started and driven off.

Wendy was shaking, but she started to take another step
down.

"Mother!" Jane said protestingly. And Wendy thought
better of it. She slowly climbed back up the stairs, and
Jane went into her arms. They stood there for a moment,
each clinging to the other for support, Charlie circling
them, whining for some attention. Finally Wendy said, "I
have an idea." She led Jane into Mary's room, and Wendy
gathered the sleeping Mary into her arms. On her mother's
instructions, Jane took the mattress from the bed and put it
on the floor, and they put Mary back on it.

Getting Duncan and Gavin on the floor was more difficult, but sleeping in the drugged way boys do, the two of

them were pulled and hauled with nothing more than a "Hi, Mom," to indicate that they had any idea of what was happening to them. With Charlie's help they awakened Dillon. He didn't protest but didn't want to bother shifting the mattress and rolled himself in a comforter and asked them to go away. Wendy shooed Charlie into his bed in the boys' room and helped Jane with her mattress, then returned to Mary's room, where she took a pillow and stretched out on the floor next to her sleeping baby.

The next morning, Wendy was up at six. She didn't feel she'd slept at all, but her bones ached from lying on the floor, and she knew she probably had. She let Charlie out, and in a few minutes Evalina came in, letting Charlie in with her.

"Did you hear anything last night, Evelyn?" Wendy asked. Years ago when Evalina first had come to them, Wendy had fallen into the habit of calling her Evelyn because she'd had a close friend called Evelyn and it was familiar. Across the years it had become a kind of nickname for her that only Wendy used, a token of the bond that had grown between them.

"Yes, I certainly did," Evalina replied. "But I got up, came out, and looked at the house, and there was only the upstairs hall light on, and I thought, well it must be someone else's troubles, and I went back to bed."

"No, it was our troubles," Wendy assured her. "Someone took shots at the house."

Evalina crashed her dishrag across the edge of the sink. "I hope the master goes to court and puts those people to jail! I swear I get a curse put on them!" Evalina's grammar was not always correct, but there was never any doubt about her intent.

"Well, as soon as it's a decent hour," Wendy said, "I'm going to call Don Card and see if he'll come over. But I'll feel better if we keep the children in the house until he comes."

"Don't worry, I *fix* them something special for breakfast, and they won't even think about going outside," Evalina said confidently.

Don Card was an ex-policeman whom Donald had met very early in his career. He was an extraordinarily brave man and had once gone deep into a homeland single-handedly to apprehend a violent, homicidal criminal. Donald did a large feature on him, and in doing so had also been impressed by Card's fairness and his gift for management. He talked the paper into backing him in the private security business. It had proved a good investment for the paper and had brought Card an income and a place in society far beyond anything he could have achieved in the police force. He had remained a close friend through the years, and one Donald could call on for almost anything.

He came to the house as soon as he received Wendy's call. Wendy didn't want to scare the little ones, so only Jane and Dillon accompanied her and Don as they explored the exterior of the house. The most obvious evidence of their night visitors was a crudely painted hammer and sickle in red paint on the white fence by the gate. "Biko Commie Headquarters" had been scrawled below it.

Card shook his head and looked at the house. There were two bullet marks in the corner by Donald's study. "Look up and down the street, Dillon," Card said. "See if you find any shells. I'm going to look at those things a little closer."

By the time he got the ladder out and examined the

bullet marks, Dillon and Jane had found the five shells. When Card came down the ladder, his mouth was already set in anger. Dillon handed him the shells. Card took them, and they only confirmed his supposition.

"There's where another one went," Jane said, pointing to a pillar near the door. "On that side one went right through your window, Mom," Dillon added.

Card tossed the bullets in his hand. "It was the police," he said flatly. "Two shots here, one through your window, one by the door. Check the area around the window on the other side, Dillon."

Dillon ran off, and Wendy turned to Card. "Can you be that sure?"

Card headed for his Jaguar on the road. "Believe me, Wendy, thirty years in the police force and you know one when you see one. Tell Donald that Jim—"

"You're right, Uncle Don," Dillon called out as he ran back to them. "It's right by the living-room window."

Card opened his car door and looked back at Wendy. "Tell Donald one of us will stay here until he gets back. And I'm going to *prove* my ex-colleagues did this."

"What good will it do?" Jane called out to him.

Card was in his car. He stuck his head back out and shouted, "None! But it'll make me feel better that *they* know we know!" And he started his car.

Dillon was still looking at the broken window in his mother's room. "Geez, Mom, they must've nearly hit your bed. It's a good thing you weren't standing at the window."

Jane moved next to her mother as they waved good-bye to Card. Wendy put her arm around her. They turned to look at the window. Dillon shook his head. "They're crazy," he said.

\* \* \*

When Donald heard about the shooting at the house, he came back immediately from Pretoria. He had already made his statement to the assembled editors and cornered those most sympathetic to forcing an inquest on Biko's death. Staying any longer was of marginal value; he knew he wouldn't be able to sleep at night, anyway.

He had made up his mind what he was going to do while he was on the flight from Pretoria. One look at the house convinced him of it. He called Capetown and asked his oldest newspaper friend, Bruce McCullough, an Australian, to come to East London as quickly as he could. "I'll be there by sundown, mate," Bruce answered. And he was as good as his word.

Woods also asked the two people he felt he could trust most in East London: Don Card, and Biko's friend, the black priest, Father Kani.

It was about nine when they came together. Evalina had fixed a big batch of spaghetti for the four of them and set a table in the garden by the lighted pool. When she placed the big salad bowl in the middle of the table, Bruce put his arms around her waist. "You know, the only reason I came up here was because he promised me you were fixing spaghetti," he whispered in her ear.

"All I know certain," Evalina replied, pulling herself loose, "is that Australians are good at eatin' and talkin', and as far as I can read, that's about all!" Bruce laughed and grabbed a beer from an ice bucket full of them. "To you, Evalina," he toasted with the bottle. She smiled at him despite herself and waited for Woods to dismiss her.

Woods checked the table. "That's fine, Evalina," he said. "It looks great, thank you very much."

When she had gone up to the house, he told them what

he had in mind. "I have a contact in Boston, U.S.A.," he began, "who says he can book me on a lecture tour all around America."

"Yeah?" Bruce said, his inflection implying, "You didn't bring me all the way up here for that news, did you?"

"The catch is," Woods continued, "I'd have to talk about Biko, his death, and the police cover-up."

They all stared at him. Don Card was the first to speak. "I think it's madness," he said categorically. "If they let you out, which *I* wouldn't do, take my word for it, they'll arrest you the minute you get back!"

"Look," Woods retorted, "I've just come back from Pretoria, and I can tell you no one's really willing to fight the government on this."

"That's why Don's right, old mate," Bruce chimed in as he served himself a heaping plate of spaghetti. "They're mad enough about what you've done here. You should read the Afrikaner press in Capetown. You start stirring up trouble overseas and—"

"*Here* or *there*," Woods interrupted, "we've got to force them to have an inquest. They can't arrest me *there*, they can't *gag* me there, but a lecture tour in the States *will* stir up pressure they'll *have* to listen to."

"If you were a lawyer, you know," Father Kani said thoughtfully, "getting support for the law, in actual fact that's one thing. But you're going to talk about *Biko!* I tell you, Donald, they won't stop at niceties."

"Kruger lied," Woods argued. "If Bruce can get those pictures out of the country, we can *prove* it. He's on the hook. If we expose him, they're going to have to admit how Steve *really* died!" The others looked at him dubiously. They didn't question the facts; they questioned his estimate of the government's will. "My friends," Woods began archly, "I'm going to go. If one of you will stay in the house with Wendy and the kids, I'm not worried. In fact, I think the more publicity I get, the safer I'll be."

His conviction convinced them that he was going to go, not that he was right.

Woods booked his flight to Boston via New York. He went through Bea Davis's travel agency with only Bea handling the paperwork or knowing he was leaving the country. Then the day before he left, he printed the pictures Ken had taken of Biko in the morgue, with a scathing editorial demanding an inquest. The government seized some copies of the paper and prohibited the pictures being republished in other papers.

He took a local flight under a false name to Pretoria to catch the plane to New York. Bruce met him at the airport and assured him that copies of the pictures had been sent to the news agencies and to key papers in England and the United States.

As they walked toward passport control, Donald was supremely confident he had the government over a barrel. Bruce remained a doubter. "I just hope I'm the only one planning to meet you when you return," he gibed. "If Kruger sends some of his boys, the next thing we may read is that you went on a hunger strike!"

Woods smiled. He took out his passport and grabbed the briefcase Bruce had been carrying, juggling them with a newspaper and the cigarette he was smoking. "When I come back," he said, "you'll be asking for my autograph."

"Fat chance," Bruce quipped, and banged his fist on Woods' arm in farewell. He stood watching as Woods slipped his passport to the passport control officer. There were two armed soldiers flanking the booth. This was the moment. If the government had put a holding order out on him, he would be stopped right here. The man scrutinized Woods and the passport, then stamped it and passed it back. Woods picked it up and turned as he walked on to the security check. With a touch of triumph he grinned at Bruce. "I'll phone you when I get there!" he called.

He walked behind the smoked-glass screen separating the passengers from the main hall. As he approached the security check, a man came to his arm. "Donald Woods?" he asked. Woods nodded. "We're from Security Police," he said quietly. Woods looked up and saw two other men approaching. "Come with us, please," the man said, and lightly taking Woods' arm, guided him toward an office door. The other two men followed, and an armed soldier materialized from somewhere to take up a post outside the door. Woods heard his flight being called on the *tannoy*, and he hesitated. "Don't worry about that," the man who had apprehended him, Major Boshoff, said. "You won't be on the flight."

"But my bags are—"

"No, they aren't," Boshoff assured him calmly. "We've taken them off." And thoroughly stunned, Woods was led into a small office. It had been done so discreetly. No one would have known it had happened. He cursed himself for not making a fuss.

In the office he faced another security officer, Lieutenant Beukes. Before Woods could say anything, Beukes started reading from a warrant. "You, Donald James Woods," he began harshly, "are declared a *banned* person in terms of the Internal Security Act. Henceforth, and for a period of *five years*, you are forbidden to associate with more than one person at a time, or be in a room with more than one person at a time, except for members of your immediate family."

Woods had sighed exasperatedly when Beukes started. Now he found Major Boshoff had opened his briefcase and taken out a set of pictures of Biko's beaten face and body. The officious arrogance of it infuriated Woods, but he could only register it with a glare, because Beukes went relentlessly on. "You are forbidden to write anything, whether privately or for publication. You are forbidden to enter any printing or publishing premises of *any* kind—and are restricted for that five years to the Magisterial District of East London."

Woods shook his head. "My God," he muttered, "has Kruger gone crazy?"

"The Minister of Police, Mr. Kruger, signed your banning orders personally," Boshoff said, gloating. "And he instructed us to convey you to your home in East London immediately."

Five years, Woods thought. What would the paper do? What would *he* do? Then he saw the Pretoria morning paper on the corner of the desk. The headline read: BIKO SUPPORTERS SILENCED, INQUEST DATE ANNOUNCED. He looked up at Boshoff and thought how *fitting* for this government. They're forced to admit an inquest is proper, and then they punish the people who sought it. Well, he hated the banning, but trip or no trip, he had gotten what he was after.

It was a long, dull drive from Pretoria to East London, and at night it seemed both longer and duller. Woods slouched in the backseat of the car, his bags piled around him. Beukes drove and Boshoff was in the front beside him. For miles they said nothing, and Woods' mind flitted from the impact of this on the children to thoughts of Steve and how he had come to figure so largely in their lives.

Finally Boshoff broke the silence. "I knew Steve Biko, you know," he said with a half twist to peer at Donald. "Well, I met him once in a raid on the campus of Natal University," he said, correcting himself. "He was very intelligent—I agree with you about that."

Woods glanced at him. "Yes," he said sardonically. "He was very intelligent. Killing him was not." He turned and stared out at the darkness. "And trying to cover it up with lies was stupid."

"Well," Boshoff replied easily, "we don't know yet what happened, do we?"

"I *saw* his body," Woods answered curtly. "He died of brain damage caused by several blows to the head. Kruger knows that. He's had the medical report for weeks now."

Boshoff turned back to him again. "You *really* believe Biko was murdered?" he asked doubtingly.

"No," Woods replied. "I believe he was tortured and beaten by your people in Port Elizabeth and they went too far. But it's not the first time, is it? So maybe they *do* know what they're doing."

There was another long silence, and this one Woods broke. "And those pictures you confiscated," he said. "Fourteen sets have already been released to the world press."

Beukes glanced at Boshoff, but neither of them said anything. They drove on for another few miles, each looking into the darkness, thinking his own thoughts, until Woods spoke again. "Arresting and banning me is a stupid thing to do," he said reflectively. "Now your Minister of Police has guaranteed a world spotlight on Biko's inquest."

Woods felt he could almost touch the hostility and guilt

that flowed from the front seat. They knew what had happened to Biko. If they hadn't before, they knew now, because they'd seen the pictures and they knew what happened inside police stations. But even if what was done was wrong, they still felt that a white man who took the black side was a betrayer of his people.

The younger man, Beukes, glanced in the rearview mirror at Woods. "I've got two small children, Mr. Woods," he said quietly, "and I think about the *future*. . . . Tell me, what would you do?"

There was a disquieting sincerity and helplessness about it. Woods knew the dilemma the young Afrikaners felt they faced. In truth, it was the dilemma all whites in South Africa faced. At that moment Woods could find sympathy for Beukes and the thousands like him.

"I have children too," he answered. "But the days of a few whites running a black country are over. It's going to change—in bloodshed or partnership. . . ." He paused thoughtfully. "For your white children and mine, I hope it's in partnership."

Boshoff scoffed. "With the likes of Biko?"

The thought struck Woods like a knife. What would partnership with Biko be like, and what might it be with some others? "God," he uttered bleakly, "I hope with the likes of Biko. . . ." The car drove on, the sound of the engine and the wind taking their minds inward. Woods remembered the day he and Biko had taken a long walk across the fields near Zanempilo and they had talked of what the "new" South Africa would be like. "Donald, we don't want the whites to go," Biko had said, laughing at the idea. "Don't you read those papers I give you?"

"Yes, I know," Woods had replied skeptically, "you

want a non-racial, just, and egalitarian society. That's the dream; I'm talking about real life."

"Hell, in real life I know we need you economically," Biko had said. "But even more important, I know your ancestors came here hundreds of years ago. Even before some of *my* ancestors were in the territories. It's *your* country as much as mine . . . but mine *too*. That's our point. All that we've each got to accept is that South Africa belongs to *all* the people who live in it—not to one 'tribe' only, be it black or white."

As he saw the little towns slip by in the night, Woods prayed that somehow, some way, Biko's ideas and Biko's spirit could be kept alive.

# xiv

AFTER THREE MONTHS of banning, Woods had become pretty used to the procedures. From the movement of the police when certain things were said, they knew the house was bugged. They didn't know how many bugs there were, or where they were. All they were sure of was that the living room, their bedroom, and the kitchen were certainly bugged.

There was a black Valiant police car parked across the road with two plainclothes policemen in it, day and night. They not only checked Donald's movements but Wendy's too. The second day he was home, Woods had started typing, and within a minute the police had burst into the house. That is how they first learned the house was bugged. Fortunately Jane was at home, and in the chaos of the break-in and Charlie's barking, ineffectual pursuit of the police, there was enough time for Jane and Donald both to realize what had happened, and Jane to claim that the typing was hers. She was doing a theme for school. The plainclothesman insisted she sit at the typewriter and prove to him she could type. Woods had started to write about Steve, but his first words were about Africa, and Jane not only demonstrated her typing ability but filled the paragraph out on African history.

Woods was very proud of her that day, but from then on, he had only dared type when she was home and, by agreement, doing her homework in his study. When she was gone, Woods had to write in longhand. Many days his hands were cramped and his knuckles sore from the intensity with which he was working.

Each night he hid the manuscript, sometimes in the interstices in the bookcase, sometimes in the hollow of his cricket leg pads. Some evenings, one of his more loyal friends would come and play chess. Ken would sometimes come from the paper, and they would take a ride around town or to the ocean. The police car always followed, but it gave Woods relief from the confinement of the house and kept him abreast of the troubles and triumphs on the *Dispatch*. Despite all the difficulty he felt he had had with the board about his scrapes with the law, they had kept him on full salary and continued to run his name as editor on the masthead. He was proud of that—for himself and for them.

He had never before had the time to work so intensely on one subject. He found the discipline of trying to make Biko come alive on the page a new and exacting challenge. He was driven on by a desire to communicate, stronger than he'd ever felt. But even in his passion to get the man down on paper, he found some of Steve's ideas elusive. None more than his stance on nonviolence. Steve never interpreted nonviolence to mean *passive* resistance. On the contrary, he felt the government should be defied on every issue where fundamental justice was at stake. Like Gandhi before him, he felt there was no place for the coward in a nonviolent campaign. Whether it was a strike or a trade boycott, the nonviolent protestor faced the same physical threat a "fighter" of the System faced. He could be jailed, beaten, even killed. But in the long run, Steve felt that what he called "organized bargaining" would penetrate even the deafest of white ears. Though he always honored those who were prepared to engage in armed struggle to gain their freedom, he thought they had two great allies in a nonviolent approach. One was history. He expected the contest to be protracted and spoke to Donald sometimes of it taking twenty years, but he had no doubt that history was moving in a particular logical direction. That the System in South Africa could not last. That there was no question of the ultimate victory of one man, one vote.

Biko felt that the other great ally they had was "the rest of the world." If they struggled to make the oppression and blatant exploitation of the black majority by the white minority clear to the outside world, it would be seen as such an unforgivable sin that it could not be pardoned by civilized societies.

One of Donald's reservations about Steve's theory was that he was only too aware of how much was suffered in South Africa that the outside world would never know about, whatever sacrifices were made. Biko countered with the belief that by combining nonviolence with Black Consciousness, they were elevating the black majority in a way that ultimately made bargaining inevitable, even if there were temporary defeats.

As he struggled to put Steve's spirit and thoughts on paper, Donald could only wish he had the same confidence Steve had in the method and its results. What underlay it was a fundamental belief that people are more good than bad. At times when he stared out the window at the two policemen watching his house and thought of Steve's death, he wondered about that optimistic view of mankind. Some days the thought would bring a wry smile to his lips because he knew that even in trying to write a book on Steve, he was taking a course Steve would have called "nonviolent action."

When he finally finished it, he invited Father Kani over to the house for a game of chess. Then, without saying a word, he showed him the manuscript. The title page simply read, "Biko," and bore two pictures of Steve, one of him laughing and one of him very serious.

On seeing it, Father Kani was both impressed and alarmed. Woods had very carefully planted on the phone that Kani was to bring his photo album. Kani had been mystified by the request, but knowing Woods' phone was tapped, he assumed there was some mischief up. He now understood that Woods wanted him to smuggle the manuscript out of the house.

As they played on, Woods scribbled a couple of notes to him: one saying he wanted Father Kani to read it and to tell him if he thought he had done Steve justice; another to say that if Kani did feel so, could he possibly take it out of the country on his projected trip to England?

When they finished the game, they spent some time looking at Kani's personal photo album for the benefit of the bugs. Kani actually got some pleasure out of it, and so did Woods. It didn't relieve Kani's nerves altogether about taking the manuscript out under the scrutiny of the two security policemen, but it helped.

Three days later Kani called Woods back and said he had a couple of free afternoons; would Donald like another game of chess? When Kani arrived, they went out into Woods' garden for a little walk before they began. The garden was huge, and though they were far from the house, they still spoke in whispers. The kids were playing and shouting in the pool, providing enough background noise to make them feel secure in talking openly.

"I like what you've written," Kani told Donald, "but you're playing with fire. You think they haven't *guessed* what you've been doing since you've been—" He gestured vaguely toward the house. He had a habit of not finishing sentences when the import was clear. "In actual fact," he went on, "you know the house is bugged, one slip of the tongue, or a surprise raid on the house—" He gestured again. "Disaster. What you've written about Steve is treason, and if I get caught smuggling it out, we'd both get what Nelson Mandela's got—or what Steve—what happened to Steve. And no one would ever know—you know —*why.*"

Woods was terribly deflated. He knew what Kani was saying was right, but in doing the book he'd put those thoughts aside, thinking he would solve them when the time came. And now that it was done, was something actual, he wanted to protect it. "So you think I've done it for nothing?" He sighed.

"What I think is that you should destroy what you've written *now,*" Kani said. Woods stared at him. "Or," Kani continued tantalizingly, "get yourself out of South Africa *with* the manuscript." He gestured toward the pool. "And not just for—well, for their sake too."

Woods couldn't believe him. "Leave here—permanently?" South Africa was his home, his father's home, his grandfather's home, his kids' home.

"In actual fact," Father Kani said, "one or the other."

* * *

Woods had put too much of his heart into the book to destroy it on one opinion, however logical that opinion seemed. He called Bruce McCullough and asked him to come down and shoot some pool with him and talk about old times. "Bring me those books you promised me," he added. Bruce almost said, "What books?" and then, like Kani, he figured Woods was telling him something he didn't want the police to know. Bruce's opinion of the book matched Kani's, but instead of telling Woods to destroy it, he contacted a publishing friend in London and told him about Woods and Biko and the book. The publisher said if the manuscript reached him, in whatever way was possible, he would publish it. Bruce went back to East London for another game of pool.

A couple of days later Woods suggested to Wendy they take the kids out to the beach for an outing. It had been a long time since they'd done that, and everybody was enthusiastic. Evalina prepared a big hamper of food, and they started out early and drove to one of those glorious, unpopulated stretches of beach that abound in South Africa.

They'd been there a couple of hours, and the kids had had their fill of rough and tumble with their father and were playing off on their own—Jane helping Mary find seashells and the boys playing pirates with some old driftwood. The security police were on the hillside above them, but had come to the conclusion it was just a family day out and were lounging inattentively on the grass by their black Valiant. It was then that Woods told Wendy that they were going to have to leave South Africa. After the news Bruce had brought, his own mood was up, and he was totally unprepared for the vehemence of Wendy's reaction. "What do you mean we've got to leave?" she said angrily.

"Bruce has contacted a publisher in England—they *want* my book," Donald said with a little show of pride. "And Father Kani's right, when it comes out, they'll see it as treason. We can't stay." It was all perfectly clear.

Wendy stood and glared at him. "I don't believe this!" she stormed. "Because you want a book published, you're going to rip the kids from their schools, their grandparents, their whole life?"

"They're kids, they'll—"

"Don't you even bother to ask me what *I* want to do? We may hate the way it's run, but this is still *our* country!" Woods leaned up on his elbows; he was getting a little angry himself.

"Wendy, *you're* the radical! You want to just *accept* Steve's death? Accept what this government's doing?"

Up on the hillside, one security guard tapped the other, calling attention to the shouting match. Over the surf and the wind they could not hear the words, but the sound of the argument carried to them.

"What *more* do you want to do!" she raged at him. She was a woman secure in her nest, despite some severe difficulties, and she suddenly felt the nest itself being threatened, her children being threatened, and all for a man's vanity. "You've forced the inquest! You're *banned!*"

"Exactly!" Woods began, but she wouldn't let him continue.

"Are you so god-almighty grand that you're going to change them all on your own?"

"I'm going to do what I can!" Woods yelled back at her. "I'm a writer! You think I can just sit for five years and not put a thought on paper?"

"And to hell with us?"

"No, but—"

"Write something *else!* Is one book going to change the world?"

"Wendy—"

"And what would we do, where would we go? Donald, we've got *five* children! We couldn't take a penny out of here!"

"We'll survive, I'm not—"

"I *know* you! You're willing to tear our lives apart just to see 'Donald Woods' on a book cover!"

"God*damn!*"

"And you're using Steve's death as an excuse!"

Woods scrambled to his feet. He'd never hit her, never thought of hitting her, but at that minute he had to control himself to keep from doing something physical. But she was not afraid, and she glared back at him as fiercely as he was glaring at her. Finally he turned and strode away along the beach.

The kids, like the security police, had heard the sounds of argument. They had turned in their play—sobered, frightened—as Woods stormed off and their mother kicked at the sand.

Woods walked for half an hour, trying to cool down. He knew that part of his anger grew from the truth in what she'd said. He wanted to have a book published about as badly as he wanted anything in life. But it was only part of the truth. In his mind, Steve Biko was the greatest man he had ever met—and he had met some fairly important people in his life, from Bobby Kennedy to Jan Christian Smuts. And that Steve should die unremarked seemed to him a crime almost as great as the crime committed by those who had killed him.

When he walked back to where the family was gathered, Wendy was sitting alone, out on a little sand spit.

After all these years Woods could not help but smile at the fact that she still looked beautiful in a bathing suit. Jane saw him coming and distracted Mary, taking her off, out of earshot. God, she's so wise, Woods felt with a tug at his heart.

He splashed slowly out to the sandbar and sat next to Wendy. She was hunched over, her arms around her bent legs, not looking beyond the sand at her feet. She didn't move a muscle when he sat down near her.

"Wendy, could we talk this out?" he said quietly.

She looked over at him. She had been crying, and her eyes showed it. She looked at him stoically for what seemed an eternity, then she finally spoke. "I'm sorry I was so cruel," she said.

Woods grimaced dismissively. "No," he said, "it's true I want a book published. But"—the words came hard—"but if Steve died for nothing, if they just bury his name, if things are just going to go on getting worse—" He stopped hopelessly.

Wendy turned to him. The tears had come back into her eyes, but her voice was quiet, if deadly. "Who do you think you are, *God?*"

Woods sighed and stared out over the water. "No," he said at last. "Not God—but there's no writer who knows Steve's story or this government like I do. It's just a fact."

"There are seven of us, Donald!" she said, raising her voice slightly. "You're *forty-three* years old! What is *one book* going to do?"

Woods stared at her emptily for a moment, stopped by the rage and fear and accuracy that bubbled up like boiling mercury beneath the taut control she was trying to exercise.

She glanced over her shoulder at the security police, watching them from the hilltop. "Do you think they'll just *let* us out of here? We could all get killed even *trying* to escape—or end up in prison for years, and you still wouldn't get your 'book' published."

Donald acknowledged that, but he nodded over toward the children. "If we stay," he said calmly, "you know that Dillon—and ultimately Duncan and Gavin, too—will be called into the Army."

"All young boys have—"

"*Killing* people we know are right. Or worse, they'll end up *being* killed by people we know are right. . . ."

Wendy turned away from him, burying her head in her knees. She knew there was the possibility of truth in this too.

"I'm not God," Woods said, "but we know what this country is like now. We can't just accept it, and we can't wait for God to change it. We have to do what we can— and the book is what I *can* do." It was manifestly sincere, touching the truth he felt beyond vanity, beyond self . . . and it reached Wendy. She turned to him, her eyes watery, her face torn between love and disagreement. Finally she leaned across the sand and clutched him desperately, and he held her as her body heaved in silent sobs.

On the hilltop, the security police looked down at them.

Far across the sand, Jane played absently with Mary as she looked at the two of them with eyes full of concern.

Nothing was said about leaving South Africa, or not leaving South Africa, for more than ten days. Wendy knew Donald still wanted to, and Donald knew that Wendy didn't. Then one afternoon when Wendy was practicing scales on the piano for a recital she and a friend who played the violin were giving, and Woods was rewriting sections of the book that might never be published, the postman knocked at the door.

Mary and Charlie raced for it, Charlie winning, but Mary hauling him away to open the door.

"A package for Mary and Duncan Woods," the postman announced cheerfully. Smiling sheepishly, Mary took it and slammed the door.

"Mommy, Daddy!" she yelled excitedly. "It's for us! It's a present!" Duncan was soon at her heels, twisting the package to look at the address.

"It's true, Mom!" He beamed. "Can we open it?"

"If it's addressed to you, of course," Wendy answered without breaking her scales.

Duncan ripped open the packet and held up a T-shirt— it bore a picture of Steve Biko with the word "Steve" above it and "Biko" below. "It's a picture of Steve!" The shirt he held was a very small one, and he handed it to Mary. "Here, dumbo," he said, and Mary ran out to the patio, to where she could see herself reflected in the glass of the door. "I'll bet it fits," she said as she disappeared.

The mention of Steve had drawn Woods from his study. Duncan had taken another shirt out of the box and held it up. "Look, Wendy," Woods said lightly. Wendy stopped to glance at them. She was touched by the picture and felt a little guilty about her attitude to the book. "I wonder who's doing them?" she said.

Woods picked up the box. "He's becoming a legend. . . . It's the only good thing about his death." He turned the package over to check the label. "It can't be from your grandparents," he muttered to Duncan. "Is there a return address on the box?"

A piercing scream startled them all.

Mary was standing with the shirt half over her open-shouldered pinafore. Her head was completely locked in it. She was holding her arms straight out and screeching in pain. Woods ran to the patio, Wendy right behind him. Evalina raced out from the kitchen.

When Woods reached her, Mary was still shrieking in terror and pain, her arms outstretched stiffly. Woods lifted the T-shirt off her head and could see that the skin on her face was blotchy and inflamed, her eyes swollen and red; spots of a rash covered her arms. Still screaming, she went to rub her eyes, but Woods grabbed her hands. "Don't touch your eyes!" he yelled. "Call Dr. James!" he told Wendy. "Quick! And make sure he comes immediately!"

Wendy ran to the phone, and Woods picked Mary up and carried her quickly to the kitchen. "Drop that shirt!" he yelled at Duncan, who had followed them out to the patio.

Woods ran right to the sink. Mary went on screaming as he and Evalina splashed water on her face and shoulders. The blotches on her skin were oozing already, and more of them were spreading on her shoulders and neck. Some of them were fire-red.

Duncan had dropped the shirt as ordered but was standing in the kitchen doorway shaking his suddenly painful hands.

"What's the matter?" he said. "What is it?"

Evalina turned to him. "Never mind! Leave the shirt and go upstairs and wash your hands! *Baleka, bhuti!*" Whenever she was excited, she always slipped back into Xhosa.

Duncan was now clutching his hands to his chest, trying to rub off whatever was hurting him. "But why did they make the shirts that way?" he asked in a voice that was near tears.

"Duncan!" Woods yelled angrily. "Didn't you hear what Evalina said?" He turned back to try to soothe Mary as

Evalina poured water over her. Duncan burst into tears and wiped at his eyes with the back of his hand.

Later that night, Wendy had tucked Duncan into bed. His hands were bandaged and he had some dressing on a couple of splotches near his eyes. She held him and kissed him with a more than usual intensity. "You'll be all right, dear," she promised him. "Dr. James said it should stop burning in a day or two." That seemed a long time to Duncan, and his chin trembled. She hugged him again. "Go to sleep," she said soothingly. "The doctor said that pill would give you a good long rest." She kissed him and went over to Gavin's bed and gave him a kiss, then tiptoed out of the room.

When she came into Mary's room, Donald and Jane were still there, standing over Mary's bed, looking down at her. Dr. James had given her a mild sedative, and she was sleeping uneasily. Her arms and shoulders were bandaged, and her red-raw face was covered in a white, powdery medicine. Her closed eyes were all puffed and swollen. Jane was crying silently. "No matter how much they hate us," she whispered, "how could they do that to her?" She turned into her mother's arms, and Wendy held her tight, thinking much the same thing. She rubbed her chin on Jane's head, looking down at Mary, her own eyes ready to overflow. Finally she glanced up at Woods. "I think I want to see that book published," she said. And then the tears did come to her eyes. Donald put his arms around both of them.

# XV

THINGS HAPPENED VERY fast after that. Woods contacted
Bruce McCullough, Father Kani, and Don Card. He felt
they were the only ones he could trust absolutely. Some
others might not mean to betray him but were more liable
to do so accidentally. Bruce found the whole idea of the
Woods' escape exhilarating. By a prearranged signal,
Woods was supposed to meet him December 15. It was
early summer in South Africa, and Woods had told him to
park near a field down the road from the house. Bruce and
Father Kani were arranging for a plane to fly them to Botswana. By Christmas they might be out of the country.

When Dillon reported to Donald that Bruce's car was in
place, Woods went to the very bottom of their garden and
climbed over the wall. When he dropped down in the open
field, he checked carefully to see that there weren't any
security police parked back there to cover such a backdoor
flight. But there were none. He ran across the open field to
a side street. It had no houses on it, and he saw only one

car, which was parked at the intersection of the side street and his own street. He trotted up to the car, opened the door, and slid in.

"Holy shit!" Bruce exclaimed. "I expected you the other way!" His reaction was startled enough for Donald to know that for all his cheery exterior, he was almost as nervous as Woods about what they were trying to do.

"If I go out the front way," Woods explained, "they not only know where I am but who I'm with. And there's nothing in the banning order that says I have to go out the front door." Bruce grinned and pulled the car away, turning down Woods' street in the opposite direction from the house. Woods glanced back. He could see the black Valiant and one of the policemen lounging against it. "Well, they didn't see me," he said buoyantly.

"You ought to report 'em for neglect of duty," Bruce quipped.

"You're cheerful," Woods responded. "I take it you've got some good news."

Bruce's answer was to reach in his pocket and toss a passport on Woods' lap. "It's out-of-date, but we doctored that," he said confidently. "It wouldn't get you out of Jo'burg, but up in the sticks it ought to work as identification."

Woods had opened it to the picture and identity. *"Father* David C. Curren?" He laughed. "An Irishman! How'd you get it?"

"Old Father Kani 'lifted' it!" Bruce answered. "He said he was sure Father Curren would agree, but for safety's sake he intends to explain it to him *later*."

Woods shook his head in amazement. He looked at the picture critically. "Black hair, but apart from that, if the light wasn't too good, I suppose it could work."

"You sure those buggers aren't following us?" Bruce asked.

Woods glanced back. They'd come a fair way in open country now, and there wasn't a car in sight. "Ja, we're alone," he answered.

"Well, then, this looks like as good a place as any to get lost," Bruce announced, and he pulled the car over to the side of the road. "Let's take a look at the map."

He stopped the car and they got out, Bruce spreading his map over the hood of the car. "Trying to fly you out to Botswana is out," he began.

"But we—"

"We tried!" Bruce cut in quickly, trying to arrest Woods' alarm before it got started. "We can't get a plane with the fuel required without tipping our hand. Impossible. I tried. It can't be done."

Woods was crushed by it. If they couldn't fly out, he saw no practical way to get the whole family out. He could never leave Wendy and the kids behind, and traveling fourteen hundred miles with five kids and a wife while being pursued by the police wasn't exactly a viable idea.

Bruce was aware of all that, but he and Father Kani had worked out an alternate plan, and he wasn't going to let Donald sink into a mood of paralyzing gloom. "Grab that end of the map," he said enthusiastically. "Kani and I have got this all figured out."

Woods sighed bleakly but helped to hold down the map.

"We think New Year's Eve is the best time," Bruce began. "Everybody drunk as a skunk. You turn yourself into Father Curren and get up north of Queenstown. Kani will meet you and drive you toward St. Theresa's Mission. It's a bunch of nuns near the Lesotho border. So two priests—it's perfect."

185

Lesotho was the tiny independent republic that sat right in the middle of South Africa. It kept a nominal independence but was totally at South Africa's mercy economically. Nothing could come into it, or nothing go out of it, except through South Africa. And the South African government took every advantage of it. "People are kidnapped from Lesotho by the South African security police every day!" Woods protested. "You think they'll let me—"

"Wait!" Bruce interrupted. "Once you're in the country, and Kani says the border is only a river, you can wade across at a dozen places—"

"I'm a *priest* wading across the border!" Woods shook his head. God, it was sounding worse and worse.

"You do it at *night!*" Bruce exclaimed. "And once you're across, I'll be there to drive you to Maseru before the South African police know what's going on . . . and you *can* fly out from *there* to Botswana. The airline, if you can call it that, is run by a Canadian, with an *Aussie* and a couple of New Zealanders as pilots." He was proud of that, all problems solved by the Aussies and the Commonwealth.

Woods studied the map again. He shared none of Bruce's enthusiasm. "What about the family, Wendy and the kids?" he asked.

"Kani has got that all figured out," Bruce assured him.

Woods remained skeptical. "How are *you* getting to Lesotho?" he asked.

"I'm getting the paper to fly me in from Capetown to do a story on a three-plane Commonwealth airline in a black republic," he said cheerily. "See, while you were chasing women around in London, I was learning how to make a newspaper work for *me,* not the other way around."

Woods had to grin. He'd done his apprentice work as a

newsman in London, and that's where he'd met Bruce. Four of them had shared a flat, Woods, Bruce, and two other Australians. "If I make it," Woods said sarcastically, "my one regret is going to be giving *you* the biggest damn scoop of your life!"

Bruce scoffed. "In a pig's ass! I have had bigger scoops on an ice-cream cone!"

Woods grinned and looked at the map again. It was a long ride from East London to Queenstown. "But why do I have to get so far north before I meet Father Kani?" he asked.

"The police think arms are coming through on those roads near the border. Any car registered out of the district is checked, so Kani's going up there to get a local car."

Woods sighed gloomily. There seemed to be so many obstacles.

"Don't knock old Kani, mate. For a black guy to do what he's doing . . ." Bruce left it hanging.

"Don't worry," Woods replied, "I know the risk he's taking. I just don't see how I'm going to get north of Queenstown."

"You hitchhike, Father Curren—you bloody hitchhike," Bruce said. Woods turned to him, and Bruce smiled, but there was a sobriety to it that showed he recognized the true danger. "And that way, if you do get caught, old mate," he said somberly, "you won't take Kani and Wendy down with you."

Woods pondered that thought with all the weight it deserved. They both looked up at the sound of a heavy engine. A big hippo, an armored personnel truck, had turned onto the road and was approaching them. Bruce casually folded up the map and waved as the hippo passed. Aboard were a group of healthy, bronzed troops casually cradling their modern, steel-gray weapons as the thickly armored vehicle rumbled on. A couple of them waved back.

Woods had to wait five days for his meeting with Father Kani. They had agreed to meet at the Botanical Gardens, a beautiful park overlooking the sea. The trouble was that the park was only open to non-whites on Tuesdays and Thursdays.

Because of his clerical duties, Father Kani had a permit that allowed him into East London after dark, but both Woods and Kani felt it would draw less suspicion if they met "accidentally" in the day. Woods had occasionally taken walks in the Botanical Gardens since his ban. In working out the perspectives of the book, he had found the spacious grounds and long vistas a good atmosphere for thought. He went alone on Saturday—to reestablish the routine with the police. On Tuesday he "bumped into" Father Kani, who was having a thoughtful walk himself. They both knew it wouldn't fool anyone, but it did provide an alibi if one were ever needed, and it didn't absolutely point a finger at their relationship.

After their "happenstance" encounter they wandered together through the arboretum until they found a bench. Father Kani sat on it, and Woods paced in front of him. It was the best way for them to keep an eye on the security police guarding Woods. One direction was covered by Kani, the other by Woods, so they couldn't be taken by surprise, or overheard when they didn't know it.

"It's okay," Woods said. "They've spread out on the grass about fifty yards behind you."

"Bruce has given you the other details and things?" Kani asked.

"Yes."

"Bruce and I have told no one of the exact plan, even Mr. Card. We feel the fewer people who know the details, the less . . . you know, someone won't accidentally give them away."

Woods nodded agreement. "I don't plan to talk to anyone about it, even our closest friends," he assured Kani. "But I'm worried about how I meet up with you."

"Dead simple in fact," Kani said blandly. "We'll meet at a bridge four miles outside Queenstown on the Pretoria road. It's not a . . . you know, big bridge," Kani explained, "but it's actually the *first* bridge outside Queenstown."

"Okay, I can remember that," Woods assured him. "It's getting there that worries me."

"It's nothing to worry you," Kani said confidently. "By five o'clock New Year's Eve, all the white police will be off for parties. Wendy drives you to the edge of town. You hitchhike to the rendezvous point—it should be easy if you don't leave too late."

On that Woods did not agree with him. "If there's one *phone* call and I'm not there . . ."

Kani only smiled. "In actual fact, New Year's Eve, you've gone to bed pissed." He laughed. "Nobody'll question that! Not for you this year!"

Woods grinned ironically at the truth of that. No, nobody would question his going to bed drunk this year.

"Then, the next morning," Kani continued more seriously, "Wendy drives off to the beach . . . only she really goes to her parents in Umtata. If you make it, you phone her the minute you're in Lesotho, and she takes the children north to the border before they have time to pick her up."

Woods nodded. That should work too.

"If you don't make it . . ." Kani said gravely. Woods

189

turned to him and Kani shrugged. They had to face that that, too, was a possibility. "Well, then," he went on, "there's *no* phone call—and she gets back home as soon as she can, so she can't be accused of being a party to it."

Woods paced for a couple of minutes, running it through in his head. It could work. It *should* work. And it certainly was the safest way for Wendy. Finally he turned to Kani and smiled. They would do it.

Kani beamed in response. He was proud of the plan, proud that Woods had accepted it. Woods glanced toward the two security policemen, watching them from across the grass. "If I get out," he said, "they're going to suspect you."

Kani didn't even bother to look behind him. "Probably," he said without bravado. He knew how serious it could be. "But being a man of the cloth—it's proof they'll be missing—in my case I think they'll want it."

Woods was only mildly reassured. Kani was a brave man, taking a terrible risk. The Woods were going to owe a lot of debts if they ever got out of South Africa. He hoped the book was worth it. . . .

# XVI

DECEMBER 31 WAS A warm, sunny day in East London. As part of the plan, Wendy took the children to the beach where most of East London spent the holiday. There were kids playing in the sand all along the wide, curving littoral. People in the rolling surf, people sunning themselves, some young men in uniform tossing a rugby ball. It looked like an advertisement for all that was good about white South Africa—the sun, the sea, the carefree, healthy people.

Wendy sat on a towel in the sand, an open book in her lap, but she kept staring out at the cascading waves, a look of anxiety on her face that was in total contrast to the relaxed atmosphere around her. In twenty-four hours she would have left South Africa forever, or her husband would be in prison, for as long as they wished to keep him. Or, worst of all, they both would be in prison, with only her mother and father to take care of the children.

"Wendy!" a voice called. Wendy started. She grabbed

her book to keep it from falling and twisted to look up, shielding her eyes from the sun. It was a young woman her own age, standing almost over her.

"Alice . . ." Wendy said when she had recovered herself. "I was a million miles away."

"Yes, I could see." Alice grinned. "I didn't expect to see you on the beach at all this Christmastime."

"There's not much else I can do with the kids," Wendy said with a touch of the martyr.

Alice nodded understandingly. She was carrying a copy of the *Dispatch* in her beach bag. "I see they're still carrying Donald's name on the paper," she said comfortingly.

"Yes, they're very loyal," Wendy responded. She looked off and saw Alice's husband, Larry, walking in their direction. He and Alice were obviously leaving the beach, but he was deliberately veering off so as not to get too close to Wendy. "Hi, Wendy," he called. "How's Donald?"

"Surviving," Wendy said with a little grimace.

"Good," Larry returned. "Come on, Alice—we'll be late."

Alice made a little moue at Wendy. They both understood the snub. Alice moved off after him, but she turned to have a last word with Wendy. "I've bought tickets to your recital next month," she said. "I figure with all the time you've had to practice, you ought to be brilliant!" It was a friendly jest at Wendy's "confinement." Wendy acknowledged it wistfully.

Alice waved, then called out, "Happy New Year!" It was a distant afterthought.

"Same . . ." Wendy replied pensively.

She turned back and looked off at her brood. Jane was sitting on the side of a beached rowboat, talking shyly with a young boy while she absently petted Charlie. Mary,

whose skin still bore the marks of the acid burns, was soberly filling a hole she had dug with seawater. Farther back
from the shore, the three boys were playing cricket with
some other boys.

Even if they escaped, what would they ever find to re-
place all this? she wondered.

Back at the house, Woods was in the recreation room.
He had gone in to get the manuscript but had been distracted by the pictures around the room. It was the first
time he'd really looked at them in months. There was a
favorite shot of him and his brother outside the cricket
stand at their school. They were both in all-white cricket
gear. Donald had scored his first century, and it was for the
Schools' Cup. His brother had taken five wickets. Their
father, who thought more of sports achievement than anything else, said it was the proudest day of his life.

There was the picture of Wendy and him putting at In-
verness. It was the year they were married, and a trip to
Britain was an anniversary present her parents had given
them. And there were pictures of the kids growing up. A
four-year-old Dillon holding a rugby ball half his size. A
younger Wendy and a six-year-old Jane at the tennis club;
Gavin and Duncan, still toddlers, kicking a football.

He wanted to take all of them, every one that adorned
the walls of the room. He settled for the one of him and his
brother, and a more recent shot of the whole family canoe-
ing in the Great National Park near Durban. He took the
pictures out of their frames. They'd go in his bag with the
underwear.

Then he took his book from its hiding place in the hollow of his cricket leg pads. He looked at the pictures of

Steve on the title page. How that man had changed his
life . . . all of their lives.

When Wendy left the beach, she took the long way
home. It led them by a small black township that once was
far out of town but, as the city had grown, came to be right
on the edge of the white area. She had a longing to see that
part of South Africa one last time. Jane sat with her in the
front of the car, and the other kids and Charlie were packed
in the back with the towels and beach balls and cricket
gear.

A stretch of the road she took was an actual borderline,
with the township on one side of the road and the city on
the other. The township side was the site of a small shopping area, a row of crude wooden stores. All around them
several women sold fruits and vegetables from plastic
sheets on the ground. In the middle of the holiday, there
were many black men with the day off, and they were
crowded around the veranda of the largest store, smiling
and laughing, despite their ragged clothing and the contrast
between the paved streets in front of them and the dusty
dirt paths of their township behind them.

A police car was parked on the dirt road in the township, three black policemen and one white. They were
lounging, with the car doors open, talking among themselves and just casually keeping an eye on the activity
around the stores.

It was all familiar to Wendy, but her view of it had
changed so much in the past year. However much she
might wish to change it, though, there was a part of her
that viewed it with a melancholy nostalgia. She would miss
those smiles, the disordered vitality of it all.

They were moving slowly in a line of traffic. An old

truck was just ahead of them. It carried five or six young blacks. Boys about eighteen or nineteen, Wendy would have guessed. As they neared the little shopping area the truck slowed to a stop and two of the young boys jumped out and lugged a heavy straw basket loaded with potatoes from the truck. As they struggled with it toward the stores, the one nearest Wendy turned and smiled. "Thank you, ma'am," he said, acknowledging her patience while they were unloading.

Wendy's window was down, and she smiled back. "Don't spend all your profits from that celebrating," she said in Xhosa.

The two boys looked at her, a little taken aback by her use of their native tongue. Then the one who had spoken to her grinned devilishly and retorted in Xhosa, "We'll save some! And Happy New Year to you, too, missus!"

Wendy smiled slowly. The boy's alertness, his white smile, had reminded her of Steve. The truck pulled ahead, and with a little wave she followed it.

When they got in their own area, Wendy stopped in at a shopping center to get ice-cream cones for the kids. When they piled back in the car, Gavin leaned forward. "Can we stay up to see the New Year in, Mom?" he pleaded. "We could get undressed first." Mary and Duncan immediately chorused in, "Yeah, Mom!"

Jane darted a glance at Wendy. She and Dillon had been told the basics of the escape plan because Wendy and Donald both thought they were too aware to miss some of the preparations and might ask awkward questions that the security police's bugs might pick up. "If you *do* get ready," Wendy replied, "I've rented a film and some cartoons." This was greeted with cheers.

They were passing through their own suburb now. Beau-

tiful homes, people gathered around swimming pools and
barbecue pits, some black gardeners working here and
there. Wendy's eyes followed a police jeep with two white
policemen as it passed in the opposite direction.

"Will Dad watch with us?" Gavin suddenly asked.

Jane glanced at Wendy again. "I thought you might
want to ask Alan and Greg—"

"Oh, yeah, can we?" Duncan asked eagerly.

"Well, if you do, your dad will have to skip it, but you
know what he thinks of your choice of movies, anyway."
There were some groans and boos. Wendy's eye caught
Dillon's in the backseat. He gave her a wise look: "Well
handled, Mom."

Wendy pulled in before Alan and Greg's house, and the
three young ones bounced out with Charlie and raced
across the big lawn toward the house. "Can we stay for a
while?" Gavin shouted over his shoulder.

"No," Wendy called back. "You've got to help me un-
load the car. Just ask if Alan and Greg can come tonight."

She sagged back against her seat. There were no side-
walks or curbs in this area, just big lawns that came down
to the road. Wendy could see portions of their own house
farther along the road, and the back end of the police car
pulled off on the grass opposite it.

"Are you scared, Mom?" Dillon asked quietly. He was
leaning forward, between Wendy and Jane, his arms on the
back of the front seat.

"Of course I'm scared," she said thoughtfully, and then
she smiled and roughed his neck and shoulders affectionately. "But for your dad, not us."

"Look what they did to Mary," Jane said in contradic-
tion.

"And the gunshots when Dad was gone," Dillon added.

Wendy hesitated, then stroked his shoulder again. "Okay," she said, "I'm scared for us—and *terrified* for your father." That forced a tiny smile from them all.

Woods had packed the manuscript and the few things he was carrying in a small bag. Ironically the most suitable bag was a South African Airlines carry-on piece. He then planted the false passport on the dressing table in the bathroom, took his glasses off, and started to dye his silver hair black. He was in the midst of it when he heard the garage door being opened and Evalina greeting the kids as they romped into the house.

"We're home!" Wendy called, as much in warning as in greeting.

"Dad! I hit Dillon for a six!" Gavin shouted.

"Good show!" Woods called back as he prepared to shut the bathroom door in case any of them came chasing in to see him. He could already hear Mary and Charlie coming up the stairs.

"Daddy, I brought you some seashells!" she called.

"Take them into the TV room," Woods said quickly. "I'll look at them as soon as I clean up."

The bedroom door opened, and he started to close the bathroom door, but it was Wendy. She slipped in and closed the door behind her.

Woods put his glasses on and signaled for her to be careful about what she said. He knew the black hair could be the kind of surprise that might lead to an accidental comment. "Good day?" he asked very deliberately.

"Exhausting," Wendy said as deliberately. "But the kids want to go again tomorrow!"

"Might as well," Woods answered. "They've been so tied down by all of this."

Wendy had gone to the windows. She looked down at

the two policemen across the way. Both of them were watching the house, and one of them, seeing her in the window, casually lifted his binoculars to see her better. She pulled the drapes.

"I saw Alice and Larry at the beach," she said.

Woods turned back to the bathroom. "I must call him," he said. "Maybe he can come over and play chess with me next week." He turned back and very deliberately raised his voice. "Say, did you remember to pick up the projector?"

Wendy looked at him calmly, then threw her towel on the bed. "Oh, God!" she exclaimed. "Dammit! The kids wanted ice-cream cones, so I went the other way. We even talked about it! And it went right out of my mind. . . . I'll have to pick it up later."

Woods glanced at her, and then at the ceiling. "Dummy," he said. Then, with a lift of the eyebrows, meaning "That should do it," he took his glasses off and went back to his hair dying.

When he finished, he felt it was time to say good-bye to the kids. He was in a terry-cloth robe, and he wrapped a towel around his head. Mary came running in with her pail of seashells but stopped on seeing him. "Daddy, you aren't dressed," she said.

"No. I just washed my hair," he explained, but she'd already forgotten about it and dipped into her pail.

"This is the prettiest," she said as she held up a shell from her bucket.

Woods twisted her around and sat on the bed so that she was between his legs, the two of them facing the door. "Wow, that *is* a pretty one," Woods said. "You know, if you could find another like that tomorrow, I could put them in wood and make you bookends—for your records and things." He illustrated with his hands.

Mary was amazed. "Could you really?"

"Sure," Woods replied. "I'm getting very good with woodwork these days."

"I'll bet I can find one," Mary said earnestly.

He hugged her. "I'll bet you can too."

There was a soft knock on the door, and Duncan and Gavin pushed in. "Mom said you wanted to see us," Duncan said uncertainly. They were both looking at him strangely, the towel around his head, the bathrobe.

"His head's still wet from the shower," Mary said matter-of-factly, and the boys accepted it. They still didn't know why they were summoned.

"I hear that Alan and Greg are coming over soon, so I can't come down, and I thought you might want to say 'Happy New Year' to your old man," he said.

The boys were still sheepish, not knowing if they were in trouble, never realizing this was a good-bye. "Sure," Duncan responded feebly. "Happy New Year..." Little Gavin just smiled, too bewildered to join in.

Woods smiled at it. Then, rather soberly, he said, "I'm counting on you guys not to give your mother too much trouble tonight."

"Okay. We won't," Duncan answered.

"Fine. So... Happy New Year," he said weightedly.

They both nodded. Duncan opened the door. He poked Gavin, and they both quickly said "Happy New Year" and retreated out the door.

Woods turned from the closed door and forced a brightness he didn't feel. "Got a 1977 kiss for me?" he asked Mary. She kissed him on the cheek diligently. She was in a pinafore again, and he could see the white marks the burning had left on her shoulders. And there were a couple near her eyes too. "How about a 1978 kiss?" She kissed him very hard on the other cheek. "Okay," he said reluctantly, "you have a good sleep in the morning." He swatted her bottom affectionately and sent her out the door. His eyes lingered on that closed door for a long time.

Wendy came in later, worried about the time. She pointed to her watch, and he pointed helplessly to his wet hair. Wendy looked at him like he needed a nurse. She went to her dressing table and got her hair dryer. He started to take it from her, but she pulled it back and made him sit on the corner of the bed. She took off his glasses and started drying his hair herself.

In a few minutes it was mostly dry. Wendy's hands patted it into shape. She turned the machine off, and for a moment she looked down at his head, her hand moving through his hair, but gently, in affection. Woods took her other hand and pulled her around in front of him. For a moment their eyes held all the unspoken fear, love, and memory that was called forth because of what lay ahead of them. Finally Woods spoke. "Happy New Year," he said softly. "New Year, New Life, New Everything," it said. Wendy smiled and moved into him, cradling his head for a second as he held her. He turned his head up and their lips met, sealing their fears and hopes and memories in one bond.

Wendy squeezed him to her again, then walked to the window as Woods checked his watch. The two plainclothes policemen had gone, but a primly dressed black security policeman was on duty in their place. He was sitting on the little bench that was the non-whites' bus stop. He could not sit in the sheltered white bus stop farther along, yet he was staring at the Woods residence with the same brazen intensity his white confreres had.

Woods stepped to her side. He put on his glasses, then slipped his arms around Wendy and peeped with her through the parted drapes. "Thank God they're so predictable," he said. He could hear Father Kani's words: "By five o'clock New Year's Eve, all the white police will be off for parties."

Wendy turned to look at him. He had his collar turned, had a black suit on, and carried a black raincoat with his SAA bag. He looked the part. She took off his glasses and handed them to him. Part of the disguise was no glasses. He smiled at her caution, but she was determined not to dwell on his parting and went straight to the door to lead him out of the house.

She preceded him down the stairs. They could hear the kids playing billiards in the recreation room. Mary was pounding incoherently on the piano. Dillon caught sight of his mother coming down and distracted the two boys as Woods slipped past to the kitchen door. For a moment he was tempted to take one last peek at the kids, but Wendy took his arm fiercely. She whispered in his ear, "If they see you and say one *word*..." She pointed to the ceiling, and Woods reluctantly gave up the idea.

Wendy went into the kitchen. Jane was at the sink waiting, fighting back tears. "Where's Evelyn?" Wendy asked. "In her room?"

"No, I sent her to the Corders' to borrow hamburger buns," Jane answered. "She got bloody cross with me."

Wendy opened the door and signaled Donald to come on in. Jane looked at him in his priest's outfit and almost smiled through the anxiety and heartache she felt. Jane was the most imaginative of all the children, and her mind called forth all the possibilities, especially the disastrous ones. Woods was going to say something to her when the phone suddenly rang. For a moment they all froze, and then Donald took the kitchen extension. "Hello," he said cheerfully. "Oh, Terry—Happy New Year to you too.... No, the buggers are always listening, but don't let that stop you.... No, I'm rapidly getting pissed here, so it'll be a good New Year's regardless.... Yeah, well come over when you get back. We'll raise one for liberty.... Same, mate." Donald looked at them all, raised his eyebrows in relief, and hung up. Dillon had come into the kitchen in the middle of the call. He'd carefully shut the door behind him and stood in it so no one else could come in without bumping him first. Now that the call was over, he made a little gesture of approval about Donald's attire. Woods smiled at it, then looked up at the clock. He couldn't read it without his glasses, but Wendy knew what the gesture meant.

"Well," she said, "I've got to go and pick up that damn projector—I might as well do it now."

Those were the words for going. Water flooded Jane's eyes. Dillon looked a little pale. Woods went to him and gave him a hug around the shoulders. Dillon smiled weakly at him. Then Woods turned toward the back door and signaled Jane to come to him. She ran to his arms, sobbing in forced silence. Woods kissed the top of her head and squeezed her tightly. Then he pulled free and went to the door to the garage. Wendy had already gone out. He paused in the doorway and looked back for the last time ever—at the room...the house...his life...and then at his kids. He had to fight the water in his own eyes. He signaled thumbs-up to Jane and Dillon, took off his glasses, then turned and walked into the garage.

Wendy had the back door of the Mercedes open, and she

was waiting for him very impatiently. Woods slipped into the car, laying his airline bag before him. He covered it with his raincoat, and then he stretched out on the floor. Wendy threw a blanket over the top of him, tucking it in nervously, almost irritably. Then she closed the car door and swung open the garage door.

The black security man across the street stood up to look. It was nothing threatening. He just watched.

Wendy got in and started the car. She kept the key turned too long and made the starter grind noisily. She knotted her face, determined to keep steady, but her hand shook as she put the car in reverse and started to back out.

The black security man watched her. He had his walkie-talkie to his ear, listening to something. Wendy shifted gears with a heavy *clunk*, then pulled away. The security policeman stood watching the car disappear, speaking into his walkie-talkie.

On the floor in the back of the car, Woods was reacting to Wendy's nervous driving. He wanted to say something to calm her, but he didn't dare speak until they had pulled well away from the house. But it was Wendy who spoke first. "I hope there aren't any drunks out yet. I'm so nervous, I'll run right up the curb if anything goes wrong."

"Are we being followed?" Woods asked loudly.

"I don't think so," Wendy answered after a nervous glance in the mirror. "There's one car. I think it's Atman's."

Woods lay there listening to the sound of the car and the tires on the road. Everything they'd planned was going to stand or fall in the next few hours. He was more frightened than he dared admit—even to himself. He recalled one night when they were in the darkened, deserted community center, and Biko and Mapetla had come into the town illegally. Woods and Wendy were there to see what might be needed after the first repair work had been done, following the police's vandalizing. After Steve and Mapetla arrived, Woods had gone out and bought some beer, and they sat around and talked, Biko the calmest of them all. He sat with his long legs propped up on a sewing machine, smiling as Woods chastised him for "taking risks."

"Of course I take risks," Biko had replied with a casual smile. "All the time. But they're only unusual if you think we're a land at peace. In a war, people take great risks as a part of life." He looked at Donald gravely. "Well," he said, "I'm at war. . . ." And he had sipped his beer.

Lying on the floor of the Mercedes, Woods realized *he* was at war now. The thought didn't make it easier, but it gave some sense to the absurdity of driving through town on the floor of a car.

"I was afraid of that," Wendy said suddenly. "It's raining. It was absolutely clear all day, and now it starts to rain."

"Is it heavy?" Woods asked.

"Not really. It's just one group of clouds. It should pass soon. We're getting near the city limits. You'd better sit up, Father Curren."

Woods pulled himself up and grabbed the bag and his raincoat. He started to slip the raincoat on. Wendy peered up at the sky. "It's just a thundercloud. I think it'll pass."

Woods looked at the back of her head. He knew the pressure she was under. "You're a very brave woman, Mrs. Woods," he said warmly.

"No, I'm not!" she answered. "I'm a very frightened and scared woman! And don't try to bully me into anything else."

Woods smiled. She had turned the car onto the main

highway north to King William's Town. "Oh, God, we're in luck," she exclaimed. "Father Kani was right. On the holiday you won't be the only hitchhiker."

Wendy pulled the car up to the very end of the long line of hitchhikers. The rain had almost stopped. She turned around in her seat. "No good-byes," she said tautly. "Just get out, Father Curren. And I wish you luck."

Woods looked into her eyes, knowing what she was saying. He slipped on his coat. He took the bag and opened the door. "Thank ye for the lift, Mrs. Woods," he said in his best Irish accent. He closed the door, Wendy started the car away, and suddenly Donald raced after her, pounding on the window. "Wendy! Wendy!" he shouted. She stopped and rolled down the window.

"Don't forget to pick up the projector," he said breathlessly.

"Oh, my God." She sighed. "I'd forgotten all about it. Thank God you reminded me!"

Woods smiled. "See you soon," he said. It caught her. She bit her lip to keep from giving in to the emotion, sent the car ahead, and then made a sweeping U-turn back toward the city. Woods watched the car go off in traffic until it was lost in the blur.

Woods' head was turned by a small military convoy that was coming from the city. A jeep with white officers, followed by a truck with black soldiers and another truck pulling a small artillery piece. Woods watched the soldiers in the trucks tensely, seeing if they reacted to him. He knew right then that he had to fight the feeling that everyone in a uniform was looking for Donald Woods. As he was staring after them, a car pulled up beside him and honked. He jumped, startled. It was a BMW, an older one, and very unwashed. An Afrikaner farmer stuck his head out. "I'm going toward King William's Town," he said.

"Fine . . . fine," Woods said, getting his mind back to hitchhiking. "Thank you very much." And he piled in.

They drove off, and Woods shook his hair. "It's still a bit wet out there," he said conversationally.

"I wonder why the pope doesn't give you boys enough money for a car," the man said. It was mocking but dryly good-humored. Woods smiled at it tensely. He hadn't thought about *why* a priest would be hitchhiking. "Well—" he said, fumbling, "he—ah—may feel he has better uses for his money." Then he thought of a good line. "We have a parish car, of course," he went on blandly, "but it's not my turn, and since it's New Year's Eve . . ." He left the sentence dangling. The Afrikaner could figure it out from there.

"Ahh," the man said. "So that's it. I must tell you, I don't much like Catholics," he continued in one breath. "I believe God spoke in the Bible—and it's blasphemy for a man to say he speaks for God on earth." It was said with the same mocking good humor. The man was so certain of his position that he bore no malice toward those too benighted, or too perverse, to recognize the truth.

"Well, I'm very lucky you picked me up, then," Woods said wryly.

The man laughed. "Oh, I don't hold against any man— whatever his way—as long as he doesn't hold against me. Are you a true South African or one of these imports?"

"A *true* South African," Woods said before he remembered that he was supposed to be the Irish Father Curren. The Afrikaner turned to him, catching his look of discomfort.

"You look like you're ashamed of it," he said.

"No—no, not at all," Woods replied. "My—my family has lived and died in South Africa for six generations. I love every hill and valley in it." He said the last with a note of melancholy that came from the realization that he was leaving his country—probably for good.

The tone made the Afrikaner question its meaning. "You're not one of those Red priests who'd give it all away to the *kaffirs*, are you?" This was a little less good-humored.

Woods glanced at the bag on his lap and wished he could really answer that. But he stuck with his act. "Not likely," he said. "I'm a cricket player. I don't like all this fuss stopping us from beating the bloody Australians."

That drew a happy chuckle. "An honest priest!" the Afrikaner exclaimed in surprise. "By God, I wish you'd talk to your brothers of the cloth. It's the damn church schools that give these *kaffirs* their fancy ideas."

Woods smiled as he glanced at his bag. "Isn't that the truth," he said with a little more meaning than the Afrikaner could comprehend.

"They were tribes wandering around the land, never settling anywhere. We're the ones who *built* this country. If we hadn't given them something to do, they'd have wandered off someplace else. That's what they ought to be taught. It makes all this trouble." He'd turned his light on, and they were catching up to the military convoy. He nodded ahead to them.

"But our boys in the Army can handle any *kaffirs* who get out of line, just so they don't allow the Communists to give them arms." He turned and smiled at Woods. "But even your pope is against the Communists. So despite your damn schools, I expect we'll make out."

Wood decided he was going to hear some more along

this line in the next few miles, so he relaxed and listened to the Afrikaner's accent for memory's sake.

The guard was changed at Woods' house at about ten o'clock. It was a white duty officer who drove the next black security policeman to the post and picked up the man he was replacing. The man coming off explained that all the drapes had been pulled in the living room. But he'd seen them setting up a movie projector. The white duty officer looked at the house. You could see bits of light from around the drapes in the living room and the venetian blinds in the study. Upstairs, there were some lights too. "It's okay," he said to the new man. "Just keep your eyes on the place—and *don't* go to sleep!"

In the house, Dillon was showing a cartoon. It was in the living room where the big Christmas tree still had its place in the corner. The kids were all in their pajamas. Mary was sitting on Evalina's lap. Duncan and Gavin were sprawled on the floor with their friends, Alan and Greg. "That's the Road Runner!" Mary whispered loudly, pulling Evalina's face around to the screen.

"Yes, isn't he som'thin'!" Evalina responded, hugging Mary until she squealed. But Evalina's eyes went right back to Jane, who was prowling restlessly around the billiard table in the recreation room. *Come in here,* Evalina mouthed to her. Jane shrugged and pointed to Dillon. *When he puts the film on,* she mouthed back. There was a sudden thud upstairs, and Evalina's eyes went anxiously to the ceiling. Jane moved quickly to her side, anticipating what would follow.

"Maybe I should go help," Evalina whispered.

*"No,"* Jane answered too emphatically. "I mean, Mother's probably just taking his shoes off." Evalina was

still bothered, but Mary pulled her face around to the cartoon again.

Wendy had lost her grip on a large suitcase she was taking down for packing. She waited nervously for some reaction to the thud, but she heard the kids' laughter go on, and no footsteps on the stairway. She'd already packed the things she felt were absolutely necessary for the kids. It had been so hard to choose what should be left behind. She only took one reminder of South Africa for them—a rugby pennant with a player in full stride, a small South African flag at an angle near the top, and across it all the words, THE SPRINGBOKS. Even choosing it had affected her. What strange and powerful loyalties sports created.

She stood and looked around their own bedroom. What to take? She went first to her dressing table. They could take almost no money with them, because they hadn't dared tap their savings account for fear of alerting the authorities. So her jewelry was going to have to do for spending money, until one of them got a job.

She pulled open the top drawer and took out a necklace of pearls, a ruby brooch with little diamonds around it. As she rummaged through the other things to separate the real from the costume jewelry, she came upon a picture she had slipped into the drawer long ago. It was one of the children at poolside with a beaming Evalina standing behind them like a proud mother hen. She paused and looked at it again. Gavin had a tooth out. Jane still looked androgynous in a bathing suit. And Evalina . . . Wendy felt a sudden pang of remorse. That face, that devotion. Her mind went back to the courtroom in Pretoria when Steve had been asked by the prosecution lawyer, "But why do you use a phrase like 'Black is beautiful'?" Steve had answered, "Because black is commonly associated with negatives—the black market, the black sheep—anything which is supposed to be bad."

"Then why do you use the word," Judge Regter had asked. "I mean, you people are more brown than black."

"Why do you call yourselves white?" Biko had replied blandly. "You're more pink than white." Wendy remembered that there was utter silence in the court; she and a number of other people were fighting smiles because Judge Regter was so pink as to be almost rubicund. Finally the judge blinked and said, "Precisely." Wendy had wanted to laugh, but Steve had responded with words she would never forget.

"Whatever *we* do, we *will* be called black in the inferior sense by some. And it is precisely because of that that we choose to use the word positively. To alter its negative image. To challenge the very roots of the black man's belief about himself. To say, 'Man, you are okay as you are.'"

Wendy looked at the picture of Evalina and thought of those words. Her vision blurred, but she put the photo in the box with her most valuable jewelry.

# xvii

WOODS DID NOT have an easy time going north. The Afrikaner farmer had let him out at the intersection of a small road in the middle of nowhere. Woods had signaled, waved, whistled, done everything but get down on his knees and pray, as one car after another passed him by. In sheer desperation he had started walking. He turned at the sound of a motor approaching and waved his hand, pointed at his priest's collar, but like all the rest, the lights swept past him. Then, about two hundred yards up, it pulled over to the side of the road and stopped. Woods couldn't believe it at first; then the truck, for that's what it was, began to back up. He ran along to it.

As he got closer he could see that it was an old Bedford loaded with empty chicken crates. He pulled open the door on the passenger's side. "Where you headin', Father?" the driver asked. He was a black man in overalls who looked like he'd spent the day working.

"Well, I'm going toward Queenstown, but I'll go as far as you're going," Woods answered quickly.

"Come on in," the man said with a smile. His name was Jason, and he was returning to a farm north of King William's Town after delivering chickens to a catering supplier in East London. Woods put one foot in the cab, and suddenly a mangy little brown-and-white dog started yapping at him. Jason grabbed him and shoved him down in the seat. "Don't mind him," he said, "he just makes a lot of noise—he doesn't do nothin'."

Woods climbed in, and Jason veered out onto the road again. His dog was sniffing at Woods and wagging his tail. "Why's a Father traveling at night like this, hitchhiking?" Jason asked, then laughed quickly, to be sure Woods understood that no offense was intended.

"Well, I didn't expect to be doing it," Woods answered. "But priests have troubles, too, I'm afraid." His tone carried all his pent-up anxiety at the time he had wasted trying to get this one ride.

"Oh, yes, sir, I can believe that!" Jason laughed. "But I tell you somethin', Father, it's very hard to see you in those dark clothes. I couldn't tell what you were at first."

Woods worriedly glanced down at his black outfit. "Yes," he said thoughtfully. "I'd better get out under a light next time. Maybe you could let me off in Stutterheim."

Jason laughed. "Yes, sir, Father. As long as you ride with me through King William's Town," he said. "Those white kids will be dru-unk tonight. Maybe they give me trouble, but with a white Father . . ." He laughed again. It was his way of dealing with whites, and trouble. Laugh. He glanced over at Woods, and Woods smiled back that he understood.

They drove a little while, and Jason chose to make absolutely sure no offense was seen in his remarks. "Certainly when it's not New Year's Eve it's a fine town," he said. Then he laughed again. "I've met some good people from King William's Town!"

Woods looked out at the dark road. How many good people had he met in King William's Town? "Yes," he said reflectively. "So have I. . . ."

For some reason his mind went, not to his first meeting with Biko, but to the inquest he had fought hard to get. There was the medical evidence of the blows Steve had received, the details of that ruthless ride on the floor of a Land Rover to far-off Pretoria, the contradictory testimony of the police, and yet he could still hear the magistrate's verdict: "The findings of the court are as follows: one, that the deceased, Bantu Stephen Biko, a black man aged thirty, died on September 12, and the cause of death was brain injury, which led to renal failure and other complications; two, that on the available evidence the death cannot be attributed to any act or omission amounting to a criminal offense on the part of any person." And with the tap of a gavel he called the inquest closed.

It was the first time Woods feared that South Africa would never make it without bloodshed.

They drove on through the night, and Woods' eyes became used to the darkness of the cab. On the dashboard in a weathered but gaudy plastic frame, Jason had a picture of a group of kids standing before a crude brick dwelling. They were lined up—smallest right, tallest left—all barefoot, ragged, but most of them smiling.

"Those your children?" Woods asked.

Jason glanced proudly at the photo. "Yes, sir. I got seven. Was eight, but Sarah, she died. Sweet little girl." He was pleased at being asked.

Woods eyed him with a teasing grin. "You're still a young man. You're going to end up with a *big* family."

And Jason rocked back and forth with laughter. "That is the truth!" he exclaimed. "My wife and me, we always try to have our week off together, and sure as sin, every year, she gets pregnant!" And he laughed again.

"Where's your wife working?" Woods asked.

"Up in Jo'burg. I got a permit to look for a job up there once, but unless you wanna work in them mines, the *baas*, he don't have to pay you hardly more than your bus fare to work. I couldn't send nothin' back to the homeland for my kids."

"They're in a homeland, are they?"

"Yes, sir," Jason replied. "Ciskei. My wife's cousin— uh-oh!" And he started laughing. A very forced and anxious kind of laugh. Woods looked ahead at what had caught Jason's eye.

They had entered King William's Town, and some white youths were spread out across the street in front of them. They were celebrating, shouting "Happy New Year" to one and all. Their mood wasn't nasty, but they were looking for fun, and the old truck, with its load of empty chicken crates, seemed heaven-sent.

Jason slowed a little, but he knew he didn't want to stop. For a moment it looked as though the boys were going to let them through without incident, but then one of them threw an empty beer bottle at the chicken crates, and it bounced off and landed on the road with a pleasing crash. Another bottle was thrown, and then another. They had separated enough to let the truck through, and Jason kept right on driving and right on laughing. But as they came even with the last boys, one of them grabbed a rope tied around the chicken crates and hopped a ride. The others cheered and started to give chase to get rides of their own. The boy's hold on the rope was tilting the whole load of crates, and it looked like they'd topple any second.

Jason was still ho-ho-ho-ing, with a weaker and weaker will, and Woods was frantic at the thought of an incident here that might bring the police. Finally he could take it no more, and he opened the door and leaned out, shouting back at the boy on the truck, "Get off, you damn fool! I'll break your goddamn neck!"

The boy stared at him—openmouthed and stunned— and he slowly dropped off the side of the truck. The other boys were still running and shouting in pursuit, but the boy who had first grabbed the rope pointed to the truck in amazement. "There's a white priest in with that *kaffir*," he warned.

Satisfied that the pursuit was over, Woods pulled back around and slammed the door. He was suddenly aware that Jason was staring at him—*his* mouth agape too. Woods realized that his choice of words hadn't exactly been priestly.

"I—ah—I suppose I'll have to say penance for that out-burst," he said as primly as he could.

Jason burst into laughter again. "Yes, sir! You going to! But you got me through King William's Town, so I think God must be with us!" His laughter rolled on into the night.

At the house Wendy had finished her packing and come down to be with the kids. Mary had gone to sleep on Eva-lina's lap, but the others were wide awake, watching the film. She had hardly settled when there was a knock on the door. Jane looked at her worriedly; Charlie growled but was held back by Duncan. Wendy signaled Evalina to stay put with Mary and walked anxiously to the door herself.

When she opened it, all she faced was a smiling, and somewhat drunk, Don Card. He was dressed in a tuxedo with a white silk scarf around his neck. "Hi," he said cheerily. "I've come to have a New Year's drink with Donald!" Before Wendy could stop him, he had pushed into the hall and given her a clumsy kiss on the cheek. "Happy New Year!" he said tipsily.

Wendy could see why it was a wise decision not to let anyone but those directly involved know about the escape. In this mood Don might have told Kruger himself! She grabbed his arm and turned him back to the door. "Don," she said firmly but good-humoredly, "he's gone up to bed. He's had too much already!"

"Good," Card declared as he resisted her shove to the door. "Wake him up! It'll serve him right—drinking on his own!"

"Don, really, I can't," Wendy insisted. "He's out. Besides, the kids have two friends in there. He couldn't come down."

"I'd meet him in the kitchen," Don pleaded. "Just the two of us. And as an ex-policeman, I guarantee you, no law would be broken."

Wendy grabbed his arm again and with feminine persuasion led him out the door. "Come on, you big buffalo, get out of here," she chided. "Come around tomorrow night. He'll *need* company then."

Card reluctantly accepted that he wasn't going to have a drink with Donald. But when he got out of the house again, his boozy cheer turned to boozy earnestness. "I've been to one police ball," he said, "and I'm going 'round to another."

"Well, if you don't run into anybody, then I'm sure you won't get arrested for drunk driving," Wendy said, and waved good-bye.

Card glanced into the living room where the kids were gathered around the movie, and he signaled Wendy to him very confidentially. Wendy went to him reluctantly. He put his arm around her shoulder and started to walk to his car. "Wendy," he said very seriously and very quietly, his eyes on the black security policeman across the street, "they've been talking. They hate Donald—he's made them look like fools. They figure he's gotten away with murder in court." He stopped and turned to her. "They're going to get him."

Wendy felt a chill from her head to her feet. "What do you mean?" she whispered as calmly as she could.

"They know someone like Donald isn't sitting around doing nothing," Card replied in the same hushed tone. "They figure they're going to catch him writing. I got a feeling they're going to raid the house when you least expect it."

Wendy's anger was heightened by her tension. *"Are* they?" she said acidly.

It went right past Card. He bent and got into his car. He closed the door and rolled down the window to speak to her. "I'll keep my ears to the ground," he whispered with obvious concern, "but if they ever find him writing, or find something he's written—if they can legitimately get him into those police cells, just once . . ." He looked up at her, and there was no question that he felt the danger. And it turned Wendy's mood from defiance to abject fear.

"How can you *mix* with them, Don?" she asked with loathing.

Even drunk, its corrosive disgust got to Card. "Wendy,"

he said in expiation, "I was a policeman when I was eighteen. Before Donald set me up in security, it was my whole
life. My oldest friends are still police." Wendy was looking
at him, shaking her head, unaccountable tears running
down her cheeks. Card saw them and knew, he thought,
the tensions and fear she was experiencing; but he knew
something of the other side too. "All cops aren't bastards,
Wendy," he continued gravely, "or I can tell you, more
would have happened to this household than ever has. . . ."
But he could not face the pain in her face and he lowered
his head. "The trouble is," he explained, "if people get a
license to run wild, the scum come to the top . . . and even
the nice ones lose their incentive to be nice."

There was a moment of silence, with only Wendy's
choked snuffles a lingering evidence of their conversation.
Card turned on his lights and started the engine. He looked
up at Wendy again. "Tell Donald to play by the rules," he
pleaded solemnly. "Tell him not to take one chance." He
reached out and squeezed her hand—and drove off.
Wendy watched him go, then looked across at the black
security policeman. He was just standing in the dark,
watching her. She turned back to the house.

Wendy walked up and down the garden for several minutes after Don Card left. She tried to pull herself together
and make something good out of his visit. It convinced her
more than ever that they were right to leave. Now they
must only do it safely, and that depended, in part, on her
keeping her emotions under control.

She walked back to the house about twenty minutes before midnight. She went in through the kitchen door and
went directly to Donald's "wine cellar." It was just a cupboard, but he did keep a fair supply. There were three bot-

tles of champagne, all expensive. She took one out and placed it in the freezer, then got an ice bucket and filled it with ice cubes.

By the time the magic moment came, she was in the living room with the chilled champagne, trying to get the top off. "Hurry, Mom," Gavin exhorted. "It's almost time!" The television was on to a New Year's party, and a second hand was beginning to count down the final minute. The top finally popped! There was a shout from all of them, and Wendy laughed as the champagne gushed forth.

Evalina had brought in a tray of glasses, and Wendy began filling them, a tiny sip for Mary, and something more for all the others. Jane hurriedly passed the glasses out. Dillon, Duncan, Gavin, and one for each of their guests, Alan and Greg. Wendy poured a final two—one for Evalina and one for herself. The second hand was moving fast.

"Can Daddy come down if he stays in the other room?" Mary pleaded.

"Daddy is *asleep,* which is what you're going to be in fifteen minutes!" Wendy said lightheartedly.

"It's ten seconds!" Duncan yelled.

Dillon turned the television up. People at the television party were counting down: "Nine, eight . . ." The Woods house joyously entered in: "Seven! Six!" Wendy glanced around at the house . . . at her children. What would it be like when the next New Year's came?

"Three! Two! One! Happy New Year!" they all shouted as one. They touched glasses all around, the young boys giggling at the sense of indulging in forbidden adult pleasures. Then they all took a sip. More giggling from the boys, but little Gavin ran to his mother, and Wendy clasped him to her. "Happy New Year," she said again. Duncan and Alan were hugging each other in horseplay. Wendy put an arm around each of them and squeezed Duncan. "Happy New Year." Then her eyes fell on Jane's, and they toasted each other across the room for a lingering moment.

Mary had run to Evalina and wrapped her arms around her legs. "Happy New Year," she said without being exactly sure what it meant. Evalina hugged her, then turned toward her mother. Wendy bent down, and Mary ran into her arms. "Happy New Year, Mommy!" she said excitedly. "And a Happy New Year to you, my darling," Wendy replied, holding her especially tight.

Wendy looked up. Dillon had kissed Evalina on the cheek, and Jane was next. From her kneeling position Wendy watched Evalina's beaming face as Duncan and Gavin came to pay their respects too.

Woods was standing alone under a streetlight in Stutterheim when the ringing of church bells and the horns and shouts from a party nearby told him he had entered a new year of his life. He had been looking at his map and worrying about the time when the celebrations started. He saw some lighted houses; there was a party in a building near him with well-dressed young couples dancing to a band. It was a neat, wealthy little community. The distant shouts and laughter reminded him of Steve dancing in the *shebeen*, so happy and seemingly carefree. And then there was the day Woods had found him playing rugby, miles from where the police thought he was.

"I got my summons today. I think they're trying to break up our friendship." Woods could remember the words.

"I don't know," Biko had answered with that knowing

grin of his. "A few months in jail might be just what you need to prove your credibility."

Woods was jerked from his reverie by the roar of a Land Rover turning the corner and pulling up next to him. A patrol policeman jumped out, glanced at the startled Woods, and went around to the back door. "Okay, in you go, Father!" he said flatly.

Woods was staggered. "But I was just—"

"The locals told us you were trying to get to Queenstown," the patrolman said impatiently. "We're about to cover that stretch of road. If we don't run into any trouble, we should get you there in a couple of hours."

Woods sighed with relief. "Bless you, my boy," he muttered as he got in the back. Patrolman Louw closed the door. The driver, Patrolman Nienaber, turned to glance at Woods. "You going to the Mission?"

"That's right," Woods replied as they started off.

"Well, if it's not an emergency, I'd spend the night in Queenstown if I were you," Louw said.

"Oh, I'm sure I can find a lift," Woods protested.

"You might find some black terrorists too," Nienaber remarked.

*"Here?* In the Eastern Cape?" Woods exclaimed.

They both turned to look back at him. Was he kidding?

At the house, Wendy was lying on their bed, fully clothed. She looked at her watch, the ceiling, the empty space beside her. The door pushed slowly open, and Charlie came in looking as mournful as she felt. She petted him, and he lay at the side of her bed.

For a moment she just looked at the ceiling vacantly, but she decided it was a good time to put the suitcases in the car. She took the big one with all the kids' things down

first. She was alive to any noise. She didn't want any of
the younger ones to wake and see her with a suitcase and
ask questions. Charlie bounded down the stairs after her,
and she shushed him.

By the time she got in the garage, Charlie was convinced they were going someplace, and he circled Wendy
eagerly, begging and whimpering. With her mind on him
and the noise he was making, Wendy slammed the trunk lid
too hard. She slapped at Charlie's nose, then froze, waiting
for some reaction.

Across the street, the security policeman had heard the
noise and stood, wandering over toward the house. But the
noise wasn't repeated, and he shrugged his shoulders and
returned to the non-white bench and sprawled on it.

In the house, Wendy had Charlie by the collar, leading
him across the kitchen. When she got out into the hall
where the stairs were, she let him go and he bounded up
the stairs. She could have killed him, but he stood at the
top, wagging his tail, waiting for her to come up. She
shook her head but couldn't help smiling at him.

Once he'd gotten over his initial fright when he was
picked up, Woods had remembered he was supposed to be
an Irish priest. They had started talking about South
Africa. It was all good-humored, with Woods leaning over
the seat between the two patrolmen and giving them a
slight accent as he went along. Nienaber had made the
mistake of calling South Africa one of the free countries of
the world.

"Free?" Woods had exclaimed. "By God, man, *no* one
in South Africa is free. The blacks—well, you know for
certain how 'free' they are. And you whites, it's almost as
bad. You spend fortunes on guns and police, and yet I'm

damned if you don't all live with the fear of terrorism. And I say, until you create a little justice, it's just going to get worse."

"Justice?" Louw responded. "You sound like the bloody Americans. They slaughtered all the Indians; now they're telling us how awful we are because we want the blacks to have *passes!* Justice!"

Woods had to smile. "All right," he said, "but if you five million whites were to kill off twenty million blacks, you'd have to ship twenty million back from someplace to do all the bloody work for you!"

Louw grinned wisely. "Well, Father, that's exactly what we're doing," he said. "We're shipping them *out* to the homelands, and then importin' them back in to work!" Nienaber chuckled.

"Well, that may seem very clever to you, old son," Woods replied. "But how long do you think the cockeyed world's going to buy that one?"

"We should give a shit—oops, pardon me, Father—but whether the world buys it or not makes no difference," Louw argued. "They need our manganese and chromium and stuff, and they're going to accept anything we tell them as long as we sugar it up a little."

"Don't you believe it, my boy," Woods retorted. "The one thing that will ruin South African mines and industry is a long, drawn-out civil war. If that starts, your fine country will be back to the Stone Age in more ways than one. You think England and America haven't figured that out?" The rest had been banter, but this carried a note of true conviction with it that bothered both the patrolmen.

"*Ach*, man," Louw stated with a touch of bitterness, "I'm really glad you came to this country, Father. While we're out here gettin' shot at, it's nice to know we got people like you behind our backs."

"Don't misunderstand," Woods protested affably. "I know what you boys are doing isn't easy. I just think you're shooting at the wrong enemy."

"*Ja*. Me too," Nienaber chimed in. "I think we ought to be zeroing in on a few Irish *priests!*" He smiled drolly, but Louw burst into laughter. A real joke! He turned back to Woods and offered him a cigarette.

"Have a smoke, Father." He grinned. "And you just leave South Africa to us."

Later they turned into a small road that led to a township. There had been a fight in one of the houses. Louw and Nienaber had gone into the house. The clock on the Land Rover's dashboard already read two-forty, and Woods was growing increasingly apprehensive. Outside, one black man was standing in the search position against a wall. There was no electricity in the township, and Woods could only see what was revealed to him by a couple of hand-carried kerosene lamps. There was still some angry shouting and some crying, but Nienaber finally came out with one man who had his hands handcuffed behind him. Nienaber put him in the back with Woods, securing his hands with a chain and lock to a metal rail along the side.

Woods slid along, closer to the driver's seat. Louw finally came out of the house and handcuffed the man who was propped against the wall. He brought him to the Land Rover and secured him opposite the other man. They both had blood on their clothing, and the man who'd been against the wall had a blood-soaked bandage on his face. Nienaber brought two thick knives, a machete, and a heavy fighting chain from the house. He dumped them on the floor near Woods. They were all bloodstained. He didn't say anything, he just looked up at Woods.

The two patrolmen got in the cab and started to pull away. As they went down the little township street, their lights revealed the faces of dozens of blacks, some watching them stoically, some glaring—none of them friendly. "You still want to go beyond Queenstown?" Louw shot back to Woods.

Woods looked at the clock. Two-fifty. He turned back, and his eyes caught the eyes of the man opposite him. They were angry, sullen eyes, made more fierce by a scar that ran from the corner of one eye down across his cheek. Woods was reminded of Biko's softer eyes, looking at him with that same kind of penetration. "Black people don't have any hope," Biko had said. "They don't see any way ahead, they are just defeated persons. They live with their misery, and they drink a hell of a lot because of their misery. I want to give them hope—before their resentment gets to a point where people are prepared to use any means to attain their aspirations."

Woods looked into the sullen man's eyes again. He felt like saying, "I'm trying to give you hope too." But it was clear that the man was not in a mood to listen to white Irish priests on this night.

# xviii

IT WAS OVER an hour later before Woods finally stepped
down from a big cross-country truck at the spot he hoped
was his meeting point with Father Kani. It was raining, and
the black driver of the truck really didn't think he was
doing the right thing by letting the priest off here in the
middle of nowhere. "You sure you want out here, Father?"
he said dubiously.

Woods looked around uncertainly in the darkness and
rain. "Yes. Yes, this is fine," he said. "Thank you very
much." As the truck pulled away, its lights revealed the
little bridge up ahead that was his marker. The water was
very high and reflected the lights of the truck as it went by.

Woods circled in the darkness, and then he saw car
lights flick on and off from a little copse off the side of the
road. Woods was a little uncertain because of his blurred
distance vision, so he fumbled to get his glasses out of his
bag. The lights flicked again, and this time he was con-

vinced. He shoved the glasses back in the case and started across the muddy ground to the trees.

As he neared, he could make out the silhouette of a man. The man turned on a flashlight to help guide Woods' feet over the strange terrain. When Woods got very close, he could recognize Father Kani. "I expected you three hours ago!" Kani scolded. "It'll be light in an hour!" He lifted his flashlight to Woods' face. *"Tyeni!"* he exclaimed. "In actual fact, it does change you!"

"What's changed me is getting here!" Woods retorted. "When I wasn't shit-scared, I was standing in the cold waiting to be! It's a wonder the hair dye didn't turn gray!"

Kani laughed and opened the car door. "This ground was fairly dry when I first parked here," he said a little worriedly. "It's going to be trouble—you know, actually getting out of here." Woods got in and Kani started up the car. He put it in first, put his foot down, and the car skidded and swerved. Woods wanted to tell him to let up on the gas, but Kani was one of those drivers who thought power was the answer to all problems, and he just floored it. With a *swoosh* and a lurch, they slid out on the highway, and Kani weaved back and forth, getting it straight without once letting up on the gas. Woods began to wonder if the most dangerous part of his trip wasn't still ahead of him.

Back in East London, Wendy was sitting in the kitchen. She was on her third or fourth cup of coffee. She'd lost count. Charlie was at her feet. He was lying still, but his eyes were open, moving from side to side, expecting something to happen on this strange night. Wendy looked up at the clock: four-thirty. She had given up any thought of sleep.

\* \* \*

Father Kani's car went racing past St. Theresa's Mission. Woods saw the sign on the wall. They had lost some time when a police car pulled off a road right behind them and followed them for about five minutes. It seemed an eternity to Woods, but finally the police had turned off on another side road, and Kani had made the sign of the cross and put his foot down. The road was fairly straight, and there was almost no other traffic. A few trucks coming in the opposite direction were all they saw.

They had driven another five or six miles past the Mission when Father Kani turned in on a dirt road. "This goes right to the river," he said. "From here it will be easy for you to . . ." And he made one of his vague gestures.

When they got to the river's edge, his gesture stood for nothing, because they faced a wide, raging torrent, spilling and swirling with the aftermath of the rain. They both got out of the car and walked numbly to it. Woods dropped his bag dispiritedly. "God," he muttered emptily. "'I could wade across it.'" He looked up and down the river. There were hills on the other side, green and wet. You could see why Lesotho was called the Wales of Africa. What you couldn't see was a place to cross.

Kani had examined the other way cursorily. It was too fast and too wide, as far as he could see in the dim light. "When do you have to make the call?" he asked anxiously.

"Ten o'clock," Woods answered. "If I'm late, she'll go back." Just the thought of that spurred him on. He turned to Kani with fresh resolve. "Now, for God's sake, get out of here. You'll end up spending ten years in jail if you're seen with me."

"*Hayibo!*" Kani protested. "I didn't come this far to . . ." And he made one of his vague gestures again.

Woods pointed to the horizon where the sky was beginning to lighten. "Now, look," he said, "it's getting light. And that's Lesotho right over there! I'll *get across!* Now *go*—before we're seen together!" Kani was undecided. The lightening sky clearly worried him, but he felt he was leaving Woods before he'd finished his job. Woods waved him away and grabbed his bag. When he picked it up, he almost lost its contents. He circled it in his arm quickly. "Damn!" he exclaimed. "I split the bag!" It seemed like the last straw.

"In actual fact," Kani said dispiritedly, "it's turned into a balls-up, hasn't it?"

Woods started moving along the river. "We've done all right," he said. "I'll find somewhere I can cross. Just get out of here!" He waved again and pushed on through some brush as he followed the course of the river.

Kani glanced up at the sky again. Light was appearing behind the hills. He should leave. The car was more likely to draw attention at this hour than either one of them. "If you get desperate," he shouted, "go to one of us! Use Steve's name!"

Woods was moving on, the ground was muddy, the river curving but still wide and strong. The terrain ahead was half open, so that he might easily be seen once it was light. He clutched the bag under his arm and waved back. "See you," he called. Then, as an afterthought, "See you in London!"

Light in her open window awakened Jane. She had deliberately left the shade up so she would be awake early. She could hear the piano downstairs, and she slipped on her slippers and her robe and went down to see.

It was Wendy at the piano, her hands just going over

and over the scales, her anxious mind taking solace in the sheer familiar mechanics of it. When Jane pushed open the door to glance at her, she looked up. Thank God she had Jane to share it all with. Jane leaned against the door frame, just watching and listening as the room grew gradually lighter.

The sun was still very young in the sky, and the birds were noisy in their chorus to the new day. Woods felt he had to try to get across the river at whatever cost. He had found no place where the river narrowed more than the spot he and Father Kani first saw. So he picked a spot where there were some trees on the other side that might give him help as he neared that shore, then he took off his shoes and tied them around his neck, and holding his SAA bag on his head, he waded into the water. In a couple of feet the water was around his knees. It was slippery and muddy underneath, and he probed ahead cautiously for another step. When he took it, the water swirled around his waist. He kept moving slowly. The whirling water crept up his chest with every inch he took forward. When it was around his armpits, he was only a third of the way across. The water was moving so fast, he knew he would have a hard time swimming across the river even if he didn't have the bag, but he certainly couldn't risk its contents to a fight with that river as it now was. The broken bag would take water the minute it was exposed to it. Cautiously he turned around and slowly worked his way back to the bank. He looked at his watch. It was 6:05.

The sun was now higher, and Wendy had gone into the boys' room. She woke Duncan first. He resisted it like all boys do, but he was old enough to accept that it couldn't be avoided. She went over to Gavin's bed and whispered in his ear. "Gavin . . . Gavin. We're going to the beach early. Come on, honey."

Gavin looked up at her, put his arm around her neck, then closed his eyes and cuddled down again. Wendy pulled herself loose, tickled his ribs a little, and said, "Come on, up!" She went to the door and turned to Duncan, who was moving . . . slowly. "Nudge him in a couple of minutes," she said. And then deliberately, "And be quiet. Your father's sleeping in."

She went out in the hall and found Mary walking toward her, still in her pajamas, clutching her well-worn Raggedy Doll. "Evalina isn't in the kitchen," she said plaintively, like the whole world had suddenly gone wrong.

Wendy bent to her. "I'll get her," she said as she hugged her. "You go find Jane and ask her to help you get dressed."

Mary touched her wrist. "You've got your pretty watch on."

Wendy caught her breath. It was the sort of thing she didn't want the bugs to hear. "Oh," she said lightly, "my other one's running slow. Now hurry, go find Jane. We want to be the first ones on the beach." Mary wandered off sleepily to Jane's room, still clutching her doll tightly.

Twenty minutes after Woods had tried the river crossing, the two black hands of Tami Vundla held the title page of his book.

After pulling himself from the river, Woods had stumbled on a small settlement of houses. They were obviously the living quarters of farm workers. By sheer chance, he had knocked at Tami's door. Now he sat with an old blanket wrapped around his shoulders, watching Tami read as his own pants and shirt were drying on a line over the wood stove in the dark little room. Tami's wife and five children sat around the room, silently watching them both.

The elderly, wizened face of Tami Vundla examined the two photos of Steve Biko. Tami could read. Not well or fast. But he pored over the first page of the manuscript and then went to the very last and started reading that.

Woods had told Tami roughly what he was doing and why. But he was so unexpected a caller, his mission so unlikely, that Tami had listened mutely and skeptically. He couldn't afford to insult a white stranger, even a mad one. It was his expression of immutable doubt that led Woods to the idea of showing him the book itself. It added some physical credence to the wild story. Tami had first regarded it like some dangerous explosive, but Woods took the wrapping off and exposed the two photos of Biko. He talked of Biko's arrest and how his paper had revealed his death to the world. Some of these things Tami had heard of. In the end, he had taken the book from Donald and sat down to examine it.

When he had scanned the last page, he put the book in his lap again, studying the photos of Steve. At last he spoke. "If there is no more rain," he said, "there will be places to cross tonight."

Woods was a little relieved. At least he believed him. "I can't wait," he said anxiously. He looked at his watch and did not have to act his panic. "I don't have time," he said. Tami didn't move. Then Woods got a desperate idea. "How far is the Telle Bridge?" he asked.

"Likude," Tami answered. No hope in that. "Nine, ten miles," he went on. "You cannot cross there."

"I have a false passport," Woods said. "Maybe I can. I'm so close, I can't fail now. . . ."

Tami rose and carefully put the manuscript back in Woods' bag. He zipped closed the top, then took off his own belt and wrapped it around the bag to keep the contents secure. It was a gesture Woods was sure put Tami on his side.

"Is there someone we can trust who has a car?" Woods asked.

Tami sat back down. His face never lost its look of calm sobriety. "I trust *me*," he replied. "And *I* have a car." And suddenly his sober face cracked into a devilish grin. He smacked his hand on his wife's leg, laughing at Woods. "You, master editor Donald Woods, escaping," he roared. "Botha will shit himself! Vorster will shit himself! *Kruger* will shit himself! *Masiqube!*"

He could not stop laughing. His wife laughed, his children laughed. Woods put on his still damp clothes and pushed the rollicking Tami out the door. The car was parked in a pile of weeds behind a little shed. It looked like it hadn't moved in years. Woods shooed some chickens out of the way and got in. There didn't seem to be an undented piece of metal on the machine, but when Tami turned the key, the motor kicked over, and on about the third try it held. Tami's children and the children from the other little houses had gathered around them now. Tami grandly waved them out of the way, and the car lurched forward, shedding dust, weeds, and odd pieces of bark. Tami was not an expert driver, and the car didn't help as it sputtered and backfired out onto the road. Tami smacked his hand on Woods' bag and laughed from his heart up. "You will make it!" he yelled over the protesting engine. "You will make it, and the Boers will *all* shit themselves! *Mayibuye iAfrika!*" Rise again, Africa!

And Woods hanging on to the jolting car, echoed him, "*Mayibuye iAfrika!*"

In twenty minutes they came to a wide sweep in the road. Tami slowed the car, gradually bringing it to a stop on brakes that Woods suddenly realized were in the same condition as the rest of the car. Tami turned off the motor, and when he did, the sound of rushing water could be heard. "The bridge?" Woods queried. "Where's the bridge?"

Tami pointed off through the foliage at the side of the road, in the direction the road curved. "Through there," he said. He was much more restrained now, clearly frightened and sobered by the proximity of authority and danger.

Woods got out. All was quiet. It was almost an ominous silence. He went to the edge of the road where Tami pointed, and pushed through the brush. He'd only gone a few feet when he could see that they were on a rise. The road curved down to the river and the Telle Bridge. He was only a few hundred yards from it. The guardhouses and customs houses were visible on this side of the border and on the Lesotho side.

Woods scrambled back to the road. Tami was standing in the front seat, waiting for his word. Woods smiled.

"You find it?" Tami inquired.

"Yes, I found it," Woods assured him. "Someday when things have changed, I will come back, and you and I will have a beer together, Tami."

"Yes, Master Donald Woods," Tami said soberly. "I wait for you."

Woods grinned and waved good-bye. As he went into the foliage and started down the hill, he could hear Tami's

noisy, struggling car being turned around and driven off.
He broke out of the foliage about a hundred yards from the
customs and passport shed. There was a large wire fence
separating the shed and the bridge from the road. Woods
went up to it. It was padlocked. He shook it, but there was
no sign of anyone. God, what did that mean? Woods wondered. Was it only open on some days?

He turned apprehensively at the sound of an approaching vehicle. It was coming quickly, and its motor sounded
like that of a Land Rover. Woods looked at his clothes.
They were all wrinkled from the soaking, and covered with
dust from the run down the hill. He brushed at them the
best he could. The speed of the approaching vehicle worried him. Was it someone with a message about him? Had
they caught Father Kani?

Movement across the river caught his eye, and he saw a
black official in short trousers moving around outside the
smaller Lesotho passport shed. It seemed so excruciatingly
close.

The Land Rover came around the curve at the top of the
hill. Its markings *were* official. Through the windshield he
could see a large figure at the wheel. He looked for a line
of escape, but there was none. In coming all the way to the
fence he had cut himself off from the hill. He stood there,
trapped, as the Land Rover raced toward him. It was
within yards of the fence when its brakes were applied and
it slithered to a stop in front of Woods. A black man in a
knit cap and a light brown uniform was at the wheel. He
stared at the gate, then shouted out the window at Woods,
"It's locked?"

"Yes," Woods said hesitantly.

The man looked at his watch. "It should be open," he said. "It's seven o'clock!"

At least it seemed that the man wasn't after him. Woods checked his watch. "Not quite," he said.

"Jesus!" the man exclaimed. Then he immediately looked at Woods and apologized. "Sorry, Father." He opened his door and stepped down onto the ground. In doing so, he revealed the markings on the Land Rover: LESOTHO POSTAL SERVICE.

Woods sighed with relief. "It's all right, my son," he said amiably.

The man looked at him, seeing him really for the first time. "What are you doing on foot, Father?" he asked quizzically.

"Well . . ." Woods fumbled. "A—a friend brought me, and another is picking me up across the river. I've—I've got to get to Maseru for a ten-o'clock mass."

"You'll, be lucky!" the man said. "The rain's messed up those roads somethin' bad." He looked Woods over again and seemed to approve. "Here, Father, put your bag in here. I'll give you a ride over." He reached out, took Woods' bag, and put it in the cab.

Woods was immensely relieved. A ride across would make his position look much less anomalous. "Thank you," he said. "Thank you very much. My name's Wo— *Curren*. Father Curren." He offered his hand.

"My name's Moses," the man said brightly.

Woods stared at him, dumbfounded. "Moses?" he repeated blankly.

Moses smiled. "Yes, sir."

Woods glanced across the river. "Yes, of course," he said serenely. "It would be, wouldn't it?"

* * *

There was activity at the Woods house at this hour too. Outside, there was another changing of the guard. Again a white officer was driving, but he was replacing one black security officer with another one. He glanced at the house. "Anything?" he asked. The officer coming off duty shook his head. "They're up, that's all." The white officer nodded, gave a routine admonition to the new guard—"Keep alert"—and drove off.

Inside the house, there was a lot of tension. Wendy was in the kitchen putting sandwiches and fruit into a picnic basket for the car. Her nerves were on edge, and the sleepless night hadn't helped. Neither did the fact that Evalina was in one of her moods. She was doing the breakfast dishes and wheezing in annoyance because Wendy had told her they weren't going to take the dog to the beach. Charlie was whining, sensing that something was wrong in this flurry of activity, and every time he whined, Evalina wheezed.

Little Gavin came through the kitchen heading for the garage. He was carrying a rolled towel, his swim suit, and an inflated inner tube. Charlie ran quickly to his side. "Say good-bye to Evelyn," Wendy said.

Gavin stopped and looked at her. "Why?" he asked.

"Just to be polite!" Wendy snapped. "Charlie, *sit!*" she commanded, and pointed to the spot by her feet.

Gavin shrugged, mystified by the request and his mother's sharpness. "See you later, Evalina," he said obligingly.

Evalina turned to him, avoiding Wendy's eyes. "Don't pick a fight on your little sister," she admonished. "If I don't have that dog at my heels all day, I may make a cake for when you get back."

Gavin's face lit up. He looked at Charlie, who was looking at him, whimpering eagerly. "Why can't we take Charlie?" he asked.

"We're not taking Charlie!" Wendy declared impatiently. "Now go on. *Charlie!*" she shouted angrily. The dog had risen at the mention of his name, but Wendy's tone drew him back to her feet.

Dillon had entered the kitchen. He was carrying a couple of cricket bats and his towel. He shepherded Gavin out the door, then glanced back at Evalina. "So long, Evalina," he said. "Like the Americans say, 'Have a nice day.'"

Evalina scowled across at him, not understanding these farewells. "Get out," she said in spurious dudgeon. "If I do make a cake, I'm going to put the cherry icing on it so *you* won't eat more than one piece!"

Dillon smiled a little wistfully, then turned and followed Gavin out to the car.

Jane came in with Mary, who carried only a little pail, a shovel, and a sun hat. Jane moved briskly over to Evalina. She was wearing sunglasses, and she tipped them up to plant a kiss on Evalina's cheek. She kept right on walking to the garage door. "Don't let them tease you, Evalina," she said, fighting to keep her voice from breaking. "See you when we get back." The tears were tracing down her cheeks below the sunglasses by the time she got to the door.

Duncan stuck his head in from the hallway. "Mom," he shouted impatiently. "I can't find my trainers!"

"Have you looked under the television?" Evalina called out. Duncan looked at her, turned, and walked back to the hallway.

Wendy bent to Mary. "Give Evelyn a kiss," she said, "and then tell Dillon to open the garage door."

Mary ran to Evalina. Evalina bent down to her, but she was still showing her irritation at Wendy. Mary wrapped her arms around her neck and kissed her. "Don't you get sunburnt," Evalina cautioned.

"Nope," Mary said brightly, and headed for the garage. "Come on, Charlie," she said routinely.

Charlie was up instantly, but Wendy's voice arrested him. "Charlie!" The dog sat. "Charlie's not going," Wendy explained. Mary had stopped and was just staring at her in puzzlement. "Go on," Wendy said, well versed in methods of distracting children's attention. "Tell Dillon to open the garage."

It worked. The command diverted Mary's mind from perplexity to action, and she pushed out the door.

Duncan came running in, carrying a pile of towels and wearing his trainers. "Thanks, Evalina," he called in passing.

When the door banged on him, Wendy glanced at Evalina. The hamper was packed now, and there were just the two of them in the silent kitchen. Wendy went to the refrigerator to add a bottle of cold drink. "The master's sleeping," she said. "He had a bit too much to drink last night. If there're any calls, just take the number and tell them he's not to be disturbed."

She put the bottle of orange in the hamper and turned to Evalina—for the last time. Evalina kept her back to her, scrubbing the dishes with angry emphasis. "Evelyn, don't be cross with me about Charlie," she pleaded. "He's such a nuisance at the beach, I can't read—I can't do anything."

"He's always gone before," Evalina said stonily.

"I—I just want one day without him," Wendy entreated. "Is that all right?"

The stiffness in Evalina's shoulders softened a bit—a

small concession, but she still would not look at Wendy. Wendy bit her lip, hating their parting to be like this. She took up the picnic hamper and backed to the door to the garage. Charlie was whimpering, begging at her feet. She bent to him, roughing his neck, hating the thought of leaving him too. "He'll be good, I'm sure," she said, giving him one last squeeze.

She stood up, but Evalina still wouldn't look at her. Tears came to Wendy's eyes. "Don't spoil the master with too big a breakfast when he wakes up," she said in a light-hearted reference to an old family conflict.

A huffy wheeze was Evalina's only response.

Wendy looked at her with an affection that had had its birth even before Jane was born. Her eyes swept the kitchen, then came back to Evalina. "Good-bye Evelyn . . . see you later." And she pushed out into the garage and closed the door behind her.

The black Security Officer was surprised to see the garage door open so early. He stood and frowned with uncertainty as the Mercedes slowly backed out. He glanced at his watch. Something must have got them up very early on New Year's Day. He got a good look at all the children, packed into the back with their beach things. The mother and the daughter were in the front seat.

Wendy had had to stop and take hold of herself after she left Evalina. The young ones were pushing and shoving in their usual way, so she didn't have to worry about them noticing her blotched face, but she wanted to show strength for Jane and Dillon.

By the time she got the car out onto the road, she had recovered enough of that strength to glance back at the house she would never see again. There were so many memories there, it was almost impossible to conceive that they wouldn't return again that night—or any night.

Jane sat beside her, rigidly staring out to the front of the car, tears rolling down her cheeks beneath the sunglasses.

Finally Wendy pulled the car away.

The security officer brought his walkie-talkie to his ear and began to speak into the mouthpiece.

# xix

AT THE TELLE BRIDGE, the morning somnolence had passed. It was seldom a very busy place, but there were two or three small trucks waiting in line on each side of the river.

On the South African side, Moses and Woods were the first in line. They waited at the counter of the passport shed while the two passport control officials did all the bureaucratic things such people do before they actually turn their attention to the public. Files were taken out, pencils sharpened, drawers opened. Moses watched it all with smiling impatience, Woods with nerves that seemed on the verge of breaking.

Finally one of the officials turned to the line and looked like he was ready to do his job. "Take the father here first," Moses said magnanimously. "We're *both* in a hurry."

Woods passed his passport over. The official pushed a form at him, then flipped through Woods' passport. Woods watched him tensely while pretending to read the form.

"You're always in a hurry, Moses," the official said banter-ingly. "I never will understand why it takes four days for a letter to get from Queenstown to Maseru." The other pass-port official laughed. He was reading a telex message coming across in the rear of the shed.

Moses threw his official passport on the countertop. "You know why?" Moses said. "Because ya have to spend so much time sitting outside your gate, that's what the trou-ble is!"

The passport official at the counter set Woods' passport down and picked up Moses' and stamped it without really looking at it. Woods started to fill out the form he'd been given, but his eyes kept going back to his passport, sitting there like a time bomb on the counter.

"We've got to check our instructions, Moses," the offi-cial at the telex machine gibed. "Who knows, the security police might be looking for a certain Lesotho postal in-spector."

"That's what takes the mail so long!" Moses retorted. "Your security police got to read half of it before they let it through! You don't think we know what's goin' on, but we know, we know."

During this ritual exchange, Woods finished the form and passed it back across the counter. In doing so, he no-ticed the wedding ring on his finger. He quickly withdrew his hand and surreptitiously pulled off the ring. He hoped none of the truck drivers in the line saw him.

The official glanced at Woods' passport again, and then the completed form. He hesitated a moment, then stamped them both and handed Woods back his passport.

Woods moved to follow Moses out of the shed, but the passport official stopped him before they made the door. "Father," he called. Woods turned, ashen. "You're a brave man, Father," he said flatly. He was just staring at Woods. What was this, some kind of deadly game? "Driving with Moses, I mean," the official said. "I wish you luck, Father, you'll need it." The blood started to return to Woods' face, and he felt his legs could move again. Moses scoffed at the officials and held the door wide for Woods. Woods forced himself on, trying to keep his balance and to look as casual as he could.

Outside the shed, the black frontier policeman was standing by the cab of Moses' Land Rover. He was holding Woods' bag, still held together by Tami's belt. Moses ran around to get in the other door, but Woods just stared at the frontier policeman.

"Is this your bag, Father?" the policeman asked.

"Yes," Woods answered stiffly.

"What's in it?"

Moses was already at the wheel, watching impatiently.

For a moment Woods was speechless, then he shook his head dismissively. "Oh, just some clothes, shaving things, a Bible." He made it sound as inconsequential as he could.

"I *thought* I felt a book of some kind," the policeman said, and burst into a smile at his own acumen. He handed the bag to Woods. Woods nodded lifelessly to him and made it to the Land Rover. Moses pushed the door open for him. Woods got in, the motor was started, and the frontier policeman lifted up the boom. Moses gunned it forward, and Woods waved to the policeman as they went by.

His eyes followed their progress across the bridge; the demarcation line at the border in the middle of the bridge grew closer and closer. Finally the Land Rover was over it, heading toward the gate on the Lesotho side.

Woods put his glasses back on at last, and leaned his head back against the seat. His eyes were closed when they were waved past the Lesotho guard post. But as they started past the Lesotho passport shed, there was a whistle and a shout. Moses slowed the Land Rover and finally came to a stop. Woods looked out anxiously, but the Lesotho passport official was looking past him to Moses.

"There's been some trouble on those roads, Moses! There's a message for you!" Moses pulled the Land Rover over to the side of the road and hopped out. He looked back in at Woods. "I won't be long," he said.

"Moses!" Woods called out to stop him. Moses stuck his head back in the window. "Moses, do you think I could make a phone call from here?"

Moses laughed. "You're in *Lesotho*," he said. "There's no telephone here, unless you want to go back to the South African side. *They* got a telephone."

Woods shook his head. "Can I telephone along the way?"

Moses smiled and seemed wildly amused again. "What do those people want a phone for?" he asked rhetorically.

Woods suddenly had a terrifying thought. "Aren't there any phones in Lesotho at all?" he asked hesitantly.

"The next place with phones in working order is Maseru," Moses answered. "And even there, it's only government offices and a couple of big businesses you can be sure of."

"The embassies, maybe?"

"Probably." Moses laughed. "But if you want to call quick, you better go back and call from over there."

"No, no. Maseru will do just fine," he assured him.

Moses nodded and trotted off to the Lesotho official at the passport shed.

Woods opened the door of the Land Rover. He looked down at the ground. The ground of Lesotho. He stepped down on it. He turned and looked back across the river. There it was, South Africa and the South African Frontier Police, the South African Customs and Passport Shed, and here he was in Lesotho. He turned and looked over the hills and land around him. *I've made it. I'm free, Steve Biko!* he said to himself. *God, if you were only here with me today, my friend.*

He thought of the time he and Steve had walked in hills like these, around Zanempilo. They had talked of freedom that day too. "The worst prison," Biko had said, "is the one they make you build around yourself. That's why those kids in Soweto, refusing to be taught in Afrikaans, are taking chains off their minds no one will ever be able to put back. That's why I'm as free as you are, Donald, whatever they do to me." God, how he wished he could share *this* freedom with *that* man now. He turned, and turned again, bursting with it. And suddenly he started to dance—an old African tribal dance he had learned as a boy. And to its rhythm he kept repeating, *Oh, God—oh, God—I made it! I made it!*

He wheeled in the dance—and caught Moses and the Lesotho official staring at him out of the corner of his eye. He stopped and turned slowly to them. They were looking at him, openmouthed and dumbfounded. Woods smiled weakly. "I learned it as a boy," he explained.

They remained baffled. Woods shrugged insouciantly. *What the hell. Who wants to make sense today!*

Wendy had been on the road for some time before the younger kids realized they weren't headed for the beach. When Duncan finally yelled, "Mom, I think you're lost!" Wendy at last told them what was happening. "So you see," she finished, "Daddy was really traveling all night."

"But why are we going to Granny's, then?" Duncan asked.

"I didn't bring my pajamas!" Mary suddenly blurted out.

"Your pajamas are in the back," Wendy told her. Then she caught Duncan's eye in the rearview mirror. "Because if your Daddy gets across safely, he's going to phone us there—and then we're going to join him and fly to England."

Gavin leaned forward on the seat. "What's going to happen to Charlie?" he asked in a frightened, apprehensive voice.

They all looked at Wendy, waiting. What she had to say was not much easier on her than it was on the children. "I've left a note for Evalina," she said tautly. "She's going to take him to the Bricelands."

Jane just glanced at her. There was a long moment. "What about Evalina?" she asked softly.

Wendy paused. Her eyes seemed to focus inward. "I don't know," she said finally. "Daddy's left her as much money as he could." She bit her quivering lip and drove on.

Back at the Woods house, there was another changing of the guard. This time two white security officers were replacing the single black who had been on duty. There were two cars, theirs and another one, to pick up the guard they were replacing. After a word with the departing officer, they pulled their car over onto the grass opposite the house and parked. The driver sprawled out in the car; the other man got out and strolled to the edge of the Woods house and then back to the other end. Satisfied, he walked back to the car and called in to headquarters.

* * *

In Lesotho, Moses had driven Woods along the main road to Maseru. Woods had been appalled to learn that there were five different routes to Maseru, and since none of them were paved, Bruce might have been on any one of them. How the hell was he supposed to know which? He also found that the warning about Moses' driving was justified. He was one of those drivers who make a lot of assumptions, like nobody is going to be going over a hill at the same time he is, that a curve will not keep on bending. Woods was grateful when they came to a meeting of two of the roads and there was a mud-splattered car sitting in the apex of the junction.

"Is that your man?" Moses asked without cutting his speed.

"Maybe," Woods answered.

Moses slithered to a stop on the wet road. Woods grabbed his bag, jumped out, and ran to the car. If it had been Bruce, he felt the horn would have honked by now. He ran on, simply to be sure. When he got there, he saw a figure slumped behind the muddied window. He peered closer. It *was* Bruce. Sound asleep.

Woods pounded on the window. "Hey! Hey! Wake up!"

Bruce stirred groggily. Woods raised his hand in benediction. "Bless you, my son," he shouted. Bruce blinked his eyes, staring in bafflement. "Wake up, you sleepy Aussie bastard!" Woods yelled.

That did get through. Bruce pushed the door open and grabbed Woods by the shoulders. "Christ, I'd given you up!" he bellowed in relief.

Woods twisted to look back at Moses. "Thanks, Moses," he shouted. "It's the right one!"

"Good luck, Father!" Moses called back. "Hope you make it!" And he pulled away.

Still clutching his bag, Woods pulled free of Bruce and ran around to get in the passenger side of the car. "We've got to move!" he barked. "He tells me the roads are awful."

Bruce checked his watch. "Christ, eight-thirty!" he exclaimed, and scrambled to get back in the car. "It took me two hours coming down yesterday, and I really pushed this thing!"

He started the car, swung it out onto the road, and in the first four hundred yards Woods knew he was in the hands of a real driver. In no time they were coming up on Moses. Moses pulled to one side and let them fly by. He waved at Woods and made an admiring face at the BMW. Bruce had shifted down, and now he shifted up as the car leapt ahead.

Evalina began her upstairs rounds by making Mary's bed. She looked around the room but couldn't find her doll. As she predicted, Charlie was at her heels all the time. She liked him more than she was willing to admit, and she talked to him like another member of the household. "Now where is that child's doll?" she muttered. "She never sleep tonight if she doesn't find it." She looked around again—no sign of it. "Oh, Charlie." She sighed in sufferance. "Well, let's go check the boys' room."

She walked down the hall with Charlie right behind her. She pushed into Duncan and Gavin's room and stopped at the door, scanning it for the doll. But she was suddenly drawn up by a couple of unaccustomed sights. The big cupboard door was open, and she could see only an empty hanger. And Gavin's bottom drawer was open and there was nothing in it.

She pushed on into the room. She opened Duncan's sock drawer. She always kept it neat, but it looked rifled, and some of the socks were missing. She glanced up at the wall and saw the marks where the rugby pennant had been pinned. Slowly, half afraid, she went to the cupboard and opened it. The boys' winter coats were gone—in the middle of summer! She bent down and put her arm around Charlie. "Something very wrong here, Charlie," she said somberly as she looked around the room, trying to figure it out.

Wendy had had terrible luck with the traffic. There was a three-mile stretch of road repairs that reduced the road to a single lane for both directions. There were traffic signals operating on it, but the delay had produced a huge backup. They were sitting in the line almost ten minutes before they could even see the light. At first Wendy took it with mild impatience. She used the time to let the kids snack from the lunch she'd prepared. Dillon poked around in the hamper and felt something strange. He pulled out Mary's Raggedy Doll. "Here, dumplehead, look what I found." He handed it to Mary, and she grabbed it and clutched it tightly. "I wish we'd brought Evalina," she said sourly.

Wendy glanced at her in the mirror but was getting too worried about the time to handle child psychology as well. She was just very glad she'd packed the doll.

By the time they finally got around the repairs and she really wanted to put her foot down, they were almost at the escarpment that divided the road to Umtata into two segments. It was a natural rift that had never been bridged. The road wound circuitously down one side and up the other. Wendy got to it behind a line of traffic slowed by a farmer's truck and an Army personnel carrier.

Time and again she tried to pass them going down but never could do it safely. As they climbed the other side she thought the Mercedes' greater pickup would take her past the slower vehicles. But no one gave her an inch to cut in, and when she pulled out to pass them all, there was never quite enough room to the next bend.

Jane was now as nervous as Wendy. She would have taken a couple of chances at passing where her mother wouldn't. "Mom, we'll never make it," she said with a touch of censure.

"We can't get in an accident! And we can't get stopped by the police!" Wendy snapped back. But even as she said it, she pulled out and gunned it past the farmer's truck, a car, the Army personnel carrier, and finally an old Vauxhall. The move had scared her to death, and she clung to the steering wheel for a moment as her heart slowed down. The hill ahead was clear, and she gradually got her breath back.

Like the others, Gavin had sensed her fear and anxiety, but he was still young enough to be unnerved by the feeling that matters might be beyond his mother's control. "Aren't we going to make it, Mommy?" he asked worriedly.

Wendy glanced desperately at the clock. "I don't know," she said tensely. "Once we get to the top, it's all flat—but I don't know."

"What if we *don't* make it?" Duncan asked.

"Duncan! I *don't know!*" Wendy flared.

The children all sank down in their seats, silently watching as the Mercedes climbed to the top of the escarpment.

\* \* \*

Bruce's rented BMW splashed through a huge mud puddle at the bottom of a turn, then spun away, surging up a hill on a long, rutted climb.

Woods looked at the clock: nine-fifteen. He had the map out and looked down at it as they churned up the hill. "Oh, Christ, over forty miles of this," he muttered. He leaned his head back on the headrest. "I can't have gone through all this, just to have to turn around and go back again," he said dejectedly.

Bruce glanced at him but said nothing. He had powered the car to the top of the hill; now he braked in case there was other traffic. When he saw it was clear, his foot went down again, but as they came to a little turn he slithered to a stop. They had skidded into a herd of goats. "Oh, *shit!*" Woods exclaimed.

"Goddamn," Bruce snapped. "Come on, get them across!" He was already out of the car. Woods followed, and the two of them started beating the herd across the road as the baffled shepherd watched them helplessly.

Wendy had at last gotten the car on the flat, and she was driving faster than she'd ever driven. The three boys were all leaning on the back of the front seat, watching tensely as she raced along. Duncan was the first to see it. "Mom —police," he said calmly.

The police car was now visible to all of them, coming at them from the opposite direction. Wendy let her speed swing down to fifty-five. "Kids, get down in the seat," she said. "We don't know if the police are looking for a Mercedes with five children in it." The three boys crouched down.

The police car neared, and then passed, the two policemen just glancing at Wendy and Jane. Wendy watched them in the rearview mirror, keeping her speed down, glancing at the clock: nine forty-five. Then she put her foot down again.

The boys felt the acceleration and peered up, looking out the back window at the disappearing police car.

Mary was in the corner of the backseat, holding her doll to her. When Duncan's face loomed up before her, she smacked out at him—it was just an expression of the tension in the car. Duncan lifted a hand in threat to her, but he didn't strike back.

The dirt roads turned to tarmac on the outskirts of Maseru. Bruce and Woods bounced off the dirt road and onto the tarmac at 9:56. They could see the buildings of the city ahead. "By God, I think we're going to make it!" Woods shouted. He slapped Bruce on the back; he had driven like a veteran rally driver.

Bruce grinned, but he kept his eyes on the road and continued with his battle against the clock and anything the roads of Lesotho could throw at him. They glided through the outskirts of the town, flying past donkey-drawn carts, a few old cars, and some even older trucks. As they came near the center of town, Woods was looking for someone who might have the information he needed. "There!" he suddenly shouted. "That man at the curb!"

Bruce swerved the car into the intersection just in front of a tall, well-dressed man. In this black republic there were almost no whites, and this man was a true native. He wore a pin-striped suit and carried an umbrella. Woods jumped out of the car and raced to apprehend him. "Excuse

your government for political asylum," he replied. He had finished dialing, and he looked over at Moffat inquiringly.

Moffat was still a bit perplexed by it all, but he bowed at that request. "Our pleasure," he responded with a little smile.

"What time do you have?" Woods said, looking at his own watch.

"Just after ten," Moffat replied with a glance at his.

Woods listened anxiously to the rings at the other end.

In Umtata, Wendy's mother hurried in from her garden to answer the phone. "I've got it, dear," she called to her husband. "Yes, hello," she answered when she picked up the receiver. As she did, the sound of a car turned her head and she saw the white Mercedes pull into the driveway. "Donald!" she exclaimed. "That was good timing, dear! She's just arrived." She waved at the car and listened, then, "No—no, she's just pulled into the driveway." She leaned to the open window, taking the receiver from her ear.

"Wendy! Wendy!" she called. Wendy's stepfather, Harold, was at the car, but Wendy heard the call and started moving toward the house as the kids piled out. Wendy's mother went back to the phone. "Donald," she said with some concern, "you haven't quarreled, have you, dear? She's got all the children with her! No, no—you'd better not say anything, she's coming now."

Wendy had come in the room. She was staring at the phone, half afraid, half elated. Jane and Dillon came in right behind her. Mary scooted past them all and ran into the arms of her grandmother. Wendy's mother hugged her and held out the phone with one hand. "It's Donald," she explained cheerfully. "Isn't that a coincidence!"

Wendy was still afraid to take it. Was he in Lesotho, or had he failed to get across? "Go on, Mom," Dillon urged. Wendy moved slowly to the phone.

"What's the matter, dear?" her mother asked anxiously. "Is something wrong?"

Wendy didn't answer. She took the phone like a sleepwalker. "Donald?" she said leadenly.

"Wendy," Woods replied in relief and triumph. "I'm— I'm where I expected to be! Come as quick as you can." He noticed a clock on Moffat's wall. It read 10:04.

After all her control, Wendy finally gave in to a flood of tears. She turned to Jane and Dillon. "He's there—" she choked. "He got across." Jane ran to her. "Oh, Mom!" she exclaimed as she buried her head in her mother's shoulder. Wendy sniffled and put the receiver up to her ear again. "Donald, Donald," she said, trying to halt the tears. "Do you still think we should head for the Telle Bridge crossing?"

"Yes," Woods answered emphatically. "It's a sleepy little place, I can tell you. From Umtata you'll have good roads most of the way, but just hurry before—well, just hurry!"

"We're on our way!" Wendy promised exuberantly. "I love you!"

"I'm a priest," Woods responded. "You can't talk to me like that. Hurry!" Moffat was staring at him in shocked confusion when he hung up.

Wendy wiped at her tears, a smile still on her face. She turned to the kids. "You all go to the toilet—quick!" she ordered. "Mom, have you got any fruit and biscuits and things?" she asked.

Her mother simply headed for the kitchen, with Mary

still in her arms. "Regina!" she called. "Come along quick! I think we need some help." Regina, her black maid, came out of the kitchen, smiling as she saw the kids.

"We'll drive you," Wendy's mother shouted over her shoulder.

"There isn't room," Wendy shouted back.

# XX

JAMES MOFFAT ACTED with swiftness once he understood
what Woods' problem was. They would need Lesotho permission to fly out of the country. Chief Jonathan, the Lesotho head of state, had been very courageous in standing
up to South Africa, but his country's very real dependence
*on* South Africa limited his possibilities a great deal.
Woods' case would have to be put to him very delicately.
Moffat contacted the one man in Chief Jonathan's inner
circle whom he knew would be sympathetic toward a liberal white South African. The man was John Monyane,
and at Moffat's urgent request he agreed to come to the
High Commission that afternoon.

When he arrived, Moffat gave him the general details
and handed him the book on Biko, which he himself had
scanned in the intervening time. Monyane had met Woods
and Bruce graciously, but he had listened to Moffat without
any show of commitment or sympathy. As he took the
book he glanced at the two of them; again, the look was

more testing than committed. He looked at the two pictures of Biko on the cover, then flipped a few pages and read a paragraph, then a few more, and another paragraph. He spent perhaps ten minutes reading here and there in the book while Woods paced nervously across the other side of the room, glancing out now and then at the rain that had been falling since noon.

Finally Mr. Monyane folded his glasses, then rose and carefully put the book back on Moffat's desk. He avoided Woods' eyes until he sat down again. Then he looked at Woods without saying anything. Bruce looked at the two of them and felt the situation called for a catalyst. "They can't stay here," he said. "They'd never be safe from the South African police." It was an unpleasant fact that the South African government often sent their police into Lesotho to kidnap wanted suspects and take them back across the border. There was a certain political pretense on both sides that it didn't happen, but anyone who followed such things believed it to be true.

"We had hoped to fly to Botswana," Woods added. "The sooner, the better."

Monyane frowned. Behind the commissioner's desk was a large ceramic map of southern Africa, somewhat impressionistic, but showing how completely surrounded Lesotho was by her vastly larger neighbor, South Africa. Monyane pointed to it. "To fly anywhere out of Lesotho," he began, "you have to fly over South African territory. And they demand that all planes leaving here land in South Africa before going on."

Woods was crestfallen. He looked over at Moffat. Wasn't there some way? Moffat was first and foremost a professional diplomat. He shrugged helplessly; the law is the law. It angered Woods. "If we flew out anyway, could they *force* us to land?" he asked challengingly.

"They have no shortage of military planes," Monyane said dryly.

Woods felt cornered, but there was one thing he knew for sure: He had to get Wendy and the children someplace safe once they got across the border. When the security police found that they had fled the country, they would do whatever they could to get them back. He turned to Moffat. "If all goes well," he declared, "my wife and children will reach Telle Bridge in a few hours. At least we could be there in case—"

Monyane cut him off. He gestured to the windows. "In the rains," he said, shaking his head, "impossible." He read the concern in Woods' eyes. "We *will* telegraph to have your family met at Telle Bridge," he promised. "And I will see that they have a military escort until they're brought here."

It was something, but it still left Woods disconsolate.

In the deepening twilight, two new security policemen were on duty in East London outside the Woods house. One was leaning against the car, the other was in the front seat listening to music on the radio. The one outside poked the other's shoulder and nodded to the house. An upstairs light went on, and then the light in Woods' bedroom. The policeman in the car reached for his police radio set.

Evalina had turned on the lights. The dog was following her as she went to Jane's room, drew the drapes, and turned the light on there. Desolately she walked out into the hall again. In her hands she was carrying Wendy's note. She looked at it once more, then folded it and carefully put it in her apron pocket. "Come on, Charlie," she said glumly. "We go and light up the living room...then maybe we have some of the master's whiskey." She smiled at the thought, but it was a melancholy smile. She trudged down the stairs with Charlie at her heels.

The rain was heavy at Telle Bridge. A big truck was waiting at the boom on the South African side when Harold's VW minibus pulled up by the passport shed. They had left the Mercedes because Harold had reminded Wendy that they couldn't take it across the border without elaborate customs formalities. She would have to walk across, but that was one of the smaller problems.

Wendy stared out through the undulating patterns of rain on the windshield. There were three or four frontier police moving around, and another one was checking the back of the truck. She turned back to Harold and her mother. "Well, here we go," she said as cheerfully as she could. "Come on, kids." She stepped out and grabbed Mary, carrying her on the run to the shelter of the passport shed's porch. When all the children had made it, she handed Mary to Dillon and pushed open the door.

There was a new crew on duty now, and the big, heavy-set passport control official at the counter lifted his head from the manifest of the truck he was checking through. "What have we here?" he mumbled in Afrikaans. As they all straggled in, he looked at them, half amused, half annoyed.

Wendy shook the rain from her hair and faced him nervously but with a somewhat aggressive show of confidence. "I'm just taking the children over on a little holiday," she said.

The official shook his head at human nature; some people do the craziest things. He took the passport she had held out to him and pushed a form at her. "They all under eighteen?" he asked.

"Yes," Wendy answered tightly.

"Then you can put their names on your form," he instructed her. He turned back to the truck's manifest. "You picked good weather for a holiday, all right," he muttered with a wink to the truck driver.

Wendy was staring at the form; there was one part of her mind that didn't hear him at all. "Well, they say it changes every half hour," Jane interposed, "so by the time we get over, it may be fine." The official grimaced; there was some truth in that all right. He started stamping the manifest.

Wendy looked at Jane in stunned admiration for her cool. Jane smiled demurely and directed her mother's attention back to the form. Dillon leaned over her shoulder and whispered, "Mom, you've got my birthday wrong." Wendy pushed his hand away. The passport control official had given the trucker his manifest, and now he moved in front of Wendy. She smiled at him nervously, signed the form, and pushed it across the counter to him.

He scanned it quickly. "Oops," he said, "you haven't put down your husband's name." He took his own pen from behind his ear to write it in.

"O-oh—" Wendy stammered. "James." The kids looked at her. Donald's middle name was James.

"Okay, and his middle initial?" the official asked.

There was a pause. "D," Wendy said positively. She said it because she could think of nothing else. Jane glanced at her, then touched her arm reassuringly.

As the official was counting the children against the list on the form, the telex machine suddenly started chattering. Wendy jumped at the sound. Then she watched in anxiety

as the other passport control official got up from his desk
and went to the machine.

Her attention was brought back when the official dealing with her stamped her passport and handed it back.
"Have a good holiday." He beamed at the kids. "And try to
stay dry."

Wendy returned his smile nervously and grabbed Mary
again. Mary had picked up the passport stamp; Jane pried it
from her hand and put it back on the counter. Wendy sent a
guarded look at the official by the telex machine as she
went out the door. His colleague had turned to him and
asked, "Anything?"

"I wish they'd get the bloody signal straight," the official at the machine grumbled. "They're trying to tell us
something."

As Wendy ran to the minibus, her mother stepped out of
it and put up a little compact umbrella. "Here, dear," she
said, "I found this in the side pocket."

Wendy moved under it and turned to Dillon. "Get the
suitcases," she said. "And hurry." She took the umbrella
from her mother's hand. "It's so stupid," she chastised herself. "I didn't bring anything for the rain."

Her mother touched her arm consolingly. "Everything
will be all right. Here," she said, pressing some folded
bills into her pocket, "you take this. It's not much, but you
can't arrive in England with five children and no money."
Wendy kissed her mother's cheek and glanced out at the
frontier police, who were standing in the rain in their plastic capes watching them. There were large lights on the
passport shed, and they cast long shadows that made everything look menacing and uncertain.

At the back of the minibus, Harold was helping the boys
with the bags. Dillon and Duncan were carrying the big

ones, Gavin the two small ones. Harold reached in the van and took out an old plastic raincoat. "Here, Dillon," he said, "I only use this for emergencies. You boys put it over your heads."

Dillon and Duncan each held one side and lifted the raincoat over their heads. They bumped as they walked, but at least they were sheltered from most of the rain. Gavin was wearing a big straw beach hat.

When they struggled up to the front of the minibus, Wendy was terribly aware of how strange it must all look to the frontier police. "We must go," she said.

Her mother clutched at her, kissing her, kissing Mary. "You write to us, my darling," she said as she stepped back. She was already crying as she turned to kiss the other kids.

Harold gave Wendy a hug and kissed Mary. "Give our love to Donald," he said. "Be *careful*. We love you."

Wendy nodded, her own face pinched in the pain of this parting.

Harold bent to give a kiss to Jane. Then he took the hat off his head and gave it to her. Jane hugged him, then trotted ahead to her mother.

There was a black frontier policeman at the boom. When the odd little procession started to approach the brighter lights of the barrier, he looked at them all askance.

"Someone's meeting us on the other side," Wendy explained with as much reasonableness as she could.

The policeman lifted the boom when they were all gathered before it, Wendy and Mary under the umbrella, Dillon and Duncan under the "tent" of Harold's coat, Jane with Harold's hat on, Gavin with the wide straw beach hat. And all of them loaded with luggage of one kind or another.

They moved out on the bridge, and then Wendy glanced

back. Her mother and Harold were standing next to their minibus in the glaring lights and the rain, staring in numb agony at them. "God bless you!" her mother called. Wendy waved the umbrella, then moved on again with the children.

The frontier policeman at the boom was joined by two other policemen, all of them looking off doubtfully at the little procession on the bridge and wondering about the emotion in all these good-byes.

At the same time the passport control official who had stamped Wendy's passport was peering out the window of the passport shed, cupping his hands over his eyes at the glare of the lights and clearly very surprised to see them all *walking* across the bridge in the rain.

On the bridge they were getting soaked despite the efforts to protect themselves. Jane suddenly called, "Mom?" Wendy looked over at her. Jane nodded to the middle of the bridge. There was a painted line that marked the border. Jane smiled at her mother, then planted the first step across the line.

Wendy felt a wave of relief when all of them were across that four inches of paint. She lifted her eyes and looked across to the other side. There was only one very modest light there, but underneath it stood a young man holding a huge umbrella. He broke into a bright smile when Wendy looked at him. As they drew closer, they could see a Lesotho government Land Rover behind him, and two soldiers sitting in the cab out of the rain but smiling toward them too.

Jane shifted her load and put an arm around Wendy's waist. Wendy leaned down and kissed the top of her head as they walked on toward the huge umbrella.

* * *

That first night, after he got the telegram that his wife and children were in Lesotho, Woods washed the dye from his hair. He turned his collar around and bought a colorful native tie. The next morning, he and Bruce went out to meet Mr. McElrea, the owner of the three plane airline that flew out of Lesotho.

Bruce gave him the whole story, one colonial to another. The Canadian, McElrea, said he had one plane he would risk for the flight. Its pilot was a New Zealander named Richie De Montauk. If Richie was willing to fly out without landing in South Africa as the regulations demanded he did, McElrea was willing to turn a blind eye to the whole incident.

"You can see Australia didn't get all the criminals," Bruce said jovially when Woods was floored by the generosity of the gesture. Richie was called in and, without a moment's hesitation, agreed to make the flight.

Woods went into the operations building to call Moffat. He felt it was safe to tell him, and he still needed him to make sure Wendy and the kids were being brought from the Telle Bridge.

Woods underestimated Moffat's friendship with Mr. Monyane, because the minute Woods hung up, Moffat phoned Monyane and told him what was planned.

Woods and Bruce stayed at the airport while Richie and two mechanics serviced his plane. McElrea got a weather report and made up a flight plan that would take them southwest of Johannesburg—not the usual way—and dog-leg on into Gaborone, the capital of Botswana.

Woods was pacing on the grass in front of the little operations building at the airstrip when a limousine bearing the British standard appeared on the paved taxiway beside the operations building and came right out on the airstrip.

"Bruce!" Woods called. Bruce was lying on a bench sunning himself in a new and gloriously sunlit day. He sat up and saw the limousine come to a stop right in front of the building. The windows were tinted, so you could only see the driver. But one of the back doors opened, and Jane and Mary came running at Woods, shrieking and calling, "Daddy! Daddy!"

Woods started toward them when Gavin and Duncan came roaring around the front of the limousine from the other back door. "Dad!" they shouted. "We made it!"

Woods stopped in his tracks and bent down, holding his arms outstretched to receive both groups. As they ran into him and he hugged them, Wendy and Dillon got out of the limousine. Now it was Dillon who felt choked up. He looked at his father as Woods picked up Mary and Gavin and stood. He winked at Dillon. "Well done," he said. Dillon shrugged it off but was plainly touched.

Woods turned to Wendy. She held his gaze a moment, then marched right to him. "Welcome to exile," he said as she paused before him. She simply squeezed past the kids and kissed him.

Bruce laughed. "Hey, now that you're all here, I'm going to phone in that scoop, mate! Don't scare them too much about getting out of here," he added with a nod to the airplane.

Woods shook his head joyfully. "Bruce! No mention of Father Kani or Tami," he cautioned.

Bruce looked back at him acidly. "I'll tell you who I *will* mention, and that's Steve Biko—but I bet the South Africans won't!" He waved. "Don't worry, mate, I'll make a hero out of you!" he shouted, and disappeared into the operations building.

The security policemen on duty outside the Woods house were the usual daytime crew. One was leaning on the top of the car, gazing at the house; the other was sitting on the front seat with the door open, just listening to the radio. There were the bleeps for noon, and the newscaster said, "This is Radio South Africa. Here is the twelve-o'clock news." The policeman turned the volume up a bit. "An Australian news report has stated that the banned editor of the *Daily Dispatch,* Donald Woods, has escaped into Lesotho by swimming the flooded Telle River by night."

The two policemen were staring at the radio in stunned incredulity. The newscaster's voice went on. "His family had preceded him, crossing into Maseru to be present at the British High Commission when Woods arrived. The Minister of Police, J. T. Kruger, was unavailable for—"

But the two security officers had broken for the house, leaving the car door open, the radio rambling on as they burst through the front door.

Richie's plane, a Britton-Norman Islander, was finally ready. Richie idled the engines as the family started to board. Woods had pushed open the door, and Dillon handed him his SAA bag with the text of *Biko* in it. "You should have bought a new bag to go with your tie, Dad," he said as he watched Woods grab Tami's ragged old belt.

"Oh, no," Woods replied. "This goes with me—just as it is—all the way."

"Hey, wait a minute!" Bruce yelled. Woods turned; the whole family was strung out behind him, Wendy's and Jane's hair being blown by the wash from the idling prop.

Bruce held a camera. "This is a moment you want to remember!" he yelled. "Get in there all together." They crowded in for him. "And smile!" he demanded buoyantly. They obliged, and he took the picture.

"Come on, now," Donald said, hurrying them along. He started to help Dillon lift the big suitcase aboard.

"Donald!" Wendy suddenly called. Woods turned, and he could see Moffat and McElrea hurrying toward them. Woods took Jane's arm. "Help Dillon get the bags stowed, and then get them all strapped in." Jane moved up to help Dillon, but she glanced at the adults with a worried frown.

Woods intercepted Moffat and McElrea just past the edge of the wingtip.

"The South African government has gotten wind of the flight," Moffat said. "They've refused transit for the plane, and they've said they'll force it down with jets if you fly anyway."

Woods was stunned. He glanced at Wendy and Bruce.

"I think they're bluffing," McElrea interjected. "With all the media attention now that the escape is known, I don't think they'd dare. It would look pretty bad."

"Listen," Bruce retorted, "they've shown what they think of the press. And if they do get downed, you might have a plane impounded, but for Donald it's . . ." He left it hanging, but it didn't need emphasis now that Donald had really made the government look like fools.

The engines of the plane thundered as Richie tested them. "Have we got a chance at all?" Woods yelled at McElrea.

"It's cloudy," McElrea answered. "Richie's a clever pilot—I'd say a chance! But the longer you wait, the longer they have to plan something!"

Woods hesitated a moment. He looked at Wendy. Her

face was noncommittal—not yes, but not no, either. Woods looked out at the sky, his face knotted in indecision . . . then he said, "'In a war, people take risks.' If Richie will go, *we*'ll go!"

The engines had revved up to full throttle and had been pulled back to idle. The children were all in the plane. Richie looked impatiently from the cockpit window. McElrea trotted over toward him. But before they could see the outcome of that conversation, Bruce had called their attention elsewhere. "Oh, shit!" he yelled over the engine.

A large black limousine flying the Lesotho standard was approaching them across the tarmac.

Before it pulled to a stop, McElrea had run back to them. "Richie will go," he shouted firmly.

The door to the limousine opened, and John Monyane stepped out. The chauffeur jumped out and handed him a manila packet and a small handbag. "Mr. Woods," Monyane stated, speaking out over the sound of the engine. "Our prime minister, Chief Jonathan, has arranged to get United Nations passports for all of you." He handed the manila packet to a dumbfounded Woods. "He has also decided that I should accompany you on your flight." Again, Woods was overwhelmed. He didn't think they even knew of the flight!

"It might make the South Africans hesitate," Monyane continued. "We're not sure. But I'm afraid it's the best we can offer."

Woods could still hardly believe it. "A friend of Steve Biko's is a friend of ours," Monyane declared. "But now I think we'd better hurry." And he started them all toward the passenger door.

When the plane took off down the little airstrip, there

was a party to see them off. Moffat and his wife, McElrea, the British chauffeur, and the Lesotho chauffeur. And last but not least, Bruce, who stood in front of them all, waving his arms back and forth.

Inside the plane, Woods and Jane waved back. Monyane was seated next to Richie, Dillon was with Woods, then Jane and Duncan, and finally Gavin and Wendy, who held Mary on her lap. It was a crowded little plane and took a good part of the airstrip to get airborne. Once they were aloft, Woods leaned forward. "How long before we're over South African territory?" he shouted at Richie over the straining engines.

"About thirty seconds!" Richie shouted back. "Maseru's right on the border! I'm not going to go where they expect me," he went on, "but then, they'll expect that too!"

They all peered about the sky, looking for other aircraft. When Richie had reached a fair altitude, he suddenly banked and dived a bit lower. Woods leaned forward in concern. "Don't panic!" Richie shouted. "I just thought I'd make use of those clouds for a while!"

The plane flew into a bank of fluffy clouds. They continued like that for some time, in cloud and out. Each time they came out, everyone strained to look up, down, on each side, for other aircraft.

They were in a long bank of clouds when Richie suddenly responded to a squawk from his headset. He pushed it tighter on his ear to hear better. "Roger, hang on . . ." he said into the mike at last. He turned back to Woods. "They've picked up the flight," he yelled. "They're demanding to know who's aboard! McElrea thinks we have to give some answer!"

Woods hesitated, but before he could think of anything, Monyane tapped Richie's shoulder. "Tell them one Lesotho official," he shouted, "and seven holders of United Nations passports!"

Richie smiled. Donald nodded to him, and Richie turned back to repeat it on the radio. Woods patted Monyane on the shoulder in gratitude.

They played hide-and-seek in the clouds for what seemed an eternity. At first their hearts started to beat faster every time they broke into the open, but then, as each time found them safe, fear loosened its hold on them, though they didn't slack on their vigilance.

At last they broke into sun, and Woods knew by the time that they must be close to Botswana. He checked above them, below, to the right and left. Dillon, who had done the same, signaled "okay." Woods looked down at the passing terrain—the lush farmland, cattle grazing on hills, a farm house, little shacks for the laborers . . . a stretch of beautiful open land . . . a kraal—and in his mind he could hear the sounds of that countryside, the cattle, the clicking of sticks, the drums, the African voices raised in song. He remembered Wendy's words on that day at the beach when he'd first told her they had to go. "We may hate the way it's run," she had said with tears in her voice, "but this is still *our* country. . . ." How much in him still felt the truth of that? It would always be his country, he knew that, even as he saw it passing under him for what might be the last time in his life.

He looked down at the bag in his lap and felt the bulk of typed pages. It was so ironic that Biko, who, apart from Wendy, he most associated with South Africa, had been his reason for leaving South Africa. He knew that one thing they both had shared was a love for the country as strong as a personal love.

He looked out again. They were flying over a small

town, and there, a little bit outside it—looking, from the air, like chicken coops—were the houses of the black township that served the little city. Big or small, every city had its township. He heard Steve's voice in his head. "Have you heard about Soweto?" it said, full of excitement and cheer. Woods had been in his office, and Biko had called him from his little office shed in King William's Town.

"Yes," Woods had answered. "And remember, you're talking on the *telephone*."

"Just tell me," Biko had laughed. "Is it true?"

Woods had smiled. It was one of the most pleasurable days he had had since meeting Biko. "The schoolchildren in Soweto are on strike," he had said a little playfully. "They are citing something called Black Consciousness, and they have refused to study in Afrikaans, refused to be trained simply as servants to the System." He had grinned. "The name Biko has been uttered here and there."

"It's the beginning of the end, Donald," Biko had replied. "Change the way people think, and things can never be the same. What's the government reaction?"

"Tense," Woods had answered a little less playfully. "Troops have been sent in 'to restore order.'"

Biko had passed it off. "Hell," he'd said lightly, "they're *kids*—they may shout a little and break a few windows . . ."

And Donald's mind was suddenly filled with the terrible images of Soweto that had come by newsreel, and by photos across his desk.

Kids, he thought ironically. There was that first day, when thousands of those kids had marched, jumping and prancing under their crude, hand-scrawled banners reading, TO HELL WITH AFRIKAANS! FREEDOM! DON'T SHOOT, I DON'T

SPEAK AFRIKAANS! And in their bright, and maybe somewhat cocky, thousands they had come face-to-face with the barricade of police. All of them armed, all of them supported by security vehicles of all kinds, from simple police cars to the huge army hippos.

And those cheering, dancing kids, who had broken nothing more serious than their school attendance records, were told their march for freedom was an "illegal gathering" and were ordered to disperse. The order wasn't even heard by most of them, and wasn't likely to be obeyed by any of them. It was, after all, the Afrikaner law they were trying to change.

The order to disperse was repeated and again it hardly dented the cheering, singing throng of schoolchildren. Police guns were lowered, tear-gas canisters were readied. Maybe God could answer which happened first: the launching of tear gas by the police or the throwing of some stones by the students.

One thing was certain, the stones were thrown at armed men who were in, or in front of, heavy military vehicles. The tear gas was launched into a crowd of youngsters whose only weapons might have been some loose stones in the street and whose only protection was something in cotton or polyester that they wore on their backs.

But within seconds of the burning tear gas creating chaos in the massed throng of closely packed children, gunfire came from the police military. Much of it was not gunfire in the air. Youngster after youngster was shot in the back as he or she was running away from the police.

Then the stones came in earnest. And the gunfire continued to fell twelve-year-old kids, fourteen-year-old kids. And for days a battle was joined. The young broke and burned and vandalized in an expression of hatred for the

System, in revenge for those of their kind who had been killed. The police and army charged and clubbed and shot, as though their victims did not belong to South Africa but were some invading horde from another world.

When it was over, Soweto had lost some of its "best" buildings to fire; many cars and buses had been destroyed; hundreds of windows had been broken.

And over five hundred children had been killed, over four thousand wounded.

Like all battles, it was a theater for great acts of heroism. Children hauling friends to safety across a field of open fire. Older brothers of fourteen defying gunfire to try to rescue wounded little brothers of eight.

Like all battles, it produced examples of man's inhumanity to man, woman, and child that were hard to believe. Police cars "toured" the dirty streets of Soweto, shooting children, male and female, as some kind of legalized sport. The children were running; they were no threat to those who shot them; they had been proved guilty of no specific crime.

The brutality, the stubbornness, the misunderstanding that begat Soweto still hung over the country like some choking, miasmic cloud.

Woods knew, and Biko believed, that men's minds could be changed. Could enough of them, *would* enough of them, change before that charred and lethal Soweto of those weeks became a microcosm of all South Africa?

Woods' hands clutched and held the pages of the manuscript in his bag. What a cost had already been paid! Biko, the official verdict read, "died of injuries from falling." Mapetla "hanged himself." "Official verdicts" like that accounted for the deaths of dozens and dozens of men who had sought to lead South Africa out of that cloud. Were there enough martyrs to make it happen yet?

"Dad, look! Up ahead. A city!" It was Duncan's voice that was calling Woods from his reverie.

He looked out of the plane. "Yes, that's it," he said. "Across the river. We've made it. . . ."

And his eyes turned back to that beautiful land of his birth, and he heard that huge chorus of sound at Biko's funeral:

> God bless Africa,
> Raise up her name . . .
> Hear our prayers
> And bless us . . .
>
> Bless the leaders,
> Bless also the young
> That they may carry the land
>     with patience,
> In their youth, bless them.
>
> Bless our efforts
> To unite and lift ourselves
> Through learning and understanding,
> And bless us.
>
> *Woza Moya! Yilha Moya!*
> Come, Spirit! Descend, Spirit!
> *Woza Moya Oyingewele!*
> Come, Holy Spirit!

And the plane banked and turned its nose down to land.